Connor gripped her hand almost to the point of pain, and she glanced up sharply.

The intensity of the gold stare she met sent a tremor through her.

"So marry me now. I want you and Savannah both to have my name."

Darby's heart lurched. "What?"

"It's what we'd planned before I went into WitSec. We can get a justice of the peace or the hospital chaplain to come—"

"Connor, stop." She wrenched her hand from his and shook it to get the blood circulating again. "Think about what you're saying!"

"I don't need to think about it. It feels right. It is right." Determination and conviction set his jaw and shone in his gaze.

Her pulse raced so hard her head spun. At one time, marrying Connor and growing old with him had been her heart's desire, a dream within her reach. Now he was offering her another chance at the dream that had been snatched from her. She should be grabbing on with both hands. But she couldn't.

How could she marry a man she knew planned to leave her in a few days?

Dear Reader,

The Return of Connor Mansfield is the first of a new trilogy about three sexy brothers from my fictional town of Lagniappe, Louisiana. The Mansfield brothers—Connor, Grant and Hunter—will rise to the challenge of life-threatening danger with courage, loyalty and honor, and will find that true love is worth fighting for!

Connor is up first as he risks his life to claim his daughter, make a life-saving gift and win back the heart of the only woman he's ever loved. This was a heartbreaking tale to write—a gravely ill child is every parent's worst nightmare, next to the death of the child—and I found myself rewriting and struggling at times to tell it just right. I hope you enjoy Connor and Darby's story. Watch for Hunter's story in the next few months!

Happy reading,

Beth

THE RETURN
OF CONNOR
MANSFIELD

Beth Cornelison

HARLEQUIN® ROMANTIC SUSPENSE

ISBN-13: 978-0-373-27854-1

THE RETURN OF CONNOR MANSFIELD

Printed in U.S.A.

Books by Beth Cornelison

Harlequin Romantic Suspense

Special Ops Bodyguard #1668
Operation Baby Rescue #1677
^*Soldier's Pregnancy Protocol* #1709
^*The Reunion Mission* #1717
Colton's Ranch Refuge #1724
^*Cowboy's Texas Rescue* #1746
Colton Christmas Rescue #1780
#*The Return of Connor Mansfield* #1784

*The Bancroft Brides
^Black Ops Rescues
#The Mansfield Brothers

Other titles by this author available in ebook format.

Silhouette Romantic Suspense

To Love, Honor and Defend #1362
In Protective Custody #1422
Danger at Her Door #1478
Duty to Protect #1522
Rancher's Redemption #1532
Tall Dark Defender #1566
The Christmas Stranger #1581
Blackout at Christmas #1583
  "Stranded with the Bridesmaid"
The Bride's Bodyguard #1630
P.I. Daddy's Personal Mission #1632
The Prodigal Bride #1646

BETH CORNELISON

started writing stories as a child when she penned a tale about the adventures of her cat, Ajax. A Georgia native, she received her bachelor's degree in public relations from the University of Georgia. After working in public relations for a little more than a year, she moved with her husband to Louisiana, where she decided to pursue her love of writing fiction.

Since that first time, Beth has written many more stories of adventure and romantic suspense and has won numerous honors for her work, including a coveted Golden Heart Award in romantic suspense from Romance Writers of America. She is active on the board of directors for the North Louisiana Storytellers and Authors of Romance (NOLA STARS) and loves reading, traveling, *Peanuts'* Snoopy and spending downtime with her family.

She writes from her home in Louisiana, where she lives with her husband, one son and two cats who think they are people. Beth loves to hear from her readers. You can write to her at P.O. Box 5418, Bossier City, LA 71171, or visit her website, www.bethcornelison.com.

For my dad. Thanks for all you've done for your family through the years!

Thanks to Emma Welch for sharing her cat, Toby. I was happy to celebrate the love and loyalty of her furry friend as Darby's faithful feline companion.

Thank you to Allison Reed for her winning bid in Brenda Novak's Auction for the Cure of Diabetes 2012 to be featured as a character in this book.

Prologue

Through the thick fog of a Louisiana autumn morning, Victor Gale watched his prey from an abandoned hunter's blind. Raising his rifle, he peered through the scope and drew a bead on his target's head. Hatred gnawed his gut like acid, and his muscles hummed with tension and anticipation. Other men had used this camouflaged blind to hunt deer. Victor hunted a man. A traitor. A liability to his family, his livelihood, his freedom.

Last year, Connor Mansfield had found evidence of Gale Industries' side business, had stolen company records to show the FBI and had testified for the prosecution at William Gale's trial. Mansfield's betrayal had cost Victor's father everything. For that, Mansfield had to pay. He had to be silenced. He had to die.

Their father had taken the fall for the family to protect Victor and his brother, James, so retribution against Connor Mansfield fell to his sons. Victor relished the duty.

As quietly as the mist curled through the woods, Victor tracked Mansfield's progress from his truck to the small cabin, a hunting camp deep in the pine forest of central Louisiana, waiting for a clear shot through the trees. He had to take Mansfield out before he went inside.

Before he lost his chance.

Mansfield hesitated at the cabin door as if reluctant to go inside, but a fat cypress obscured Victor's line of sight. Damn it!

When Mansfield finally slipped inside and out of view, Victor growled his frustration and spit on the ground. He might not get another shot for hours, not until Mansfield left the camp. Unless…

Victor considered approaching the ramshackle cabin, peeking in the window and shooting Mansfield from closer range. But he risked being seen or heard, tipping Mansfield off, leaving evidence near the scene that could trace the kill back to him.

No. Better to have patience. Wait him out. Catch Mansfield when—

A deafening blast rocked the woods as the cabin erupted in a massive fireball.

The concussion of the explosion knocked Victor off his feet. Rang painfully in his ears. Thundered in his chest.

Debris rained down around him, piercing the thin walls of the hunter's blind and stinging his skin when it hit. When all fell quiet again and his shock eased, he scrambled to his knees to peer out the blind's slit of a window.

The cabin Mansfield had just entered was in ruin, the remnants ablaze. Stunned by the turn of events, Victor stared, his head buzzing from adrenaline and the damage of the loud blast.

Finally he pulled out his cell phone and punched in his brother's number.

"Is it done?" James asked without preamble.

"Yeah, but…I didn't do it."

"What are you saying?"

"The freakin' cabin exploded. Maybe a gas line leak that went up when he hit the light switch?" Victor shook his head, still gawking at the carnage. "No way he survived that blast."

Silence answered him.

"Did ya hear me, man?"

James's sigh rattled through the phone. "Yeah. I guess fate took its own revenge."

Victor grunted, a tickle of suspicion pricking his neck. "Maybe, but…I don't like it. I smell a setup."

"What kind of setup?"

"Don't know, but…I think I'll stay and watch the place. See who shows up—whether they recover a body—how this gets handled." Victor pinched the bridge of his nose, dreading the long hours of sitting cramped in the hunter's blind, getting eaten by mosquitoes. But he had to be sure.

"Fine," his older brother said. "I want a full report of everyone and everything that happens out there the rest of the day."

Resigned to the task and more mosquito bites, Victor stayed and watched as the cops and fire department arrived and put out the flames. Grim-faced men in FBI jackets came next. A coroner's hearse hauled away a body bag. And an attractive redhead drove up, broke down in hysterical tears and was stopped from approaching the smoldering remains of the cabin by two FBI agents.

When the scene was deserted several hours later, Victor rolled his aching shoulders and dialed James again to report in. "Did Mansfield have a girlfriend?"

"Yeah," James said. "A redhead. Name's Darby something. Kent, I think. Yeah, Darby Kent."

"She showed up. Seemed pretty torn up about his death."

James grunted, then fell silent again for several nerve-racking seconds.

Victor braced himself. He knew what was coming next.

"Find Darby. Follow her. See if she meets up with him. If the explosion was part of a setup, she's the key to bringing him outta hiding."

"You want me to take her out?"

"Naw. She's nothing to us. But if she meant anything to him, and he's still alive—"

Victor glanced at the burned-out husk of the cabin. His brother had a point. Family had always been Mansfield's weakness. But Victor disagreed with James on one point. If Mansfield was still alive, pulling a hoax, Victor wasn't as squeamish as his brother about collateral damage. If Darby Kent led him to Mansfield, he'd kill them both.

Chapter 1

Four and a half years later—Dallas

Sam Orlean looked up from his laptop when he heard a knock on his office door.

His boss at Tri-State Insurance strode in and slapped several files on his desk. "These just came in. They're Roy's accounts, but he's on vacation. All three have reached over a hundred thousand in claims in the past month and need a policy review, follow-up calls."

Sam glanced at the sticky note on the top file that Roy had left.

Male, 87, two weeks in intensive care—complications from flu
Female, 3, cancer

Sam's gut wrenched. The cases that involved children were always the toughest to handle. The third notation read:

Woman, 37, staph infection post-hysterectomy—
extended hospital stay

Sam's job didn't usually include medical claim reviews.
He was in the auto claims department, but the company
was small enough that covering for a different department
wasn't unusual.

"What exactly am I looking for in the review?" he
asked.

"Just look at the paperwork, check for duplicate charges,
tests run without supporting documentation from the doctor. Just make sure everything we've been billed for is
on the up-and-up." His boss gave a little wave as he left.
"Have fun."

Sam leaned forward to drag the files closer, gritting his
teeth in frustration. Days like today, he really hated the job
the U.S. Marshals arranged for him. In his old life, when
he'd been an accountant, he'd dealt with numbers. Numbers
made sense. But insurance meant factoring in people—
little girls with cancer and old men dying from complications from the flu. Even auto claims often mean human
suffering. Spouses killed by drunk drivers, reckless teens
who learned hard lessons and would never walk again.

Given any other feasible option, Sam would leave this
job. He'd complained to Marshals Jones and Raleigh before, requesting a new position doing something else, and
was given the bureaucratic runaround. His new identity
couldn't bear any resemblance to his old one. New name,
new hobbies, new hometown. New career.

As they had when he entered the program, his handlers
had fed him the line that went, "no Witness Security Program participant, who has followed security guidelines,
has been harmed while under the active protection of the

U.S. Marshals." Translation: if you want to live, stop complaining and do what you're told.

Acid gnawed Sam's gut as he shuffled the files and opened the one on the case that would be toughest. Three-year-old girl with leukemia. Chemotherapy started. Doctors placed child on bone marrow transplant list. No match found on maternal side of family. Father deceased. No siblings. One paternal uncle was a partial match, but her doctors were still hoping for a closer match from the donor registry.

Sam sighed. He'd heard how rare it was to find a bone marrow donor with enough matching genetic markers outside of a patient's immediate family. The poor kid and her mother were facing an uphill battle. A heartbreaking fight against an ugly disease.

His chest tightening with sympathy, he flipped the page and found the policy history.

Date policy purchased: January 18 of last year.

Clicking his tongue in his mouth, hoping he could find enough supporting information to approve the claims without bothering the mother for further paperwork, he flipped back to the first page, looked for the date the first claim was filed. March 2 of this year. A little more than two months ago. He turned back to the summary page Roy had left to see the total paid out so far and gave a low whistle. Cancer treatment wasn't cheap.

As he flipped back to the front of the file, his gaze snagged on the name at the top of the form. The name of the mother, the policy owner: *Darby L. Kent.*

Sam's heart rose to his throat. What were the odds that there were two Darby Kents? Slim.

He checked the woman's address: 1209 Cypress Court, Lagniappe, Louisiana.

Icy dismay washed through him, chilling him to the

bone. It was *his* Darby. The woman he loved. The woman he'd had to give up when he entered the Witness Security Program more than four years ago. If he closed his eyes, he could picture her as she'd looked the last time he'd seen her, an autumn breeze lifting her copper hair from her oval face. One errant wavy lock had blown across her green eyes, and she'd laughed as she brushed the strands behind her ear and blown him a kiss from her front porch steps.

He rocked back in his chair, slamming a hand through his hair. Through the haze of shock, his brain began clicking other facts into place.

Darby had a baby. A sick little girl. Three years old. Almost four.

He checked the child's birth date and dragged a hand over his mouth as he did the math. The little girl would have been born…eight months after he left. Eight months after the U.S. Marshals faked his death, and he'd become Sam Orlean. Eight months…

The file read *Father deceased.* But he wasn't dead.

A shudder rippled through him. The drone of blood whooshing through his veins buzzed in his ears.

It was a near certainty…

He was the baby's father.

The hardest part about being a mother was seeing your child suffer and being absolutely powerless to ease her pain.

Her heart giving a tender throb, Darby leaned forward to stroke her daughter's tiny brow, knit in discomfort even as she slept. If Darby could have been the one getting stuck with needles and dealing with the nausea from the chemo treatments, she would have switched places with Savannah in a second. But all she could do was watch her baby soldier through the treatments and procedures she was too young to understand.

Please, God, don't take my baby, she begged silently for the millionth time. She'd lost Savannah's father four and a half years ago, before she'd even realized she was pregnant, and thought she wouldn't survive the pain. When she'd learned she was having Connor's baby, she'd pulled herself together and rebuilt her life, focused on raising the miracle that was Savannah. An unexpected posthumous gift from Connor.

Connor. Another sharp pang twisted in her chest, and she forcefully shoved down the suffocating ache. She had to be strong for her daughter.

In her purse, her cell phone trilled. Darby set aside the sketch pad on her lap—drawing had always been her best stress reliever—and swiped tears from her cheek as she shuffled through her bag. The caller ID showed the insurance company with which she'd bought health coverage, and Darby tapped the answer key.

"Hello," she whispered, hoping not to wake Savannah. She rose from her chair beside the hospital bed that swallowed her daughter and crept quietly to the hall to take the call.

After a brief silence, a man asked, "Ms. Kent?"

"Speaking."

"This is…uh, Sam Orlean with Tri-State Insurance." His voice had a funny nasal pitch to it as though he had a bad cold or something.

"Yes, Mr. Orlean, what can I do for you?"

"I'm…calling about your recent claims."

She didn't like the hesitation in his voice. A knot tightened her gut. "Is there a problem?"

"It's standard procedure to do a policy review when claims reach a certain level. The company needs to verify the claims so that your daughter's treatments can be covered."

A nervous sweat rose on Darby's top lip. "What kind of concerns do you have?"

She tried to keep the note of panic out of her voice, but even the suggestion that the insurance company would deny her claim made her lunch churn and threaten to come up. If her claim for Savannah's treatments was turned down, the expense of chemotherapy, the hospital stay, the CT scans, blood tests, doctors' appointments… She'd go bankrupt paying for it all. She couldn't possibly afford—

"Can you tell me when Savannah—" his voice cracked, and he paused to clear his throat "—first showed signs of illness?"

Darby frowned, wondering what had the man so anxious, but also wary of his questions. She poked her head back into Savannah's room to check on her. Still sleeping, if fitfully. "She had been acting droopy, tired and cranky for a few weeks back in February. I assumed she was catching a cold or maybe had an ear infection. You should have a receipt for the trip to her pediatrician in her file for around the sixth."

"Yes, I see it." He had her recount other trips to the doctor, tests that were run and details of the treatment regimen that was started once Savannah's leukemia was confirmed. "And how far into the chemo treatments are you?"

"She'll be finished with her first round by the end of the week." Darby drew a deep breath and switched the phone from one hand to the other. "What is it exactly that you want to know, Mr. Orlean? What is it the company is taking issue with?"

He sighed heavily, and something about the world-weary sound tickled a memory, triggered a gut-level response. She knew it was ridiculous, that she'd never met the insurance man who worked in the company's Dallas office, but she knew that sigh…somehow.

"We're simply verifying the charges filed with us, cross-checking with standard treatment expenses, double-checking that your policy covers—"

"You're looking for fraud." Even the hint that the company might try to deny her claims or cancel her insurance, take away her ability to pay for Savannah's treatments, made her knees buckle, and she slid to the cold tile floor.

"Well, we do have to be alert to the possibility of fraud, yes, but—"

A buzzing rang in her ears, and she leaned her head back against the wall and closed her eyes, fighting to keep her breathing measured and even.

Stay calm. Stay strong. I have nothing to hide, nothing to worry about…

"But as I said, this is simply a policy review—"

Darby groaned and dropped her head to her hands.

"Ms. Kent, are you all right?" One of the nurse's assistants squatted beside her in the corridor, laying a cool hand on her arm.

Darby shook her head, searched for her voice. "No," she rasped, wanting to deny everything about her current circumstances. "No, no, no."

No, her daughter couldn't be sick, couldn't be dying. No, she didn't have the will, the strength left to fight an insurance company for the medical coverage they'd promised. No, she wasn't all right. She hadn't been truly right in almost five years, since Connor died.

Tears prickled her sinuses and dripped on her cheeks. She waved the nurse's assistant off with a tremulous smile, then wiped her face with a thumb. "I swear to you, Mr. Orlean. If something about the claims filed by the doctors or hospital is off, I'll do my best to get things straightened out." She heard the rustling of papers on the other end of the phone line. "To be honest, I haven't paid close attention to what's been filed and where claims stood. I've had my hands full just taking care of my daughter. Thank God I work for family, so I can get the time off—"

"You changed jobs?" he interrupted, his tone not quite so nasal this time.

"Uh…yes. Last January. Just before I bought the policy. But I am employed, if that is part of your concern. I won't miss any premium payments."

"I—um, no. That's not… You're working for Mansfield Construction? But your art…um, your file says you are an artist."

She wrinkled her brow. If the company wasn't concerned about her ability to pay her premiums, then what business was it of his where she was working?

"Yes, I do the billing and clerical duties for Mansfield Construction. They're a small company a friend owns." While she'd much rather be doing something with her art for a living, working for Mansfield Construction gave her a steady income, health insurance and, because the owners were her daughter's grandparents, understanding and job security when she needed time off to take care of Savannah—a benefit that had been particularly welcome since Savannah's diagnosis a couple months ago.

Mr. Orlean sighed again, and another hint of the familiar whispered down her neck. She shoved to her feet, feeling a bit stronger now, past the initial shock and dread of impending doom. She peeked in the room to check on Savannah, then pulled the door closed and resumed her position in the hospital's corridor. "If that's all, sir, I need to get back to my child—"

"Wait! I…" He cleared his throat again. "I still need

to verify some things to satisfy the company's questions about your policy."

She straightened her spine, suddenly exhausted by the man's endless questions. "Look, Mr. Orlean, I've paid my premiums on time, and if your company has questions about charges filed by the hospital, you should talk to the billing department. Not me. And if you try to deny my claims based on a clerical error or technical glitch and put my daughter's health in jeopardy, so help me, I'll sue your company ten ways to Sunday!" All her pent-up frustrations with Savannah's illness, her helplessness to ease her daughter's pain, her sense of being alone in the most important battle of her life boiled over. "If you think I'm going to lie down and let you walk all over me, you've got another think coming!"

A chuckle filtered through the line.

Darby saw red. "This isn't funny! Do you think I'm kidding?"

"I know. I'm sorry, Darby. I…"

She stiffened hearing him use her first name, as if they were best friends. Hearing the way his Southern accent softened the hard *ar* in her name to *Dahr*-by. The way Connor used to say her name.

Pain clutched at her chest as Connor's face flickered in her memory.

In the pause of the conversation, Mr. Orlean had apparently sobered. His tone was darkly serious when he asked, "What is Savannah's prognosis? What are the doctors telling you about her treatment options, about her… chances—"

Darby felt the blood drain from her face. The best way she had of dealing with Savannah's illness, the *only* way she had of not going stark raving mad with worry and grief and fear for her daughter, was to take things one day at a time. She couldn't think about the long term, the odds of Savannah surviving her cancer, or she'd become so burdened with despair that she couldn't be the mom Savannah needed *now*.

"I'm not sure why that matters to you at this point. Whatever the doctors feel is necessary and best for Savannah should be covered, regardless of how long it takes or whether she—" Her voice broke, and she paused for a reinforcing breath. "Or whether she responds to the treatments."

"Of course. If Tri-State clears your policy after our review, we will cover—"

"If?" Darby shrieked then, clenching her teeth, she growled, "Listen here, buster. Don't you screw around with me! I need that coverage to save my daughter's life!" Just saying the words brought a rush of unwanted emotion, and moisture filled her eyes again. "Don't take away my only means to give my baby the medical care she needs!" So much for the tough-cookie act. She was begging now, tears in her voice and the words. Pitiful.

Her shoulders slumped as she gave in to the tears, surrendering to the roller-coaster emotions that had her head spinning these past several weeks. She was a mess, and she had to pull herself together in order to be the rock, the comfort, the mother Savannah needed.

"Please, Ms. Kent, don't cry. I'm so sorry this is happening to you." The man's nasally voice softened with compassion. She almost believed his sympathy was real. "This is all standard company procedure. I promise. Please know that I will do everything I can to see that all of your claims are processed in a timely manner. I want your daughter to recover. Truly I do."

Darby couldn't answer. Her throat was too clogged with emotion to breathe, much less speak.

"I'm sorry for upsetting you. I know you're dealing with a lot." He sighed again. "Alone."

She frowned. How did he know she was alone?

"I wish…" he continued in a low voice, the nasal twang gone again. "I wish I could do…something to help. I—"

Darby stilled. Her heartbeat slowed. Without the nasal affectation, his voice sounded so familiar. She shook her head. It was just her turbulent emotions playing with her mind. Wishing. Longing…

"Actually, there is something you can do," she said.

"What's that?"

"Get yourself on the National Bone Marrow registry if you aren't there already. The doctors say my baby's best chance to beat this disease is a bone marrow transplant, but we need a donor. Her uncle was close, but not close enough." Darby sighed. "It's a long shot you'd be a match, but maybe you'll be able to save some other mother's baby."

Silence answered her request.

"Mr. Orlean? Are you there?"

"Yes…I'm—I'll do that. I'll get on the registry this afternoon. I swear."

"Good. Thank you."

"I…have the doctors said…would her father have been a suitable match?"

A chill tripped down Darby's spine, along with regret and fresh waves of grief. "Kind of a moot point since he died before she was born. That information should be in her file."

"Yeah, I guess… I—"

Darby shifted her weight, uncomfortable with the personal nature of Mr. Orlean's questions and tone. "Why do you ask?"

"I just…well, I thought, maybe…" He fumbled awkwardly, the nasal voice back. He sounded truly contrite, and Darby closed her eyes. The man sounded as if he really cared about Savannah's plight, and she appreciated that he wanted to be more than just a cold company drone at the other end of the line.

"For what it's worth, I bet he'd have been a match," she blurted, not knowing why she was going down this road with a perfect stranger, other than the fact that the subject had preoccupied her mind for weeks. "She inherited so much from him. From his dark hair and light brown eyes to his stubborn streak."

What if Connor were alive? Would his marrow have been able to save their child? She shook her head and shoved the what-if aside. She'd never know that answer. Connor was gone.

I bet he'd have been a match.

Connor rocked back in his desk chair and squeezed his eyes shut. Frustration and regret gripped his chest and twisted painfully. His daughter needed him. Needed his marrow.

"I have nothing to base this on other than my own speculation, of course," Darby went on, the sadness in her voice almost more than he could bear.

When she'd started crying earlier, it was all he could do not to blurt out the truth and jump on the first plane back to Louisiana.

"But Savannah got so many other traits from her father, why not marrow type, too?" She paused for a humorless laugh. "And since Connor's brother has some of the same markers and is a partial match, it seems reasonable to me that Connor would be a closer match. Right?"

Connor. He gritted his teeth, swallowing a groan of anguish. She'd unwittingly confirmed what he suspected, but hearing his name on her lips again was a sweet agony. The precious details about his daughter were like manna that he feasted on, but painful to hear, as well.

He had to clear his throat before he could speak. "Sounds reasonable." He grimaced, realizing he'd forgotten to mask his voice again.

She grunted, and he heard shuffling noises. "I'm sorry. I don't know why I'm boring you with all this. I need to get back to Savannah. I think I hear her waking up."

He heard a door squeak, a muffled, "Hi, Miss Priss. Did you sleep well?"

Connor held his breath and squeezed the phone, treasuring the tiny glimpse of the life he'd left behind. The life he ached for every waking minute and dreamed of every moment he slept.

If he slept.

A tiny, distant voice answered. Sweet, plaintive, so young. "It ouches, Mommy."

Savannah. His daughter.

His baby needed him.

But going back to Lagniappe, leaving WitSec and reclaiming his old life would be suicide. More important, he could put Darby and Savannah in jeopardy.

"I have to go," Darby said. "I don't know if I've helped you settle anything, but I hope…well, that you'll do the right thing. Goodbye, Mr. Orlean."

He heard the click of the call disconnecting, then sat staring at the phone in his hand for long minutes after Darby was gone.

Do the right thing. Years ago he'd done what he believed was the right thing and "died" in order to protect his family and Darby. Now, to save his daughter, would he have to come back from the dead?

Connor went to a local medical lab that same afternoon, requested his blood be analyzed for bone marrow matching and gave the lab directions to send his contact information along with the results of his test to Savannah's doctor in Lagniappe, flagged for comparison with Savannah's blood. Roughly thirty-six hours later, his cell phone buzzed while he was in a morning meeting. Seeing the name of Savannah's doctor on his caller ID, he excused himself from the meeting to take the call.

"Mr. Orlean, this is Dr. Allison Reed in Lagniappe, Louisiana. I received a set of test results yesterday from a lab in Dallas that you asked be compared with a patient of mine."

"Yes, ma'am. Darby Kent's daughter, Savannah. Am I a match for a bone marrow transplant?"

"As a matter of fact, you are a fairly good preliminary match."

Connor gave a silent fist pump, and his heart rate leaped. "That's great!"

"I have to ask, how did you know you might be a match?" Dr. Reed asked. "What prompted you to send us your results?"

"I…" He hesitated, knowing he couldn't tell the doctor he was Savannah's father without blowing his cover. "I didn't know. More like hoped I'd be a match, I guess. So what's the next step? What do I need to do?"

"I understand that you are in Dallas, but if there was any way you could come to Lagniappe, I'd like to have a face-to-face consult with you and do a few more blood tests."

"Go to Lagniappe?" His heart sank. Returning to his hometown, even for a little while, meant risking someone recognizing him. Meant putting his new identity on the line. Meant putting his life—and potentially Darby's and his family's lives—in danger if one of the Gales' henchmen spotted him. "Can't I have the blood tests here? Can't I make the marrow donation here, should it come to it?"

"Well, yes. Technically you can, but I really prefer to have at least one face-to-face consult. And if we are able to go ahead with a transplant, I'd much rather have my team harvest your marrow here. I take a very hands-on approach." She chuckled. "My husband has other names for it. But I work best when I can oversee every phase of a transplant."

"Oh." Connor pinched the bridge of his nose. *Hell.*

"Is there a problem? Is there a reason you can't come to Lagniappe, Mr. Orlean?" Dr. Reed asked. "Because if you're not fully committed to the possibility of being Savannah's donor, it would be better that we not raise the family's hopes—"

"I'm committed," he interrupted. "I'm absolutely committed." He'd figure out a way to get to Lagniappe, whatever it took. Maybe the U.S. Marshals, who'd set him up with his new identity, could provide him a cover or a disguise to get him in and out of Lagniappe when needed. "When do you need me there?"

"Can you be here Friday?"

"I'll find a way."

"Good," the doctor said. "In that case, I'd like you to get more blood drawn tomorrow. I'll send you the address of the center where you should go. They'll start a more detailed DNA study and send me the results in time for your consultation here Friday."

Connor clenched his teeth, dreading the meeting with the U.S. Marshals, fearing what might happen if his cover was blown. But he had a daughter. A sick little girl who needed him. He *would* go to Lagniappe—hell, he'd eat glass or take a bullet to the gut in order to save his daughter's life.

Chapter 2

"I need to go back to Lagniappe." Connor cast a side glance to the men on his couch as he paced his small living room in Dallas. "Just for a day or so."

"You can't do that, Sam," Deputy U.S. Marshal Gerald Raleigh, a fiftyish man with thinning hair, a long, jowly face and the body of an aged football player, countered. "The program only works if you—"

"My name is Connor. Not Sam," he argued, feeling peevish.

Raleigh sighed. "Connor Mansfield is dead. You're Sam Orlean now, and if you want to stay alive—"

"I understand what going back there means. But I found out today that I have a daughter."

Raleigh exchanged a startled glance with his partner, Deputy U.S. Marshal Jamal Jones. "How did you hear about your daughter?"

Connor stiffened and faced Marshal Jones. "You knew about Savannah?"

Jones, an African-American of approximately Connor's age, with closely shaved hair and a short Vandyke, didn't answer, but the twitch of muscle in his jaw and self-conscious lift of his chin said all the federal marshal didn't.

Raleigh dragged a hand over his face. "How did you find out?"

Connor bit out a curse. "You knew, and you didn't tell me? What right did you have to keep something like that from me?"

"For exactly this reason," Raleigh said. "That part of your life is over, Sam, and knowing about your daughter would have only made it tougher to—"

"She's sick. Or did you know that, too, and not tell me?" He divided a glare between his handlers and ground his back teeth until his jaw ached. "She has cancer and needs a bone marrow transplant. I may be her best chance for a match."

Jones shook his head. "I'm sorry, Sam. But Gale's men are still a threat to you. They could be watching Darby Kent's house, waiting for you to show up. We've been monitoring Darby since you entered the program, in case Gale or his men made a move on her. That's how we knew about the baby."

Connor shook his head, confused, a chill coiling in his gut. After everything he'd sacrificed to protect Darby, could Gale's men *still* be watching her?

"Why would they watch Darby if they believe I'm dead? She had nothing to do with Gale's prosecution. You said you tied up all of the loose ends. I'm officially dead, right? So why—"

Jones raised a hand. "Connor Mansfield, witness for the state, *is* officially dead. And as long as you stay dead, there is little chance Gale can find you. You are safe, and Ms. Kent will be safe."

"But if you suddenly come back from the dead," Raleigh added, leaning forward and poking the coffee table for emphasis, "your cover is blown, you become a target again and you put Darby and her daughter in the line of fire."

"*Our* daughter. She's my flesh and blood, too!"

"Exactly." Raleigh spread his hands. "So why would you put her in danger by returning from the dead? Think about her safety—"

"I am thinking of her!" Connor shoved his hands through his hair, gritting his teeth in frustration. "Savannah could die if she doesn't get my marrow!"

Jones stood and jangled the keys in his pocket. "You don't know that you're a match."

"What if I am?" Connor blew out a heavy sigh. "I have to *try* to save her. I can't sit here, knowing she needs me, knowing I might be the one who could save her life and not do anything!"

"I understand your frustration and concern, Sa—"

"Do you?" Connor spun to face Raleigh. "Do you *really* understand? Giving up the woman I loved to enter the program nearly killed me. Not a day goes by I don't think about chucking it all and going back, consequences be damned. Darby's safety is the only reason I haven't gone back before now. My life means nothing without her."

"Sam, I know it is hard to leave behind—"

"You had no right to withhold the truth from me!" Connor jabbed a finger toward Raleigh, punctuating his point. "If I'd known I had a daughter on the way, I don't know if I'd have ever agreed to entering WitSec without Darby."

Jones shook his head. "We've explained why that was a bad idea. To make it believable that you'd died—"

"—the woman I loved had to believe I'd died, too. Yeah,

yeah. I remember your reasoning, but…" Connor turned to pace again. "But things are different now. My daughter is sick. I have to go back." He planted his feet and squared his shoulders. "I have an appointment Friday with Savannah's doctor. There's a chance I could be a marrow donor for her, and the doctor insisted on a face-to-face consult and more tests."

Raleigh shook his head. "Sam…"

Connor firmed his resolve. "I have to try to help Savannah."

"Even if it puts all of your lives at risk? Not just yours, but Darby's and Savannah's. Your brothers. Parents. Anyone close to you could be at risk, because Victor Gale hasn't forgotten the man who brought down his father's money laundering scheme and put ole Pop behind bars. He has a history of vigilante justice and revenge against those who cross his family."

"I'm aware of that, but I *am* going. The question is, will you help me get in and out of town without detection?" When his handlers hesitated, Connor dropped heavily onto a wingback chair and propped his elbows on his knees, his face in his hands. "I'll be careful, use disguises. But I can't sit here, knowing I have a daughter who needs me. Savannah will die without a transplant." Connor gritted his back teeth and revisited the option he'd rejected years ago, for Darby's sake. "Is it too late for Darby to join Wit-Sec with me?"

Even as he asked, his gut tensed, knowing what a difficult move that'd be for Darby to make. Asking her to give up her life, her family, her home to be with him would be so horribly selfish. Did she even love him anymore? Perhaps she'd moved on, found someone else…

Raleigh grunted. "Hiding a child who's as sick as Savannah would be highly dangerous, full of pitfalls. Besides the high level of medical care she needs, tracking you through her medical records, through treatment facilities would be far too easy. There'd be too many doctors and nurses and other patients involved who could talk and blow your cover, even if accidentally…"

"So then I have no choice. My mind is made up." Connor divided an even stare between the two marshals. "I know the risks. I hate the risks, of course, and I'll deal with them somehow. But my baby needs me, so I'm going home. I'm going to save my daughter."

That Friday, with help from her longtime friend and almost-brother-in-law Hunter Mansfield, Darby packed Savannah's bags, preparing to take her daughter home following the last chemo treatment. When her cell phone rang and the caller ID showed Dr. Reed's office, she assumed the call was about Savannah's discharge papers and directions concerning her at-home care. Darby answered, relieved to have the chance to ask questions. She hadn't felt this nervous about taking Savannah home from the hospital when she was a new mother with a one-day-old baby.

Hunter had Savannah distracted, animating her stuffed rabbit to make her laugh as Darby took Dr. Reed's call. "Hello?"

"Darby, it's Jillian Evans in Dr. Reed's office."

"Oh, hi, Jillian." Darby smiled hearing the friendly voice of the nurse who'd been so helpful and supportive in recent months. "We got Savannah's discharge papers, and we're just getting ready to leave the hospital now."

"Oh, great, but…that's not why I'm calling."

Darby heard an odd note of apprehension in Jillian's voice, and her gut immediately clenched. Bracing for bad news—God, she was tired of bad news—Darby said, "Go on."

"Well, Dr. Reed asked me to call you about some rather confusing information we have regarding a potential donor for Savannah."

Darby's spirits lifted. "You have a potential donor?"

Hunter's head jerked up, and she met his hopeful gaze as she listened to the nurse explain.

"Well…yes. Dr. Reed will call you later to tell you more about that, but…" Elation made Darby's head spin, and her heart pounded so hard she almost missed Jillian saying, "But his test results show something that has Dr. Reed puzzled."

"Puzzled? What's wrong?" Like being on a roller coaster, her stomach swooped, her mood crashing from high to low again. *Here we go. The bad news…*

"The DNA tests that show that he is a strong candidate as a donor also say, with statistical certainty, that he is Savannah's father."

The air froze in Darby's lungs. "Wh-what? That's impossible. Connor is dead."

Hearing his brother's name mentioned, Hunter rose to his feet and hurried over to Darby, pressing his ear close as she tipped the phone for him to listen in.

"That's what Dr. Reed understood from your records, which is why she wanted me to call. Are you sure about who Savannah's father is? Is it possible this other man—"

"No! There was no one else. I don't sleep around, if that's what you're asking." Darby's hand shook, and she dragged in a breath, trying to make sense of what the nurse was telling her. "Your test is wrong. This guy *can't* be Savannah's father. Connor Mansfield is Savannah's father, and he died four and a half years ago."

"Of course we can run the test again. Dr. Reed just wanted to double-check with you, in case maybe…"

"But if the test was wrong about him being Savannah's

father—" Darby held her breath, tears pricking her eyes "—does that mean it was wrong about him being a match for her, too?"

"We'll have to see. It's just all so odd, especially since he initiated contact with us about being a donor."

Darby's legs buckled. "He did?"

Hunter squeezed her arm, supporting her, but his own face was paler than normal.

"Who is this guy? Where is he from?" she asked.

"He's from Texas, I think. Don't worry, Dr. Reed will screen him and assess if he's a nut job or if he's truly a viable donor. In fact, she's meeting with Mr. Orlean now, and she's requested new tests, pending what she learns in her consult with him."

Darby blinked. Shook her head as if she'd heard wrong. "Wait. What did you say his name was?"

"Sam Orlean. Why? Do you know the name?"

"I—maybe. It rings a bell but..." She fumbled through her memory. A classmate? A customer of Mansfield Construction? No. It was more recent. Darby looked at Hunter, and he shrugged and shook his head, silently denying any familiarity with the name.

She dredged up the call earlier in the week from her insurance company. Was that where she'd heard the name? She replayed bits of the call in her head, trying to conjure the man's name. But other pieces of the conversation were what stood out.

Would her father have been a suitable match?

I'm sorry, Dahr-by.

"Connor," she said under her breath, not daring to hope. And yet...

Her imagination raced, and just the possibility that Connor might still be alive made her dizzy with expectation. The need to know, the demand for answers pounded through her like a tribal chant. *Connor. Connor. Connor.*

"As soon as Dr. Reed gets out of her meeting with him, I'll have her call you with—"

"Then Sam Orlean is still there, at your office right now?" Adrenaline made her pulse pound so hard in her ears, she could barely hear, much less think. *Connor. Connor. Connor.*

"He's in with the doctor, discussing his test results and—"

"Don't let him leave." She squeezed the phone tighter and hurried to grab her purse from the chair by the bed. "Stall him. I'm on my way."

"But—"

She hung up before Jillian could object and sent Hunter a pleading look as she rushed to the door. "Will you stay with her? I have to know."

"Of course," Hunter said, his expression reflecting his own shock and need for answers.

Darby jogged down the hospital corridor to the elevator. Dr. Reed's office was in a medical building a couple blocks away. She debated taking her car but decided that by the time she got to the parking garage, dealt with traffic and red lights and parked again, she'd get there faster on foot.

On the elevator, she pushed the lobby button again and again as the car descended, as if it would make the elevator go faster. She knew better, but her nerves jangled, and she needed something to do until the doors parted at the lobby. Hiking her purse higher on her shoulder, Darby flew out the front door of the hospital and made a beeline for Dr. Reed's office. She dodged people on the sidewalk, wove through cars to cross the street and took the stairs at the medical building rather than wait on another slow elevator.

By the time she raced through the door of Dr. Reed's

office, she could barely catch her breath. Though she'd run track in high school, she'd let herself get out of shape in recent months, while dealing with Savannah's illness.

She approached the receptionist desk, panting. "Sam... Orlean? Jillian said...he was...here."

The receptionist looked up and smiled at her, but when she saw Darby gasping for air and sweating, her smile fell away. "Um...he was here. But they just left."

Darby's whole body sagged, dejection sandbagging her. "He left? I told...Jillian to...stall...."

"Darby." Jillian appeared behind the receptionist, frowning and shaking her head. "I tried to keep him here, but when I mentioned you wanted to meet him, he got agitated, and they left in a big hurry."

She stiffened. "They? He had...someone with him?"

"Yeah. A big guy. Light brown hair. About fifty. Clean-cut and—"

Darby waved her quiet. "Never mind. How long ago did they leave?"

"They just did. Seconds before you got here. I'm sorry—"

Darby spun back toward the door, leaving her purse, encumbering ballast, on the receptionist's counter. Heart in her throat, she sped back down the stairs, but this time made her way toward the parking garage. She had to have at least a glimpse of this man whose DNA tests were so confoundingly wrong. Unless...

He initiated contact...

Dahr-by...

She slammed through the heavy door to the parking garage and skidded to a stop on the concrete landing. From the slightly raised vantage point, she could better see over the top of cars on this, the main deck of the garage. She swept a glance down each aisle and spotted three men, an

African American, a tall man with light brown hair and a raven-haired man with a beard, sunglasses and baseball cap.

"Mr. Orlean?" she called, her breathless shout drowned out by noise from the street below. She hurried down the steps and chased after the men. "Mr. Orlean?"

She stared at the back of the man in the cap as she ran to catch them. The broad shoulders and confidence in his stride seemed familiar, though his hair was many shades darker than Connor's.

She closed the gap between them before trying again to get their attention. "Mr. Orlean! Please, wait!"

The man in the cap stiffened, slowed. When he started to turn, the black man beside him glanced over his shoulder and pushed the dark-haired man toward a silver sedan. With the fob in his hand, the tall, older man clicked the locks off and opened the back door of the sedan. With a jerk of his head, he motioned for the man in the cap to get in the car.

They weren't just ignoring her; they were escaping from her. Puzzled and more than a bit miffed, Darby shouted again, "Wait! Sam Orlean, I need to talk to you!"

When she reached the silver sedan, the black man tried to block her path, but she shoved past him. She grabbed the arm of the man she believed was Sam Orlean as he tried to climb in the backseat. "Wait!"

He froze for a moment, dropped his chin to his chest then, straightening to his full height, he turned.

Mumbling an earthy obscenity, the older man stepped forward as if to intervene, but Orlean raised a hand to stop him.

Winded, Darby gasped for a breath and grabbed the open car door for support, her body shaking as she studied the beard-covered face. The man's coloring was wrong, his hair too dark. His eyes were hidden behind the sunglasses and shaded by the cap. And yet...

He stood stock-still, except for a slight shudder as he drew a stuttering breath.

The chant in Darby's brain screamed louder— Connor, Connor, *Connor!* Reaching up, she snatched away his cap, pulled his sunglasses off.

His jaw tightened, and he looked away, scowling at the cars parked across the aisle.

"Look at me," she whispered, and when he refused, she screamed, "Look at me, damn it!"

She grabbed his chin and wrenched his head toward her. When he lifted his eyes to hers, they were damp with tears, brimming with regret and apology. Her heart slammed against her ribs. Her knees buckled, and her lungs seized.

She knew those golden-brown eyes. Intimately. They were her daughter's eyes.

"Connor." Her voice squeaked as her throat clogged with emotion. Her body shook with unspent adrenaline, and she lifted a hand toward his cheek. He wrapped long, warm fingers around hers, moving her hand off his face and squeezing her hand. Stunned, she grappled with what her heart was telling her, while her brain rejected the truth. A hesitant joy filled her chest like helium, expanding, lifting her hope. But a darker emotion lurked at the edges of her shock. She shoved the darkness aside, not wanting anything to shadow the moment.

Tears filled her eyes as a half laugh, half sob bubbled up from her chest. "You're alive!"

He gave the slightest of nods, but that tiny confirmation sent a tidal wave of conflicting emotions coursing through her. Relief and elation tangled with disbelief. She surged forward to hug him, to celebrate their reunion. But the older man beside them caught her arm, separating them. "Not here."

She blinked her confusion, looking to Connor for answers. His expression was grim, full of grief and regret. "I'm sorry."

His apology released the darkness she'd tried to hold at bay. A chill crept from her scalp to her toes as the first flicker of understanding dawned on her. Anger and resentment elbowed past her other emotions.

He'd left her. On purpose. He'd deceived her, let her think he was dead. He'd said he loved her, but he'd *abandoned* her.

Just like her father.

Her hand flew up, surprising herself as much as him when she struck his cheek. Hard. "You bastard!"

"That's enough," the black man growled. He grabbed her, restraining her arms as he pulled her away from Connor.

Darby fought the captive arms. Furious. Heartbroken. "You lied to me! You said you loved me!" she spat at Connor.

"Get in." With a hand on Connor's head, the older man pushed him into the backseat.

"No!" she shouted, desperation rearing its head. She *couldn't* lose Connor again. "Wait!"

The older man hitched his head to the black man, whose muscular arms held her like a vise. He hitched his head toward the backseat. "Bring her. We need to contain this."

Fear clawed inside her as the black man lifted her effortlessly and shoved her in the backseat.

"What the hell?" Connor barked. "Let her go!"

When her abductor pushed into the car behind her, she toppled onto Connor's lap. He caught her, steadying her as the car engine roared to life. Panic choked her as the sedan pulled sharply out of the parking space and lurched down the garage aisle. She clung to Connor's arm for balance.

"Let me out! Please!" Tears and terror strangled her. "I have to get back to Savannah. My daughter needs me!"

"Damn it, Jones!" Connor snarled. "This was never part of the plan. What are you doing?"

We need to contain this. An ominous shiver spun through her. Who were these men, and what was Connor involved in? What was *she* now involved in?

Connor scowled at Marshal Jones as Raleigh pulled out of the parking garage onto the city street. Forcing Darby into a car against her will was not the best way to start an already difficult conversation. She was understandably confused, terrified.

"You're safe, Darby," he said and stroked a hand down her back, trying to calm her. She jerked away from his touch and sent him a dirty look. In her eyes he saw hurt, confusion, fear…but mostly fury. His return from the dead had her royally pissed.

Connor sighed, his heart heavy. Had he really thought that she'd simply fall into his arms and all would be forgiven and forgotten? That she'd still love him after so many years? That the lie of his faked death and subsequent hurt he'd caused could be swept aside merely by returning from the grave?

Using the rearview mirror, Marshal Raleigh glanced to the backseat at Jones. "What's the plan? Where am I going? Back to the hotel?"

Darby lunged toward the front seat, grabbing at Raleigh's arm. "Take me to St. Mary's Hospital! My daughter is there. We were about to take her home!"

Jones pulled Darby off Raleigh. "Not yet. We have to talk."

She wrenched away from Jones with a frown, then wiggled off Connor's lap. She squeezed onto the seat between him and the car door, pushing him closer to Jones. When Raleigh stopped for a red light, Darby scrabbled with the door handle, trying to escape. Without success.

"Childproof safety locks," Jones said evenly. "They're not just for parents anymore."

Raleigh chuckled, but Darby shot Jones a look that said she didn't appreciate his dry humor. Then her gaze shifted back to Connor, and he felt the same kick of yearning and awe he'd known every time her green eyes had met his in the past. Except now her gaze was suspicious and hostile.

"Connor, who are these people? What's going on? H-how are you still alive?"

He gave her a humorless laugh. "Wow. I missed you, too, honey. Thanks for the warm welcome home."

A fresh wave of anger hardened her face briefly before tears filled her eyes and grief slackened her features. "You jerk. Of course I missed you. I died inside when I thought I'd lost you!"

Compunction punched him in the gut. "I'm sorry, Darby. I just—"

"Sorry?" she shrieked and landed an inert fist on his arm. "We buried you! Your parents had to pick out a headstone for their son. Your brothers carried your casket. I saw them wheel a body bag out of the charred cabin. But it was all a lie!" A tear broke free from her eyelashes, and when he reached up to wipe it from her cheek, she knocked his hand away.

"Honey, I know my leaving hurt you and my family. I'm sorry. I am! Leaving all of you was the hardest thing I've ever done! If I'd had any other way—"

"You did! You could have *not* pretended to die, not devastated us, not lied to us—"

"I did it to protect you. All of you. I loved you, Darby. I didn't want to hurt you, but the Gales wanted—"

"You *abandoned* me. You don't abandon someone you love." Her voice cracked, and she turned toward the window, biting her bottom lip.

Connor mumbled a curse and rubbed his face.

After pulling the car into an alley with a tall privacy fence on one side and a department store loading dock on the other, Raleigh cut the engine. He caught Connor's attention via the rearview mirror. "I know you two have a lot of personal stuff to air out, but can we stick a pin in it for now? The more immediate problem is coming to an understanding with Ms. Kent and assuring her silence."

Darby's chin snapped up, her eyes widening. "That sounds like a threat. What do you mean assure my silence? Connor, what kind of thugs are you involved with?"

"Not thugs, ma'am," Jones said, pulling out his badge. "Deputy U.S. Marshals. Sam Orlean is under our protection as part of WitSec, the Witness Security Program."

"U.S. Marshals?" Darby ignored Jones's badge and scowled at him. "Since when is it okay for federal agents to kidnap law-abiding citizens?"

Darby's stomach swirled sourly, and she held her breath, wondering where she'd found the nerve to so openly challenge these men. The bulges under their jackets were almost assuredly guns. How far would these men go to *assure her silence?*

The man named Jones looked surprised. "You haven't been kidnapped. You're free to go whenever you like."

Darby scoffed. "Childproof locks ring a bell?"

Jones smiled and sent Connor a side glance. "Feisty."

"Just one of her many attributes," he replied.

"Marshal Raleigh," Jones said, still smiling, "would you be so kind as to unlock Ms. Kent's door for her?"

"Roger that." Raleigh pushed a button on the driver's door, and the rear door locks clicked off.

Darby blinked, startled by the turn of events. Was she really free to go, or would they shoot her in the back if she tried to leave? She glanced from the door to Jones, narrowing her eyes as she decided whether Jones was pulling a trick. She tested the door release, and it popped open. Then she paused. *Connor.*

She jerked her gaze back to Connor, the man she'd once loved and conceived a child with, and her heart staggered. This wasn't about a standoff between her and two U.S. Marshals. The important issue was Connor. Who was alive. In Witness Security. And who'd contacted Dr. Reed.

He could well be a tissue match for Savannah's bone marrow transplant. *Connor.*

She exhaled a ragged breath, shifting her gaze from one man to another. And closed the car door. "I... All right. You have my attention."

Chapter 3

Connor divided a look between Jones and Raleigh. "Do you want to do the honors?"

Jones waved a hand in deferral. "Go ahead. We'll jump in as needed."

Darby sighed impatiently. "Someone talk."

Turning on the seat to better face her, Connor scooped Darby's hand in his. For a moment, he thought she might yank it back, but she hesitated, eyeing him with a combination of suspicion and concern. "Do you remember right before I…left—"

Her eyebrow rose as if taking issue with his euphemism. *You abandoned me.*

Connor's chest wrenched. Knowing how hard Darby had taken his disappearance—no, his faked death—poured acid guilt on his conscience. He'd known she'd be heartbroken. They'd been in love, planning to marry. But he truly hadn't realized how bitter, how hurt she'd be.

He puffed out a breath and plunged on. "You remember that I testified in the federal trial against William Gale, right?"

She nodded, holding his gaze.

"Well, what I didn't tell you at the time was that the Gales have ties to organized crime. In fact, they head up a branch of organized crime that operates in Lagniappe."

She sat straighter, her eyes widening and her face paling. "Organized crime? But—"

"I didn't know about their criminal connections when I went to work for them. And I didn't learn about the criminal activity for a long time. They're quite good at hiding their illegal sidelines."

Darby held up a hand. "Wait. I'm sensing this is too big to cover in one hurried conversation parked in a back alley." She flipped her wrist and checked her watch. "I've already been gone too long. Savannah is leaving the hospital today. She was almost ready to go when I bolted out of her room to follow my hunch about you."

Connor frowned. "Who's with her now?"

"Hunter. But I have to get back. I—" She leaned toward the front seat, grabbing Raleigh's arm. "Take me to St. Mary's Hospital. Now!" She sighed and added, "Please."

Raleigh turned on the seat to face his partner. "She's right about one thing. We need to get her back to the hospital before her absence causes concern with the family or hospital staff."

Jones tapped fingers to his lips as he thought. "Okay." While Raleigh started the engine again, Jones narrowed a serious look at Darby. "Here's the deal. Witness security only works if the subject breaks all ties with his former life. No one can know Sam is still alive."

"But his family—"

"No. No one. Do you understand?"

Darby hesitated, nodded, then knitted her brow in consternation. "Wait, how is Connor supposed to be Savannah's donor if no one can know he's alive?"

"Connor can't. Connor is dead. But Sam Orlean can." Jones paused and leaned toward Darby to emphasize his point. "As long as his cover remains intact."

Darby glanced at Connor, then back to the marshal. "Only problem with that is my family, Connor's family… everyone knows Connor is Savannah's father. And because of the DNA tests he took, so does Dr. Reed and her staff. They even called me to ask about it. They were puzzled when the tests showed Sam Orlean—" she drew quotation marks with her fingers as she said the name "—was Savannah's biological father. They wanted to know if I was *sure* it was Connor who'd fathered my baby. As if I slept around and couldn't keep track of my lovers." Her tone held a bitter edge.

"That could work," Raleigh said from the driver's seat as he negotiated traffic. "You could tell the doctor you had a one-night stand while on vacation and were too embarrassed to say anything before now."

Darby's expression mirrored her outrage. "Pregnant from a one-night stand? Hell, no! I'm not that kind of woman."

"We're not saying you are. But if you could tell people that's how you got pregnant, that's why Sam Orlean of Dallas is the girl's father—"

She visibly tensed, her fury palpable. "You mean lie? If I tell people that, I become that woman in the eyes of people I love and respect."

Connor had heard enough. "Darby…"

Her gaze jerked to him, her green eyes blazing. "Do you hear what they're asking? Do you have any idea how much it would hurt your parents for me to tell them the little girl they love, the grandchild they believe was a posthumous gift from you, *isn't* really yours?"

A sharp ache speared him. The last thing he wanted was to cause his family or Darby any more pain. "I hate this as much as you do, but we have to consider all the options."

She rounded on him. "Do you hate it? You hurt us all easily enough when you faked your death five years ago! What's one more stab in the back to a family you already walked away from? The family who *grieves* for you even today!"

Connor stiffened. "Leaving you, letting my family think I was dead was the hardest thing I've ever done! I hated the idea of my parents thinking I'd died, of you going through that kind of heartache and grief. Of my brothers—" He huffed in frustration as a knot of his own grief balled in his chest. "I did it to protect you. All of you! And I'd rather that sacrifice not go to waste by blowing my cover now."

"I will not lie to the people I love. I cannot hurt them that way!" Darby poked him in the chest, then flopped back against the seat and crossed her arms stubbornly.

"Even if it means protecting the father of your child from men who want to kill him?" Jones asked.

Darby snapped her attention to the marshal, her anger clearly slipping a notch when faced with the brutal reality of the situation. Her mouth opened, as if to reply, then closed again.

Connor turned toward her, tamping his own frustration in order to keep his tone nonconfrontational. This might be his only chance to see Darby, to touch her and explain the choices he'd made, and he refused to spend it arguing. "Honey, forget about me for a minute. Yes, having my cover blown would put me at risk, but more important to me is the danger you and Savannah might be in. And my family. If the Gales find out I'm alive, they might strike at you to get back at me. They know the best way to hurt me is to hurt the people I love."

A shadow of fear crept into her eyes, and she wet her lips. "Connor, I don't want you or anyone else to get hurt, but there has to be another way. Your family can keep the secret that you're alive if—"

"No," Jones interrupted. "The more people who know, the higher the risk. We have to contain this. We need your word that you'll cooperate with us, whatever it takes, in order to keep Sam alive and your family safe."

"And we need that commitment now," Raleigh added. "We're at the hospital."

Connor glanced out the side window, and sure enough, they'd reached St. Mary's. He glanced up at the brick edifice, and his heart seized. His daughter was inside those walls. The little girl he'd made with Darby. A longing so pure and deep flooded him that he couldn't breathe for a moment.

Raleigh and Jones were still trying to impress upon Darby the importance of her complete silence, the need for her to agree to whatever lie they invented about Savannah's parentage.

"I want to see her," he blurted. Three heads swiveled toward him.

"What?" Darby asked.

He held Darby's gaze, bittersweet longing swelling in his chest. "I want to see my daughter."

Though he knew in his head all the reasons it was a bad idea, his heart shouted down the rational voice of his conscience. He might never have this chance again, a chance to meet his firstborn, the opportunity to hold her, hug her, tell her he loved her. He took Darby's hands in his, his pulse thudding unsteadily. "Let me meet Savannah. Please?"

"Uhhh," Raleigh said, dragging out the syllable to reflect his uncertainty. "Not a good idea."

Connor ignored the marshal, still holding Darby's hands and gaze, waiting. If she agreed, he'd move heaven and earth to make time with his daughter happen.

Tears filled her eyes, and she bit her bottom lip when it trembled. Hurt and anger darkened her gaze. "I want to say no. I want to say you gave up the right to see her when you walked out of our lives."

Connor tensed and squeezed her hands. "I didn't know you were pregnant."

She nodded her concession on that point. "That's why I can't justify keeping you from her. You're her father. You have a right to see her."

Behind him, Jones grunted. "Sam, we can't—"

"I am." He shifted on the seat to face Marshal Jones, determination firming his resolve. "I am going to meet my daughter. With or without your help."

Chapter 4

Clearly sensing a lengthy discussion was in the offing, Marshal Raleigh pulled away from the curb in front of the hospital and circled the block, finding another alley to park in. Jones and Raleigh took some convincing to cooperate with Connor's insistence on meeting Savannah. But with some brainstorming help from Darby and Connor, they developed a cover to get Connor into Darby's house without raising any red flags with the Gales.

"Wait. What about Hunter?" Darby asked as they headed back toward the hospital.

"Who's Hunter?" Raleigh asked.

"My youngest brother," Connor said.

"Hunter was with me when I got the call from the doctor's office asking if I could explain why Sam Orlean's DNA tests showed such a significant parental match." She glanced from Connor to the marshals. "He knows I was trying to intercept you at Dr. Reed's office to find out who you were, why the tests showed you were Savannah's father."

"All the more reason to go with the one-night-stand story," Jones said.

Darby shook her head. "He won't buy it. Hunter knows me better than that. He knows I suspected Sam Orlean was Connor."

"Then tell him you were too late to catch up with Sam," Raleigh offered. "Tell him the doctor's office realized they'd mixed up records and apologized for the confusion."

She snorted her disagreement. "I can't lie to Hunter. He'll see right through me."

"My brother is trustworthy," Connor said quietly, turning toward Jones. "Now that Darby knows the truth, maybe it'd be best to tell Hunter about WitSec, as well. He can keep it quiet."

"Yes!" Darby nodded her agreement. "Let me tell Hunter the truth. He won't believe that anyone but Connor is Savannah's father, and he reads me too well for me to lie about any of this."

In the front seat, Raleigh groaned.

Jones rubbed his face with his hand. "You understand that the more people who know who Sam is, the more risk there is of the wrong people finding out?"

Raleigh pulled to a stop once more at the hospital entrance and turned toward the backseat. "Do I need to circle the block again?"

"Hunter won't talk." Connor narrowed a certain gaze on Jones. "We can trust him."

Jones and Raleigh exchanged a long dark look, as if communicating telepathically.

Darby twisted her hands in her lap, her heart still racing from adrenaline and her brain muddled with the surrealism of the past half hour. Finally, Raleigh sighed and turned back to the front window, while muttering under his breath about hell in a hand basket.

"Okay." Jones flipped up his palms. His expression said he was far from happy about acquiescing. "But tell Hunter as little as possible until we've had a chance to debrief him and impress upon him the urgency of his silence."

Darby gave a jerky nod and opened the car door. "I understand."

As she slid out of the backseat, Connor caught her arm. "Darby." She faced him, waiting for him to continue. Emotions played over his face, clearly telling her how conflicted he was, deciding what he wanted to say, what he *could* say. As if he were torn between what was in his heart and the masquerade he was playing.

The longer he hesitated, the more irritated she grew. The Connor she knew had never hedged, never held back from sharing his heart with her. But then, that Connor was dead, wasn't he? This Connor—or Sam Orlean—had lied about his death, had stayed away for almost five years.

"See you in about an hour," he said at last, his frown saying he knew how lame he sounded.

"Right." She snatched her arm from his grip, frustrated, hurt and so angry with him she was shaking.

She hurried back inside the hospital and onto the same elevator car she'd ridden down some forty or so minutes earlier. As the doors closed, she marveled at how the elevator could look the same when her life had changed so completely in such a short time. *Connor. Connor was alive!*

The air in her lungs stalled, just as it had when she'd recognized the man with the dye-darkened beard and sunglasses in the parking garage. She braced a hand on the wall of the elevator and bent at the waist to catch her breath.

"Are you all right, ma'am?" an orderly on the elevator with her asked.

She peeked up at him and shook her head. "No. Not really."

They arrived at her floor, the door sliding open with a ding, and she straightened. Flashing a forced smile to the orderly, she stepped off the elevator, waving the hospital employee away when he made a move to help her. "No, thanks."

"Mommy!" Savannah called to her as she ducked back into her hospital room.

She managed a smile for her daughter and bent to kiss her temple. "Hi, Miss Priss."

Hunter spun to face her, his phone at his ear, his expression impatient. "Cheese and rice, Darby!" He waved his cell, thumbing the disconnect button. "Why haven't you answered your phone? I've called you at least ten times!"

"Because…" She blew out a deep breath and slapped a hand to her empty shoulder where her purse usually hung. "Crud! I left my purse at the doctor's office." Raking a hand through her hair, she dropped her shoulders wearily. "Will you stop by there to let me grab it on our way home?"

He pulled a face. "Uh, yeah. Whatever." Spreading his hands, he raised his eyebrows and huffed. "Well? What happened? Did you see him?"

Darby cut a side glance to Savannah, then scowled at Hunter. "Ixnay about Onnorcay."

Hunter looked ready to strangle her. "Just give me a yes or no. Was it him?"

"Did someone die, Mommy?"

Darby faced Savannah, her pulse stumbling. "No, honey. Why?"

"You told somebody on the phone that Connuh was dead." Savannah wrinkled her nose. "Who's Connuh?"

"Um…" She fumbled, glancing to Hunter for help. She'd put off telling Savannah about her father until she thought the little girl was old enough to fully understand the concept of death. Then Hunter's elderly dog had died a few months ago, and she'd had to explain where Bo had gone and why he wouldn't be back.

But Connor came back.

"Connor is…" She rubbed the spot on her forehead where a killer headache was forming.

"My brother," Hunter supplied.

Savannah tipped her head in confusion. "But Uncle Gwant is your bwother." Savannah had just started speech therapy that spring to help her pronounce her *R*s, when they'd been handed the challenge of cancer. *R*s would have to wait.

Hunter grinned. "A guy can have more than one brother. In fact, I know someone who has seven brothers!"

Savannah's eyes widened. "That's a lot of bwothers!" She sank back against her pillow, her face sobering, her tenacious curiosity and keen memory not letting Hunter's attempt at distraction work. "Did your bwother die like Bo?"

"Um…" Hunter stalled and looked to Darby. "Did he?"

"Priss, why don't you watch TV while I talk to Uncle Hunter for a minute." She grabbed the front of his shirt and led him into the tiny bathroom out of Savannah's earshot.

"What's going on, Darby?" Hunter asked as she closed the door behind them.

She wiped sweaty palms on the seat of her pants. "Here's the deal—and you can't tell anyone about this…"

While Darby returned to the hospital room to bring Savannah home, Connor and the marshals acquired medical scrubs, a few pieces of medical equipment and a van detailed with Lagniappe Home Health on the side panel. Soon after Darby and Hunter got Savannah home, the faux home health team arrived, and Darby ushered them through her front door. Hiding in plain sight.

"Connor!" Hunter rushed forward as soon as his brother stepped into the foyer, shock and joy reverberating in his voice. "What—? How—?"

As ordered, Darby had given Hunter only the barest of information. Connor was alive. He was in hiding with WitSec. He was in disguise and headed to her house to meet Savannah.

The emotional reunion between the brothers was bittersweet for Darby. Hiding the truth from the rest of Connor's family gnawed at her. She hated feeling as though she were buying into the lie that hurt and angered her so much, even if she understood Connor's reasoning for his choice to enter WitSec. And what did she tell Savannah about the man who wanted to meet her?

Connor exchanged a bear hug with Hunter. "It's a long messy story. One that, I'm afraid, isn't over yet."

Hunter stepped back, holding his brother at arm's length. "What do you mean, it's not over?"

Connor's eyes darted back to Darby, and he pulled away from Hunter. "I can explain, but first…"

Marshals Jones and Raleigh lumbered in carrying an oxygen tank and monitoring equipment, part of their cover as health care workers looking after Savannah.

Connor introduced Jones and Raleigh to Hunter, then the two marshals moved into the living room with their load of equipment, leaving Connor to his family reunion. Even having spent forty minutes with him in the marshals' sedan, having had time for the news to sink in, having conveyed the shocking truth to Hunter, Darby was having trouble wrapping her brain around Connor's resurrection and return. Seeing him in her house again after almost five years seemed odd. Especially since he'd darkened his hair and sported a beard as part of his cover as Sam Orlean.

Her thoughts were scrambling in too many directions at once to sort them out. Her heart thundered in her chest, and all she could do was stare at the answer to her prayers. As if he felt her attention, Connor turned his head and met her gaze. A tingle of sensation, like receiving a static shock, zipped through her as she stared back at him. She hadn't forgotten how handsome he was or how her body responded to his rugged good looks, but seeing him again, in the flesh rather than a two-dimensional photo or mistlike memory, was surreal. She felt as if she'd added a sugar high to a caffeine buzz. All her senses were on overdrive, and her emotions were supercharged, tangled and confusing.

"Darby?" The sound of his voice triggered a cascade of moth-balled memories. Her giddy excitement when he'd asked her for their first date. Nights when he'd held her and crooned her name as they made love. Her horror on that foggy morning more than four and a half years ago when she'd seen the charred skeleton of the hunting camp's cabin.

And the voice of a stranger on the phone just days ago. *I'm sorry, Dahr-by.*

How could he have abandoned her, deceived her for so many years? Hurt and anger returned with the bite of acid in her gut. She swung at him, reacting before she'd even realized what she was doing. "You left me. Lied to me!"

Her balled fist smacked his chest with all the effect of a pillow hitting a brick wall. His muscled body was still every bit as taut and toned as she'd remembered. She swung again, the fury for the lies and pain she'd suffered because of his deception and desertion surging in her, and he absorbed the blow as if he knew he deserved it.

"Darby, stop. What are you doing?" Hunter wrapped

his arms around her and pulled her back. "Calm down, okay? You'll wake Savannah."

Another stab of pain slashed through her. *Savannah.* How many times had she wished Savannah could know her father? And now he was here. To meet his daughter. Yet they couldn't tell Savannah the truth. It wasn't fair. How could she draw her daughter into the deceit? And yet, how could she tell her daughter the truth knowing Connor would leave again, return to WitSec with the marshals in a matter of days, hours? Darby knew too well the pain of losing a father, having him blithely walk out of her life.

Her shoulders shook with sobs as she turned and buried her face in Hunter's shirt. He folded her into a comforting embrace, muttering soothing reassurances.

But no words could calm her. No hug could ease her troubled heart.

Connor was alive, and she had no idea where to start sorting out the tangled web of his lies.

A cold heaviness filled Connor's chest as he watched Hunter hug Darby, soothing her. His brother had been Darby's close friend since college. She'd started hanging out at the Mansfield family home during Hunter's freshman year at Louisiana Tech, and their friendship had never faltered, even when Connor had fallen hard for his brother's friend and started dating Darby the same summer.

That Darby would turn to Hunter for comfort during a difficult time was logical. Still, seeing her in his brother's arms caused a sinking sensation to settle over him. Had the nature of their friendship changed over the years he'd been gone? On the heels of Darby's hostile reception of him, the possibility that his brother had replaced him in Darby's affections shot a chilling spear of jealousy through his heart.

They thought you were dead, he tried to rationalize,

yet the argument fell flat, did nothing to ease the swelling ache of betrayal.

Hunter is a good guy, salt of the earth, the kind of man Darby deserved, his logical mind justified. *But he's your brother. He knows how much you loved her—still love her,* his heart countered.

Connor dragged a hand along his jaw, reeling from the turn of events, stung by Darby's anger. Acid churned in his gut as he tried to sort out his next move. He had to make Darby listen to him. He had to make her understand his reasons for leaving, for letting the U.S. Marshals fake his death.

Shoving down the seesawing grief and frustration that ripped through him, Connor drew a deep breath, searching for control over his emotions. "Please, Darby, just give me a chance to explain. I never wanted to hurt you. Leaving you was the hardest thing I've ever done."

She jerked free of Hunter's arms and spun to face him, her expression cold. "So you said. But the facts remain. You left. You deceived everyone you loved."

He raised his chin and set his jaw. "My family had to believe I was dead in order to convince the Gales—"

"I'm not interested in hearing any more of your excuses. A lie is a lie. You abandoned all of us. Left us to grieve for you!" She folded her arms over her chest and pressed her lips in a thin line. Anger vibrated from her, but a sadness and vulnerability swam in her green eyes, as well. The hurt and questions reflected in her tearful gaze broke his heart. And gave him a shred of hope. Maybe in time she could forgive him for his choices.

He spread his hands in appeal. "Please, Darby, give me a chance. For our daughter's sake."

Darby jerked her chin up, fire filling her eyes, her body

going rigid. "Don't you dare use Savannah as a bargain chip! When you left me, you left her, too."

He took a step toward Darby. "Because you never told me you were pregnant!"

"I didn't know yet!" As soon as the words left her mouth, Darby closed her eyes and huffed a sigh, as if she realized she had no right to hold that argument against him.

"If I had known about the baby…" he started, but couldn't finish.

What would he have done? His life would still have been in danger—and Darby's, too, by association. He would still have wanted to protect her. His handlers in the Witness Security Program would still have argued that she had to believe he was dead to convince Gale. Her disappearance near the time of his faked death would still have sounded too many alarms with the men who hunted him for revenge.

Asking her to leave her family, her job, her friends, her *life* behind to go with him into hiding would have been too great a sacrifice for him to impose on her. Her family was too important to her. Lagniappe was the only home she'd ever known.

She lifted her eyebrows and tipped her head, inviting him to continue. "If you had known…what? What would you have done differently? Would you have loved me more? Would you have stayed for the sake of the baby?"

He heaved a weary sigh. "I honestly don't know."

"If I wasn't enough reason to stay, if somehow you didn't love me enough, then maybe it's just as well you left. I don't want you here just because of our baby." A tear spilled onto her cheek, and his heart cracked. "I needed more than that from you. I deserve more than that."

"It wasn't like that, Darby. I did love you, but—"

A shuffling sound in the hall to his right drew his attention, stopping him midsentence.

A frail-looking girl with only thin wisps of dark hair on her nearly bald head stood in the threshold rubbing her eyes. "Mommy?"

Connor's breath hung in his lungs, and his chest contracted. Tears rushed to his eyes as he took a step toward the girl and dropped to his knees. With a trembling hand, he reached for his daughter's delicate cheek and wheezed, "Savannah."

Chapter 5

Darby froze as Connor knelt before their daughter and stroked her cheek. Seeing the man with whom she'd dreamed of building a future beside the child they'd created together was an image she'd conjured so many times in her mind. And now it was real. But also heartbreaking.

Though she knew Connor would never hurt Savannah, he was a stranger to her. Connor could easily frighten Savannah if he came on too strong, too fast. Darby's heart thumped wildly, and she held her breath, watching.

"Hello, precious girl," he murmured.

Savannah wrinkled her nose and tipped her head as she studied her father and the medical scrubs. "Ah you a doctuh?"

Darby joined Connor in a crouch beside Savannah. "No, baby, this is…uh—" *Daddy.* The name stuck in her throat. Even though Connor was here for the sole purpose of meeting his daughter, the idea of telling Savannah who he was, only to rip her father away within days seemed cruel. She met Connor's golden-eyed gaze, and a shudder raced through her. The tender awe and love in his expression wrenched inside her, tripping over her anger and confusion.

Darby scooped Savannah into her arms quickly and stood, turning her back to him. She needed to set some ground rules with Connor before things went any further.

"What's wrong, Priss? Did we wake you?" She stroked Savannah's head. "Does your tummy hurt?"

Savannah shrugged and stuck her thumb in her mouth. Darby didn't have the heart to fight the bad habit that had reappeared recently. Anything that gave her baby comfort was fine with her. Her daughter craned her neck to peer over Darby's shoulder to Connor. "Where's Kaylee?"

A grin tugged Darby's lips. Savannah loved Kaylee, Grant's new baby. And she had to admit, with his hair darkened, Connor looked a good bit like his older brother. "Kaylee's at home. That's not Uncle Grant."

Darby shot Hunter a glance, looking for help, but Connor's younger brother only shrugged, deferring to her. He jammed his hands in his jeans pockets and sent her a commiserative glance.

She leaned back to meet Savannah's light brown eyes. Connor's eyes. "Remember at the hospital a little while ago, Uncle Hunter told you he had another brother?"

Savannah wrinkled her nose again, clearly skeptical.

From behind her, Connor moved into her peripheral view. The knot of frustration and overwhelming confusion tightened in her belly. "This man is Hunter's other brother."

"The one who died?" Savannah asked, her brow furrowed in obvious confusion.

"Well, that's what we thought. But we were wrong."

Darby rubbed her daughter's arm and forced a grin. "Connor didn't die after all."

"You can call me Uncle Connor," he told Savannah, taking Darby's cue. His baritone voice was pitched low and rolled over her like a warm spring breeze. "It's nice to meet you, Savannah."

When I hold you like this, the rest of the world just fades away. You are my everything, Darby. The echo from her past, spoken in the same deep, lulling tone, washed through her with a bittersweet pang.

Uncle Connor. Another lie. Connor should be more to Savannah than the uncle who passed through town once when she was almost four years old.

Savannah's *father* was alive. When she remembered the call that started today's incredible events and brought Connor here to meet his little girl, she was hit with a fresh onslaught of emotion. Fragile hope. Wary joy. Tentative expectation.

Could Connor be the key to saving Savannah's life? Darby couldn't help the tiny catch in her breath when she considered the prospect of Connor's marrow healing their daughter.

Connor shifted his gaze to Darby, and his face grew serious and direct, his eyes blazing with a purpose and passion. Clearly he'd read in her face where her thoughts had strayed. He'd always had an uncanny knack for reading her. Years ago, she'd believed that synergy meant they were soul mates. But then he'd left her.

Savannah patted her mother's face, claiming her attention. "I want some juice."

Darby shook off the painful memories, hoping Savannah wouldn't pick up on the tension in the room. Clearing her throat, she asked, "How do you ask for juice?"

Savannah rolled her eyes. Forget the teen years. Her

daughter was already a drama queen. With an exaggerated sigh, Savannah said, "May I have juice? Please!" She grasped her throat, adding, "I'm *so* thirsty!" Then, obviously an encore for their guest, Savannah wilted in Darby's arms as if she'd passed out from thirst.

Connor grinned, clearly amused by Savannah's melodrama.

"Someone's been hanging out with Peyton," Hunter said with a laugh. "I swear, where do my nieces get all this angst and theatrics?"

Savannah perked up hearing the name of Grant's oldest daughter. "Peyton is my cousin. She's six." She fumbled to hold up six fingers.

"Six," Connor repeated, his expression honestly stunned as he absorbed the truth of how his niece had aged in his absence.

"Come on, silly goose. Let's get your juice." She cast a glance to Connor as she headed into the kitchen. "Would you like to join us for a drink?"

"Absolutely." He and Hunter fell in step behind them. "What kind of juice are we having?"

"Gwape!"

"My favorite."

"Mine, too!" Savannah grinned, her eyes sparkling as Darby helped her climb into her booster seat at the table.

Darby bit her bottom lip, pleased to see how comfortable Savannah seemed around Connor, but also troubled. Her daughter adored Hunter and Grant. If she became as attached to Connor as she was to her uncles, Savannah would be heartbroken when Connor left.

She paused with her hand on the refrigerator door, a stabbing ache lancing her chest. *When Connor left...* The cruel truth was, Connor was leaving again, going back into hiding with WitSec. And whether she hated him for his lies and resented him for his desertion, she would still be devastated when he returned to his new life.

While Darby poured juice for them, Connor pulled Hunter into Darby's mudroom. "Did you sleep with her?"

Hunter faced him, a startled look lifting his brow. "Did you really just ask me that?"

Connor firmed his jaw. "Don't you think I have the right to know?"

His brother squared his shoulders. "I won't apologize for being Darby's friend, for giving her the support and comfort she's needed the past few years. Or for being a father figure to my niece. Losing you was hell on Darby. Being a single mother, juggling work and a baby has been tough, and now, with Savannah sick—"

"Answer the question, Hunter."

His brother paused, looked away and sighed. "If you were anyone else, and the circumstances were any different, I'd tell you it's none of your business. But—"

"Did you sleep with her?" Connor grated impatiently.

Hunter propped a hand on the washing machine and narrowed a glare on him. "*No.* We've never had that kind of relationship. You know that." A muscle in his jaw ticked, and he glanced away for a moment, a telling gesture, before facing Connor again. "But I asked her to marry me."

Connor stiffened. "What?"

"When she told me she was pregnant…" Hunter swiped a hand over his mouth. "We thought you were dead, bro. I didn't want her to feel she had to face being a mother alone. I thought I was doing the right thing."

"What'd she say?" Connor held his breath.

"I'd think that was obvious. She said she didn't want me to give up the chance to find my soul mate and spend my life with someone I loved. She said it didn't feel right to marry me when she was still in love with my brother."

Connor drew his shoulders back and scoffed. "Still in love? You could have fooled me." He glanced back toward the kitchen, remembering Darby's angry outburst.

"Can you blame her for being mad?" Hunter jammed his hand on his hip and arched a dark brown eyebrow. "She's got a right to be hurt. You've been lying to her with your absence for more than four years. Where have you been? How could you trick us all into thinking you were dead?"

Connor sighed and scrubbed a hand down his face. "Long story. I promise you'll get the details soon, but right now, I need to get back in there and drink juice with my daughter."

Hunter huffed. "You mean your *niece*." Sarcasm dripped from Hunter's tone. "Why didn't you tell her the truth?"

"That was Darby's call. I'd love for Savannah to know who I am. I want to hear her call me Daddy more than anything. But I won't hurt her, either. And when I have to leave again—"

Hunter straightened, his expression startled. "You're not staying?"

Connor sighed, a hollow ache throbbing behind his ribs. "I can't. If I blow my cover, all of you could be put at risk." He took a step toward his younger brother. "For what it's worth, I'm sorry. For the pain I caused you. All of the family. If I'd thought there was another way…"

Hunter's expression eased, his brow furrowing. "Mom took it especially hard."

Connor dropped his gaze to his feet. "I can imagine." Then, glancing back up, he met his brother's eyes. "How are Mom and Dad?"

"They're doin' all right. They look older. First they lost you. Now Savannah is sick. It's been difficult for them."

Hunter shook his head sorrowfully, then sent him a half grin. "Kaylee's been a bright spot, though."

"Kaylee?" Connor asked, recalling Savannah asking about the girl.

A wider smile split Hunter's face. "Kaylee is Grant and Tracy's new baby. She's two months old and cute as can be. Savannah adores her." He shrugged, a sappy grin on his face. "We all do. Peyton dotes on her baby sister, and Grant is over the moon. Tracy miscarried twice in three years before they had Kaylee. So naturally we're all thrilled for them."

Connor smiled, remembering how his older brother had gushed when his first daughter had been born. *Geez,* he thought, *Peyton is six years old now. Almost seven.*

"That's awesome. No one deserves it more. He's a great dad."

Hunter held Connor's gaze for a moment, then stepped forward to give Connor another bear hug. "We've missed you, Con."

Connor had to battle the surge of emotion in his throat before he could respond. "It's good to be back." *Even if I can't stay...*

Pulling away, Hunter hitched his head toward the kitchen. "Now get in there and get to know your own daughter."

My daughter. His pulse hiccupped in his chest as he stepped back into the kitchen.

"Sit by me, Uncle Connuh!" Savannah patted the table next to her.

"I'd be honored." He pulled out the chair beside his daughter and took a sip of the grape juice Darby had waiting for him. Savannah already had a purple mustache from her juice, and Connor chuckled. "Looks like you're wearing your juice."

"Oops!" She giggled and swiped at her face with her arm.

His own beard and mustache, prosthetics he'd put on that morning with Raleigh's help to aid in his disguise, itched. He looked forward to pulling off the faux facial hair at the first chance he got.

"Napkin," Darby said from the kitchen.

Savannah reached for a napkin, her hand flapping against the table when she came up short. Connor handed her one and pulled another for himself. He found himself staring at the fragile little girl he'd helped create, marveling at every freckle, every precocious gesture. And worrying over every obvious sign of her illness. The hair loss, the shadows beneath her gold eyes, the red needle marks and bruising on her arms where she'd obviously been stuck for blood draws and chemotherapy treatment.

Leukemia. His gut twisted. His baby had cancer. How had Darby managed these past months with that dark diagnosis? Bile churned inside him. He should have been here, should have been with Darby, sharing the burden, supporting her.

Hell, he should have been here for Savannah's birth, her first steps, her first words. When his sinuses burned with his rising grief, he gritted his back teeth, forcing down the sting of tears and regret. He hated all the milestones he'd missed, but he couldn't let his daughter see his sorrow.

Someone pounded on Darby's back door, then threw it open with a crash. "Darby!"

Connor stiffened, recognizing the voice.

"Grandma!" Savannah chirped.

"Darby, is it true? Is Connor—" His mother burst into the kitchen from the mudroom. With a gasp, she staggered to a stop when she spotted him and wheezed, "Alive."

Chapter 6

Connor shoved to his feet, caught off guard by his mother's arrival. "Mom, how—?"

"Look, Gwandma!" Savannah pointed to him, beaming proudly. "It's my new uncle Connuh."

Tears puddled in Julia Mansfield's eyes, and she raised a trembling hand to her mouth. "Oh, my God. Praise the Lord! My sweet boy."

She rushed forward, folding him in a hug. He squeezed her back, both overjoyed to see her and confused by her appearance.

"But how did you know?" Connor divided an irritated glance between Hunter and Darby over his mother's head. One of the two had to have told her, breaking their promise and blowing his cover.

Darby hurried into the breakfast area from the kitchen, frowning. "Hunter, I told you not to say anything!"

Hunter raised his palms, shaking his head. "Don't look

at me. I didn't—" He stopped suddenly, his face going slack as he groaned. "Oh, wait." He winced and sent Connor a guilty grimace. "I texted her earlier." He looked to Darby. "After you got that call from the doctor's office about the DNA test results."

Darby's shoulders sagged, and Connor blew out a frustrated breath. His mother pulled back from her embrace and gave him a puzzled look. "Why wouldn't you tell me? What's going on?"

"Uh, Savannah, honey." Darby pulled back the girl's chair and lifted her down "Why don't you take Uncle Hunter to your room for a while?"

"Mom texted me this morning wanting to know when Savannah would be going home," Hunter said, still explaining. "I told her you'd left. Told her about the call. I—"

Outside, car doors slammed, and Connor tensed.

"That'll be your father and Grant," his mother said. "I called the office on my way here, and they said they'd be right behind me."

"Julia? Darby?" his father called as he and Grant hurried through the back door. They stopped and scanned the room full of faces, their expressions eager. "Where is he?"

In seconds, the volume in the kitchen rose exponentially as everyone began talking on top of each other and emotions swelled.

"Connor! We thought you were dead!"

"I don't understand. Where have you been?"

"Mommy, can Uncle Connuh play with me? Mommy?"

"Hunter, please take Savannah to her room."

"Honest, Con, I texted her before I knew—"

From the living room, Raleigh and Jones appeared, clearly having heard the commotion. "What the hell?" Raleigh growled. "Sam, who are these people? And what part of 'you can't tell anyone you're alive' did you interpret as 'have a welcome home party?'"

Her eyes wide, Savannah shrank behind Darby as the two large men in scrubs, strangers to her, stormed in and barked at him. The fright in his daughter's eyes was the last straw.

Stan Mansfield, Connor's father, stepped toward Raleigh, his shoulders back. "I could ask the same of you. Who—?"

Connor put his thumb and finger in his mouth and whistled for quiet. "That's enough!"

Everyone settled down, facing him with startled looks.

"You're scaring Savannah," he said, casting a warning gaze to the offending adults. Moving to kneel by his daughter, he tugged lightly on her sleeve. "Hey, sweetie, sorry about all that noise. I believe your mom asked you to take Uncle Hunter to your room for a while. Why don't you do that now?"

Savannah bobbed her head, then asked softly, "Will you play with me, too?"

He smiled and stroked her arm. "I would love to. Let me finish talking to the grown-ups, and I'll be there as soon as I can. Okay?"

Hunter took his cue and lifted Savannah into his arms, tickling her side. "Come on, princess, I was hoping I'd get the chance to kick your tail at Chutes and Ladders."

"No, I'm gonna kick your tail!" Savannah said with a grin.

Darby sent him a grudging half smile. "Thanks."

He pushed to his feet and squeezed Darby's arm. "We're on the same side."

"Would someone please tell me what's going on?" his mother asked, her voice cracking. "Connor, who are these men? Why did they call you Sam? Where have you been all these years?" She paused and wiped at her eyes, then in a lower voice asked, "Are you in the CIA?"

Connor chuckled as he faced his mother. "No, Mom. Not the CIA." He took a deep breath. "I'm in WitSec."

Connor spent the next hour explaining his situation to his family, despite the marshals' objections. "They might as well hear the truth," he'd countered. "They know I'm alive, and the best way to reign in the situation now is to lay out the stakes, give them the background and our reasoning for staging my death."

When Jones scowled and paced the kitchen, mumbling sourly, Connor had quipped, "Unless you'd rather erase their memory with one of those *Men in Black* flashy sticks. You have one of those, right?"

"Can I tell Tracy?" Grant asked. "I don't like the idea of keeping something this big from my wife. She won't say anything."

"And what about my family? My mom and sisters?" Darby asked. "They should know. Especially since Savannah knows him as her uncle Connor. If he does end up donating his marrow, I'd think it would come out."

"No!" Raleigh said with a huff of frustration. "We need to shut this down. It doesn't go any further than this room." He pointed at Connor, adding, "And you should have kept to your cover with the little girl. Big mistake telling her your name was Connor."

"I told her that because she recognized the family resemblance. She knew I was a Mansfield brother before I opened my mouth." Connor tapped his fist on the kitchen table and divided a look between the marshals. "Here's the deal. Half of the family knows I'm alive. Protecting my cover made sense when we thought I could slip into town, meet with the doctor and get out again without anyone knowing the truth. I didn't consider the fact that my

DNA test would rat me out or that the doctor's office would call Darby about the discrepancy in what she'd told them about Savannah's father."

He rubbed a hand along his cheek, weighing his options, and when he encountered the prosthetic beard, he groaned and peeled it off. "At this point, I can't see any point in keeping up the charade. I say let Grant tell Tracy. Let Darby tell her family. They need to be aware of the potential threat so that they can take necessary precautions. And as Darby pointed out, if I do donate my marrow to Savannah, it will be harder to keep my identity secret."

"You really think these men, the Gale brothers, will come after you?" his mother asked.

"I do. They think I betrayed them."

"They have a history of going after people they feel have crossed them," Jones said, his jaw tense. "We have to take the threats they made against Sam seriously."

"His name is Connor," Darby said with a defiant glare.

"Not anymore," Jones countered.

"All right." Connor raised his hands, signaling for a ceasefire. "I think, despite our intentions, the horse is out of the barn as far as my cover goes."

"He's right." Jones gave Raleigh a level look, then turned an accusing glare at Darby.

She recognized the accusation and sat taller, stiffening, her expression defensive as she sputtered, "I didn't—the doctor's office called me and—how was I to know—"

"It's not your fault. No one's blaming you." Connor sent Jones a hard look and put a supportive hand on Darby's arm, which she jerked away. "But you raise another good point. Savannah's doctor needs to know the truth. My biological connection to Savannah could be relevant to Savannah's care. Also however many members of her staff as needed to contain the speculation already circulating in the office."

Raleigh rocked back on two legs of his chair, scrubbing both hands over his face. "God bless America, Sam. What happened to staying in town only long enough to talk to the kid's doctor then getting the hell outta Dodge? You can make the donation from Dallas, can't you?"

All eyes swung toward Connor, and his pulse rose, torn between what he knew would keep his family safe and his selfish desire to stay and get to know his daughter, patch things up with Darby, spend precious time with his family.

"Yeah, the doctor said I could donate from Dallas, if I proved a close enough match." A stir of reaction interrupted him, sighs of disappointment from his parents, grunts of satisfaction from the agents. He looked to Darby, needing some measure of where her heart was. Her jaw was tight with stubborn anger, but her green eyes were full of pain and discontent. "But she also said the ideal arrangement, the way she preferred, was for me to be here."

As he repeated the doctor's words, a certainty washed through him, a resolve that settled the debate warring inside him. "I want only the best for Savannah. If I can be my daughter's donor, I'll do it from here. Even if it is only marginally better logistically, I want ideal circumstances for my little girl."

Darby's expression was conflicted. The struggle between gratitude and resentment, fear and hope, grief and joy was plain in her eyes. Connor's chest ached for the hurt he'd caused her, the doubts and bitterness he was responsible for.

Raleigh shook his head, clearly unhappy with Connor's decision. "Do you understand what you're risking?"

"Of course I do. And I'm not saying I plan to wave a red flag in front of Gale Industries. I'll lay low, take precautions, continue wearing a disguise in public." He flicked his hand toward the fake beard in front of him. "Whatever it takes." He leaned forward, drilling Raleigh with a hard stare and jabbing his finger into the table. "But I need you to protect my family. I need you to make sure the Gales don't get anywhere near Darby or Savannah or any of the people I love."

"Our job is to protect *you*," Raleigh countered. "And the best way to do that is to get you back to Dallas and try to minimize the exposure from the cracks in your cover."

"I'm not leaving Lagniappe until I've done all I can to save Savannah." He hoped his tone conveyed his determination on that point. "Maybe that will be tomorrow, if I'm not a close enough match to her. But if I am, I need to know you'll do everything in your power to keep my family safe while I'm here."

Jones drummed the table with his thumb. "We're only two people, man. We're good, but we're not superhuman. We'll do what we can to minimize the threat to your family, but we can't be everywhere. You're still our priority, the witness in WitSec, and where our efforts have to be focused."

"So bring in more men. Or I'll hire private security."

Jones raised a hand. "No. No outside hires." He glanced briefly to Raleigh for some silent confirmation or perhaps giving him a chance to object. "We'll see about getting a little backup, but the department is stretched kinda thin these days."

Connor's father, Stan, had been taking in the conversation from the opposite end of the table, his arms folded over his chest and his intense scrutiny shifting from one speaker to another. Now he pushed his chair back and stood. "Bring in extra men if you want, but don't underestimate the ability of the Mansfield men to protect our own."

Grant had been leaning against the kitchen counter. Now he stepped forward, nodding. "That's right. Every one of the men in this family is trained in firearms and licensed to carry concealed. Dad spent fifteen years in the army, and Hunter spent five years in the reserves. I've been hunting since I was twelve."

"What's the saying?" Connor's mother asked. "Forewarned is forearmed."

The marshals exchanged another unreadable look.

"Well, being alert to problems will certainly help, but these men are professional killers, not common street thugs." Raleigh rose from the table. "Let me make a few calls, see about getting an extra team down here."

"Then we should head back to the hotel soon," Jones said, sending Connor a direct look.

"A hotel?" Julia said, her tone full of dismay, as if Jones had suggested they were sleeping in the gutter. "But this is Connor's home. He should stay with his family."

"We have to be *with him* in order to guard him." Jones raised one eyebrow as if driving home his point.

"And we have to be with my family in order to keep them safe." Connor sent the marshal a challenging stare. "I'm staying here. With Darby and my daughter."

Darby's head jerked up, and her gaze clashed with his. "You're what?"

"I want to know you're safe. If somehow word of my return has leaked beyond this family and the doctor's office, which is a real possibility, I don't want you here alone. What better protection than two U.S. Marshals and the man who'd die defending you?"

Darby's cheeks paled, and her eyes widened.

Connor reached for her, and stroking her chin, he whispered, "Don't look so surprised, Dar. I already died once to protect you. I'd do it again, for real, if needed."

"Oh, Connor," his mother said, her voice choked. "Don't say that! It's bad luck!" Her hand fluttered to her chest where she rubbed the cross charm on her necklace.

Darby huffed an exasperated breath and flattened her hands on the table. "Looks like the decision's made for me." She pushed to her feet. "Marshals, you can stay in the guest room. The decor is a bit juvenile, since I had in mind having my nieces and nephews staying with me when I decorated it. But the twin beds are new and should be comfortable. You—" she faced Connor, a spark of ire lighting her jade gaze "—can sleep on the couch."

Jones chuckled under his breath. Raleigh opened his mouth as if to protest, then snapped it closed. Scowling, he jammed his hands in his pockets and jangled his keys. "I feel a FUBAR in the making."

Darby pushed her chair back under the table and headed for the door. "I'm going to check on Savannah."

Savannah. Thoughts of his sweet daughter lifted Connor's spirits, which had taken a dive while discussing the serious security threats to his family. As concerned as he was by the unplanned turn of events, he couldn't regret having time, brief as it may be, with his daughter. And no matter how angry Darby was with him for his past choices, this unexpected time with her gave him a chance, however remote, of healing the wounds he'd caused her.

Chapter 7

James Gale positioned his hands over his son's, adjusting the boy's grip on the golf club. "Like this. Keep your wrists straight."

Billy did as instructed, then tipped his head back to look up at his father. "Like this?"

James grinned proudly and stepped back. "Perfect. Now swing away! In the hole!"

"Excuse me, Mr. Gale?"

James spun to face the man who approached, his jaw tight. "Not now!" He turned back to watch Billy's swing.

The chubby man he recognized as one of his brother's thugs persisted. "I'm sorry to disturb you, but—"

Billy glanced up from his stance with a startled look, interrupting his address of the ball.

James lifted a hand. "I'm sorry, Billy. Hold on." He pivoted to the interloper, his body taut. "Do you not know how *rude* it is to disturb a golfer as he takes his swing?"

"I—"

"Did you not hear me say, *Not now?*"

"It's important."

"So is my time with my son."

"But—"

James pointed a finger at the man and shot him a glare that made lesser men shiver in their shoes. "Silence. My son is taking his swing." He turned back to Billy. "Go ahead. Firm wrists."

With an uneasy glance to the chubby man behind his father, Billy addressed the ball again, swung and hit a beautiful drive that dropped onto the putting green and rolled within five feet of the hole.

James cheered and slapped his son on the back. "That's the way! Beautiful!"

Billy beamed as he stooped to pull his tee from the grass, and James faced his brother's lackey. He hoisted his bag of clubs on his shoulder. "Walk with me."

The man fell in step beside James as he strolled down the cart path toward the putting green. "Victor sent me."

"I assumed as much." James pulled off his golf gloves and poked them in his back pocket.

"Something happened today at Mansfield Construction."

James gave Victor's man—*Hollister,* that was his name—a side glance, and conflicting emotions roiled inside him. "Mansfield. There's a name I haven't heard in a while."

Connor Mansfield had betrayed his family, given testimony that sent Pop to prison. But he'd also once been a friend of James's, had been to James's house for barbecues. And had saved Billy's life when his boy was little more than a toddler.

An image of Connor Mansfield dragging Billy's limp

body from the swimming pool flickered in James's mind before he shoved the disturbing memory aside.

"What happened?" James asked.

"Victor has a mole at Mansfield Construction, a guy he pays to report anything unusual."

"Seems a waste of money." James sidestepped an ant-hill and gave Hollister another glance. "Connor Mansfield has been dead for years, and we have no interest in his family's company."

"Well, that's the thing. Victor's contact at Mansfield Construction says a call came in this morning that got Connor's daddy and big brother all riled up. They took off outta the office real quick, and when someone asked if there was a problem, the daddy smiled and said, 'Not a problem. But maybe a miracle.'"

James waited for Hollister to continue and, when he didn't, James glared at him. "That's it? That's what you thought was so important that you interrupted my time with my son?"

"I… Victor thought you should know." Hollister took a wheezy breath before adding, "Also the family all went to Darby Kent's house. Connor Mansfield's widow."

James tensed. "She's not his widow. They were never married. Do your research." He sent a scathing glare to the chubby man. "How do you know where they went?"

"As soon as his mole reported in, Victor followed up at the senior Mansfield's house. He followed Mrs. Mansfield to Darby's and parked down the road to monitor the situation." Hollister gave a smoker's wheeze, out of breath from the quick pace James set. "Outta the blue…all the rest of the family…started arriving. Along with a home health van."

"Her daughter is sick. I already knew that." James watched Billy trot up to the green and examine the lie of his ball. His gut tightened, knowing how he'd feel if either of his children were diagnosed with a fatal illness. He stopped walking and faced the chubby thug, thinking. "Do you think something happened with the girl?"

Hollister shrugged, coughed. "Could be. But…they looked happy. Excited."

"So they got good news about the girl." James slid the bag of clubs to the ground and selected a putter. "That fits with the father and brother saying there'd been a miracle."

"I guess."

James arched an eyebrow. "Anything else?"

Hollister wheezed again, gulping a breath. "Yeah. Victor thinks he recognized one of the home health guys. He thinks it could be Connor Mansfield."

The first tickle of suspicion crawled up James's back. He tapped his finger on his putter, watching Billy squat, eyeing the hole as he lined up his shot. "Interesting. He get any pictures of this home health guy?"

"Nothing clear. He kept his head down…" *Wheeze.* "Wore shades."

"Is this guy still at Darby's?"

Hollister shrugged. "Last I heard."

James grunted, stalked toward the green. Hollister followed, and James swung the club up, poking the chubby man in the gut. "We're done here. Get clear pictures of the home health guy when he leaves, follow him if you have to. I want him ID'd. Today."

The odds that Connor was still alive were slim, but he knew better than to take a chance and be proved wrong.

"Yes, sir." Hollister nodded and turned to leave.

"And Hollister?" James sneered in disgust. "You're pathetic. Get in shape, or you'll be dead before you're fifty."

When Darby reached her daughter's bedroom, Savannah was lying on the floor next to the Chutes and Ladders board, her arm pillowing her head, her eyelids half closed.

"I think someone needs a nap," she said, squatting beside Savannah and patting her daughter's back.

Hunter stretched his arms over his head and gave a theatrical yawn. "Yeah, I do. But I promised Miss Priss I'd play with her."

Darby gave Hunter a lopsided grin. "Well, you're in luck, because I'm calling a time-out on this game. C'mon, Priss, Hunter needs a nap, so why don't you get in your bed for a while, too?"

Savannah whined sleepily and looked past her mother to the doorway. "I want to play with Uncle Connuh."

Glancing over her shoulder, she found that Connor had followed her from the kitchen. Her pulse jumped, and her body grew warm from the mere sight of him, his broad shoulders filling the door and his square jaw and full lips accenting a face straight out of her sexiest dreams. She'd never been able to resist his magnetic allure, not since the first day she met him while visiting Hunter's family on a college break.

And now all that magnetism and sex appeal was going to be living under her roof for some undetermined time. Heaven help her, she couldn't fall for him again. The prospect made her hands sweat and a flutter of nerves batter her gut. She'd do well to remember how he'd disappeared from her life without a word. How he'd let her believe he was dead. He'd made the choice to let her grieve, to keep her in the dark about his plans for WitSec. She needed to hold on to the hurt and anger his actions stirred in her. Maybe then she could protect herself from the pain of his leaving again. Because he'd made it clear he would leave, he would return with the marshals to WitSec. He would walk away like he had before.

Turning back to Savannah, she forcibly quashed the piercing pain that slashed through her when she thought of Connor disappearing again. She managed a smile for Savannah and scooped her little girl into her arms. "You can play with Connor after you rest. But you've had a big day, and your body needs sleep."

"Later, Priss," Hunter said, blowing her a kiss and heading out. Savannah smiled and pretended to catch the kiss in her small hand.

Lifting Savannah was far easier than it should have been. Her daughter had been small for her age before cancer and chemotherapy had diminished her appetite and ravaged her small body. Savannah was thin to the point of feeling frail in Darby's arms, as if she would snap like a twig with the slightest pressure to her tiny bones.

She heard Connor shuffle into the room as she put Savannah in bed and arranged the covers around her. "There you go. All snuggled in."

Darby pressed a kiss to Savannah's forehead and tucked Benny, her ragged stuffed bunny, in beside her. At Savannah's feet, their brown tabby, Toby, slept curled in a tight ball.

Savannah sat up and leaned down to press her cheek to the cat's warm furry body. She gave Toby a squeeze, giggling. "Toby's sleepy, too."

"Gently, sweetheart. Don't hurt poor Toby." Darby demonstrated how to stroke the cat's fur softly, silently thanking Toby for his relaxed, easygoing nature. Never once, no matter how roughly Savannah played with him, had Toby ever raised a claw to her daughter. Toby had been Darby's companion since college, through years of struggle and life changes, a steadfast and loyal friend.

Savannah followed Darby's example, her small hand scratching Toby behind the ears. Savoring the attention,

Toby stretched and rolled on his back, exposing his belly in a show of ultimate feline trust.

Giggling again, Savannah wiggled her fingers against the tabby's belly. "Silly Toby!"

"And silly Savannah," Darby said, tickling her daughter's ribs. "It's sleepy time for you, too. Not playtime, missy." She scooped the cat up with one hand, making room for Savannah. Once Savannah was settled, she put the cat down again, and Toby cuddled groggily against her legs.

"Good boy, Toby," Darby said, stroking the cat's head. Her cat had kept Savannah company through long hours of discomfort and fatigue, and he distracted her from the pain and nausea of her chemo treatments. Just as he'd comforted her as best he could when Connor died four and a half years ago. Except he hadn't died….

"Sleep tight, sweetie," Darby whispered, and she kissed her daughter's head.

"Have a good nap." Connor brushed against her as he stepped forward to give Savannah a kiss on the forehead.

Darby swallowed hard, fighting the tears of joy that tightened her throat and the grip of hurt and anger that squeezed her lungs. Where did she begin to sort through all the revelations this morning? In just hours, her life, which had been tumultuous enough dealing with a sick little girl, had been turned topsy-turvy. And the source of the new tumult was standing beside her, flesh and blood, smelling like cedar, sunshine and tempting man.

Her pulse ramped up double-time as sweet memories assailed her of tangling limbs with Connor while his unique spicy scent surrounded her. When Connor lingered, staring affectionately at Savannah as she drifted to sleep, Darby planted a hand in his chest and backed him toward the door.

Through his shirt, Darby could feel the steady life-affirming thump of his heart and comforting warmth of his body heat. His taut muscles were a tantalizing reminder of how his hard strength had felt beneath her hands as they made love.

Huffing her frustration with herself and her traitorous thoughts, she pulled Savannah's door almost closed. She left it cracked open so that Toby could get out if he wanted and so that she could hear Savannah if she called out.

Lifting a glare to Connor, she said, "We need to talk. Alone."

Darby took Connor by the arm and guided him toward the back of the house, away from the prying eyes and ears of his family and the marshals. She ducked into her bedroom, and he followed, keeping his gaze averted from the bed where he'd made slow, passionate love to Darby so many times…where Savannah had likely been conceived.

Samples of her artwork, framed charcoal portraits and canvasses with oil-painted nature scenes, hung on her walls and lay in stacks on her work desk. The layer of dust on her art supplies spoke for how long it had been since she'd indulged in her passion.

He faced her, and Darby's hurt and anger rolled off her in waves. "Why didn't you tell me about the death threats back then? Why…" She swallowed hard. "Why didn't you trust me with the truth?"

Connor lowered himself on the front edge of a stuffed chair and leaned forward, his forearms braced on his thighs and his fingers steepled between his knees. "Originally, I didn't tell you about the threats because I didn't want to worry you. Once the U.S. Marshals' office got involved and I agreed to go into WitSec, everything happened so fast."

"Didn't it matter to you that the choices you were making affected my life, too? We were supposed to be a team! We were going to get married!"

He raked his hair back and shook his head sadly. "I know that, but I was warned that any leaks to my friends or family could blow the whole operation."

"Your faked death, you mean." Resentment was heavy in her tone as she dropped on the bed and tucked her feet under her.

He nodded, pained by her anger, understandable though it was. "You had to believe I was dead for it to work. Any hint that you weren't truly in mourning, that you had any contact with me would have tipped the Gales off."

Darby pulled a pillow in front of her like a shield and dug her fingers into it. Her mouth was pressed in a hard, unhappy line, reflecting her rising ire. "So my anguish over losing you was part of your plan? Part of the whole act to fool the world?"

He pinched the bridge of his nose then sent her a pleading look. "Darby, I've said I'm sorry. I hated hurting you, hurting my parents and brothers. But my death had to be believable. For your safety. If we could have done things differently—"

"Why couldn't you? You didn't even *ask me* if I wanted to go with you. You abandoned me!" She paused long enough to regain control over the warble in her voice and to blink back the tears that crept to her eyes.

"I couldn't ask you to go. How could I ask you to give up everything and disappear?" he asked, meeting her gaze evenly. "You would have had to leave your family, give up your job, your friends, your art—everything about your life—to go into hiding with me. You can't even keep the same hobbies, Darby. People can track you through associations, memberships, purchases..." He sighed, grief tightening his lungs. "Could you have walked away from your family, the way your father did?"

Fury flashed like lightning in her eyes. She jerked her feet to the floor, bristling. "That's not fair! Don't you bring him into this!"

"But it's relevant. You know it's true." His gaze held no malice, only brutal honesty and compassion. "Would you have said yes to me, Darby? Could you have given up art, your sketching to be with me? Could you have abandoned your family to be with me?"

A painful knot swelled in Darby's throat, and bitterness squeezed her chest, stealing her breath. She batted at the tears that tickled her cheeks. The idea of giving up her sisters, her mother...not to mention Hunter and the rest of the Mansfields, who were like family, plus her art, her job, her friends...

It was a lot to process. She stared at him blankly, staggered by the enormity of what he was asking, even if hypothetically. And realizing that everything he'd described was the very choice he'd made—to protect her. One taut second followed another. The tick of her antique alarm clock counted the passing moments like hammering heartbeats in the damning silence.

Connor's face fell, his dark eyebrows snapping together in a frown. "That's what I thought."

Darby raised her chin. "I haven't answered yet."

"Exactly. It would have been an excruciating decision for you, and I couldn't force that kind of choice on you. That would have been cruelly selfish, and I loved you too much to put that burden on you."

Darby squared her shoulders, trying—and failing—to keep her tangled, turbulent emotions at bay. "No, selfish was taking the choice from me. You always have to be the one in control. But I deserved the chance to have a say in our future!"

He held her gaze, his face reflecting deep pain tinged with regret. Finally he blinked and looked away, his forehead creasing with consternation. "I wanted to tell you the truth, even if you couldn't come with me, but the marshals were adamant. Your grief had to be real to be convincing, or the Gales would have suspected a hoax."

She folded her arms over her chest and shook her head. "And now you're back and taking choices from me again."

He frowned. "How's that?"

She laughed without humor. "You and your glorified babysitters moving into my house without so much as a 'may we?' or second thought as to how the disruption to our routine will affect my daughter."

"*Our* daughter." His tone was warm and gentle, but the simple words had the effect of a kick to her gut.

Darby raised her chin, hot tears sliding onto her cheeks. Her own father had walked away without considering her feelings. Knowing Connor had chosen to leave her once, regardless of his reasons, left the question of whether he could, like her father, abandon her again. Clearly that was his intention after the transplant. She had to remember that in moments when her heart tried to forget. "It takes more than sperm and a five-minute visit when she's four to call yourself her father."

"I know that, Darby," he said with a ragged sigh.

The pain that darkened his eyes shot a heavy sense of contrition through her, and she wished she could retract the waspish retort. Her shoulders drooped, and she rubbed the achy muscles at the back of her neck. "I'm sorry. That was uncalled for."

Connor rose from the chair where he'd been perched

and moved toward her. Her stomach bunched as he approached, and her nerves jangled with carnal awareness.

He stopped inches from her, and with his fingers tipping her head up, he met her gaze. The tenderness in his caramel eyes chipped at the icy anger she'd put around her heart.

"Every decision I've made, good or bad, I made because I thought, at the time, it was the right one. Even when the choice was hard—even painful to follow through—I did what I thought I had to, what I thought was best. Not for me. For *you*."

Her knees shook, and she had to close her eyes, steel herself as her defenses weakened.

"Even now I'm trying to do what's right. I want to do what's best for the people I love, but the variables keep changing. I'm figuring this out as I go along, Darby, but the one constant in this whole mess has always been you. You, and now Savannah, will always be my first priority."

A tiny sound, like a wounded bird, squeaked from her throat, and she pulled her chin free of his grasp. Connor gritted his teeth in frustration, feeling her shutting him out, holding him at arm's length. Her closed eyes and rigid posture screamed that he couldn't say anything that would make a difference, given her mood.

He balled his fists, wanting to hit something, wanting to yell, wanting to shake her out of her righteous indignation. Wanting to hold her and never let go. Wanting to erase the past four and a half years and start over. Wanting to take her to bed and make love to her until she remembered what they'd meant to each other.

Instead he stood there, shaking, staring at her, floundering as the seconds ticked by.

"Darby," he started again, and when she turned away, spine stiff, he snapped. He took her by the arms and backed her against the nearest wall. The move surprised her, and when her mouth opened in a startled gasp, he captured her lips with his.

For a moment, she was clearly stunned, but she quickly recovered her faculties and shoved against his chest. She tried to wiggle her mouth free, but he framed her head with firm hands and deepened the kiss. He poured every scrap of frayed emotion and four plus years of longing and heartache into his kiss. With the caress of his lips, he told her everything she refused to hear him verbalize. He showed her what he couldn't find words to say.

For several seconds, she struggled, whimpering a half-hearted protest. But before long, her shoving hands were clinging to his shirt, and her lips were responding to his, matching his fervor. Her fingers threaded through his hair, and her tongue parted his lips, seeking his. Her arms clung, her lips claimed, and her protests morphed to mewls of pleasure.

A fresh hope wove through Connor's tangled feelings, and relief loosened the knots of fear and frustration and four-year-old pain. He savored the flavor of her kiss, even sweeter now than he'd remembered, and his body hummed to life with a desire that had only grown keener over the long months without her.

"Oh, Darby, I've missed you. I've dreamed of this moment every day since I left," he murmured as he kissed her face. And tasted tears.

He jerked back to study her expression, and beneath his hands, her shoulders shook.

"Darby?" He wiped a fat drop as it rolled down her cheek.

She only shook her head and, fisting her hands in his hair, dragged him back down for another soul-deep kiss. He lost himself in her embrace, shutting out everything but the press of her lips, the warmth of her body and the pure pleasure of holding her again.

Until a loud rap on the door yanked him back to reality.

"Darby? You in there?" Hunter called from the hall.

Beneath his hands Darby tensed, and she turned her head, breaking their kiss. "Um...yeah. Is Savannah okay?"

She scooted out of his arms, and disappointment jabbed him beneath his ribs. He didn't want to let her go, didn't want to share her with the world again. After years of waiting and wanting, these few moments alone with her weren't nearly enough. As she sidled away, Darby raised a trembling hand to her mouth, then lifted her eyes to meet his. Her expression echoed the regret he felt, and his heart stuttered.

"Dr. Reed's on the phone," Hunter said. "She says it's urgent."

Darby yanked open the bedroom door to take the phone from Hunter, but when he held it out to her, Marshal Raleigh hurried up behind Hunter and grabbed the cell phone from him.

She bristled, trying to snatch the phone from the marshal. "Hey! I have an important call."

Raleigh put his hand over the receiver and said in a harsh whisper, "Cell phones are not secure. Say as little as possible and nothing about him—" he jerked his head toward Connor "—at all. Set up an in-person meeting if she wants to talk further. Got it?"

The man's bossiness set Darby's teeth on edge, but she knew his precaution was meant to protect Connor. Keeping Connor alive was her desire, as well, so she nodded. With a narrow-eyed look clearly meant to emphasize his warning, Raleigh handed her the cell phone. Hunter sized up the situation and, with a nod to Darby, eased back down the hall toward the living room.

Darby took a moment to steady her composure before lifting the phone to her ear. "Hello, Dr. Reed. Is there a problem?"

"That's what I'm calling to clarify. I understand you talked to Jillian earlier today while I was meeting with Sam Orlean. Did she tell you my concerns regarding Mr. Orlean's DNA test results?"

"She did," Darby said quickly, turning her back to Raleigh's watchful stare. "And I'd like to discuss those results with you in person if I may. Can we meet in your office tomorrow maybe? I think I can clear up some of your questions."

Dr. Reed agreed to make time for Darby and transferred her to the appointment desk. Her hand was shaking when she disconnected and met Connor's gaze.

"I have an appointment in the morning."

"*We* have an appointment," he corrected. "I should go with you. If we're going to explain the truth to Savannah's doctor, I want to be there."

Behind her, Raleigh grunted his disapproval, which Connor ignored.

"Besides, I think I owe Dr. Reed an apology." Connor rubbed his chin and twisted his mouth into a sheepish grimace. "I was not very cooperative today when I met with her, and I made have come off as hostile."

Darby slid the phone into her shorts pocket and rolled the tension from her shoulders. "All right. That's probably best."

Raleigh pursed his lips in exasperation. "Definite FUBAR in the making." He crooked a finger toward Connor. "If you insist on going into public, we need a plan. Meet me out front."

The grumpy marshal disappeared down the hall, leaving her alone with Connor again. He stepped toward her, combing his fingers through her hair as he brushed it from her face. "Now…where were we?"

A heady thrill chased through her, remembering the sweet assault of his lips and how quickly she had responded to his touch. As if no time had passed since they'd last made love. As if her body had been dormant, waiting for his kiss to wake her and bring all her senses to life again.

She twisted away from him when he ducked his head to kiss her. "We were treading on dangerous ground. That's where we were."

His brow puckered. "Dangerous? Why do you say that?"

She balled her fists and pulled her shoulders back, peeved that he was dragging her into this conversation. She'd dealt with quite enough emotional upheaval for one day, thank you. "You really have to ask? Connor, you've already said you're going back into WitSec when your business here is done. Did you really think I'd be happy having a tryst with you, knowing that's all it would be, a short-term fling?"

He blinked, his expression deeply wounded, even angry with her. "First, I don't have *business* here. I have *family*. I'm here because my daughter needs me."

The emotion in his voice pierced straight to her soul, and she ached with the knowledge of what could have been. Connor, the doting father, sharing midnight feedings and silly games designed to make Savannah laugh. Connor, the worried father, rocking their daughter when she cried and kissing skinned knees. Connor, the loving, attentive father she'd always known he'd be. She wasn't at all surprised that he'd rushed back to Lagniappe after learning about Savannah and her illness.

But it stung to know he hadn't loved Savannah's mother enough to move heaven and earth the same way to be with her. She resented the fact that his choice made her feel like the young girl who'd waited endless days for her father to return. To no avail. She hadn't mattered to her father, and four and a half years ago, she hadn't mattered enough to Connor. Darby bit the inside of her cheek, choking down the tears and self-pity that thought stirred. She stood her ground, determined not to let anyone hurt her that much again, as Connor moved closer, his eyes fierce.

"Second, I never considered our sex merely a fling and never will. It's always been about my feelings for you, about the deep connection we shared. Body and soul. How can *you* think I'd ever settle for a fling with you?" When he reached for her cheek, she stepped back, away from his touch, her heart breaking.

"So your intention is to make me fall in love with you again, so you can shatter it when you leave like you did four years ago? Rebuild that intimate connection just in time to rip it apart when you go back to WitSec?" She swallowed past the lump in her throat. "No, thank you. I think I'll pass."

"Fall in love again?" His brow furrowed, and he narrowed a stricken gaze on her. "Are you saying you don't love me anymore?"

She barked a humorless laugh. "*That's* what you got from what I said? My point is, I've hurt quite enough thanks to you and your faked death. Enough to last a lifetime. I can't go there again, no matter what feelings I have or don't still have for you."

Connor's shoulders dropped, and grief darkened his countenance. "I never want to cause you pain. I hated knowing you and my family would believe I was dead."

She jerked a nod. "I believe you. I do. And I know you well enough to know your leaving was hard on you, too. But the fact remains that it hurt. Deeply and irrevocably.

I barely survived the pain of losing you once. I can't risk hurting that way again."

The muscle in Connor's jaw ticked as he stared at her, his eyes damp. Sighing, he dragged both hands over his face. "So you're locking your heart up, closing yourself off to ever loving someone?"

"Maybe not forever. Maybe some day I'll find someone to love and share my life with." She paused long enough to gain the composure she needed to finish without her voice cracking. "But as long as your intention is to leave, to return to WitSec and disappear from our lives, then I can't let myself love *you*."

Chapter 8

After Connor joined the others in the kitchen, Darby went into her bathroom to splash water on her face and take something for the raging headache drilling her skull. Her conversation with Connor had her shaking from the inside out, and her heart felt as if it had been wrung out and beaten with a stick.

When she faced her reflection in the mirror above the sink, she found she looked as ragged as she felt. She tried to freshen up a bit, brushing her hair and dusting her pale cheeks with blusher. As she made her touch-ups, her reply to Connor echoed in her mind.

As long as your intention is to leave...I can't let myself love you. What a liar she was. She'd never stopped loving Connor. That was why his return and his plans to leave again hurt so damn much. Kissing him had only awakened memories she'd locked away years ago in order to preserve her sanity. Memories of how his touch set her body on fire and made her soul sing. Memories of the unity she felt with him on every level when they made love. Memories of how his kisses made her feel cherished, safe...and thoroughly aroused.

She rubbed her arms as lingering goose bumps prickled her skin even now. After all these months of his absence, her body still had the same reaction to his kiss. Well, almost the same. She no longer felt emotionally safe with him. And the revelation of his faked death had bruised her ego, wounded her trust in him. He could say he'd left to keep her safe, but the little girl who still lived inside her, the young teenager whose father had walked out on her family, saw Connor's departure as evidence her love hadn't been enough. That he hadn't loved her enough. That inequity stung.

Shaking her head, she roused herself from her dreary woolgathering and scoffed at the results of her touch-ups. She still looked ragged, but with coral tint on her cheeks and her hair in place. Getting rid of the dark circles under her eyes and general haggard look about her would take weeks of better sleep, healthier eating and a significant reduction in her stress level. None of which was likely to happen anytime soon.

Tossing her brush on the bathroom counter, she headed out to the kitchen, where Connor, his family and the U.S. Marshals were waiting. When she reached the breakfast room, she found Connor alone propped against the counter, his gaze taking in the scribbled artwork taped to the refrigerator across from him. Masterpieces only a mother could love. Or a father.

Her heart somersaulted, seeing his tall, wide frame filling her kitchen. The sight was so familiar and so foreign at the same time.

"Where is everyone?"

He turned toward her as she moved from the doorway. "Jones and Raleigh are settling in the guest room, I think. Everyone else is waiting for us in the living room." He paused. "Your sister's here now. Hunter called her."

"Which one? Lilly?"

Connor nodded. Of Darby's three sisters, she was closest to Lilly. Next to Hunter, Lilly was her best friend, and Hunter knew it. Nothing happened in Darby's life that her youngest sister didn't hear about and vice versa, so it didn't surprise her that Hunter would have summoned Lilly.

"And Grant told Tracy," Connor added. "She and the kids will be here in an hour or so."

Darby raked her hair back from her face. "A regular family reunion."

Another nod and a sheepish grin. "I'm supposed to be getting Dad a glass of water, but I got distracted." He pointed to pictures Peyton had drawn of Toby and Savannah. "I see our daughter has your talent for art. These are really good for a kid her age."

Darby gave him a half smile. "They would be good for a kid Savannah's age. But those are Peyton's drawings."

"Oh."

Darby pointed to a sheet with crayon scribbles. "This one is Savannah's."

Connor arched an eyebrow and glanced at the childish scribble. "Ah, so her artistic talent is more on my level."

Darby grinned. "She's not even four yet. Give her a break."

He waved a finger toward the drawing. "What is it supposed to be?"

Darby's grin spread, remembering the day Savannah had created the masterpiece. "It's a bird. With a cape."

Connor's gaze flicked to her, amusement tugging his lips. "A cape?"

Darby nodded. "It's Super Bird."

He stroked a hand over his mouth as he chuckled. "Super Bird. Got it."

His penetrating, gold gaze latched on to hers as he smiled, and her pulse danced a two-step. She and Connor had always teased and laughed so easily when they were together. His sense of humor had brightened even the hardest days when they'd dated. And it was one of the things she'd missed most the last four and a half years.

Desire thrummed in her veins, and her bones melted. Why did he have to be so blindingly handsome? Darby folded her arms over her chest, fighting the urge to throw herself at him and never let go. *He lied to you. Shattered your heart. Even knowing what Dad did to our family, he abandoned you.*

Connor dropped his gaze to the floor where Toby, who'd apparently changed his mind about napping with Savannah, was rubbing against his pants leg. He reached down and lifted the brown tabby to his arms. "Well, hello, Toby. How've you been, pal?"

He scratched her docile cat behind the ears. Toby relished the attention, completely oblivious to the betrayal, the pain Connor had caused her. She pushed aside the prick of rejection and took a glass out of the cabinet for Connor's father. "Do you still play tennis?"

"No. Sam Orlean has different interests, different pastimes. By necessity."

Darby mulled that fact, considered what life must be like for Connor, having to change everything about who he was and how he spent his time. "So what do you do now?"

And if he was Sam Orlean now, was any part of the man she'd fallen in love with still alive in him?

"I can usually find a pick-up game of basketball at the gym. I stink at it, but…" He shrugged and smiled, and she found her attention drawn to his mouth. "And I still jog. That's universal enough that the marshals thought it would be okay to keep it up." He twisted his lips as he thought, still rubbing Toby's neck with his fingers. "I've started tinkering with cars, something I used to do with Grant but gave up on when I was about fifteen."

"Mmm," she murmured, her focus shattered by the flash of heat that spun through her when she thought of those lips on hers moments ago. Their tender warmth had been so sweet, so tantalizing....

Toby wiggled and hopped out of Connor's arms, tail flicking as he sauntered away.

Darby filled the glass she'd retrieved with ice and water from the refrigerator door dispenser and headed toward the living room.

Connor caught her arm. "Will you tell everyone I'll join them in a minute? I'm going to sit with Savannah for a while."

She drilled him with a fierce look. "Don't you dare wake her up. She's just finished six weeks of chemo. Her body is exhausted. She needs her sleep!"

Connor caressed Darby's cheek, a completely unexpected gesture that silenced her warning and sent a tingle from her nape down her spine.

"I won't wake her, Dar. I promise. I just want to sit with her. Look at her. Be near her." He paused, the corners of his eyes creasing with regret. "I don't know how long I may have here, and I can't take a minute of it for granted."

With that, he silently walked to Savannah's door and tiptoed in.

Darby took Stan his water, then excused herself to follow Connor to her daughter's room.

Connor had pulled her rocking chair close to her bed, and as Darby entered he bent to press a soft kiss to Savannah's brow. Taking a seat in the chair, he gently curled his fingers around their daughter's hand and settled in, as if keeping vigil over her. He stroked his thumb back and forth on Savannah's small hand and watched her sleep with an expression of love and heartache in his eyes.

Darby stayed at the door for a few minutes, until the poignant ache under her ribs swelled so much she could barely breathe. Right now, today, she had what she'd always wanted, what she'd prayed for, what her heart desired most. Connor and Savannah, with her, together, a family. But there was no peace in the reunion. The threats to her family came from so many directions—cancer, assassins, WitSec. So many ways that her small family could be shattered.

She drew a deep shuddering breath as she closed Savannah's door. If she considered all the challenges she faced at once, the obstacles threatened to overwhelm her. Giving up was not an option. She'd simply have to face each hurdle as it arose and fight to keep the people she loved safe.

Chapter 9

The next morning, Darby held Savannah on her hip and rode the elevator to the third floor of the medical building where the pediatric oncologist had her office. Following Dr. Reed's call yesterday, she'd arranged today's meeting with Dr. Reed and Connor—no, Sam. She had to remember to call him Sam, to play the charade in public.

When the elevator bell dinged and the doors slid open, Darby adjusted the edge of the mask Savannah wore and kissed her forehead. "Remember, keep your mask on unless the doctor tells you to take it off."

"So I don't get gewms?"

Darby sighed as she marched down the corridor. "Right. So you don't get germs."

A little girl shouldn't be worried about her compromised immune system and what microbes might get her sick. She should be playing in the dirt, making mud pies and feeling the sun on her face. *Maybe someday, if Con-*

nor was a match and if the transplant was a success and if Savannah beat the cancer... She cursed all the "ifs" in her life and dragged open the door to the doctor's office.

In keeping with the disguises started yesterday, Connor and the marshals continued to dress as health care workers. They left the house an hour before Darby and arranged to meet her at the doctor's office.

When she entered the office lobby, Connor was already there. He stood in the middle of the waiting room, hands in the pockets of khaki pants, staring at a tank full of tropical fish. As if sensing her gaze, he turned.

His face lit with the smile that had won her heart six years ago, but once again, his appearance had been altered. The transformation since earlier that morning was subtle but effective. His dark brown hair had been cut significantly shorter. He sported facial hair again, as he had yesterday, this time a trim mustache and well-groomed Vandyke. Medical scrubs had been exchanged for a plaid button-down shirt to complete his Sam Orlean persona. His light brown eyes were hidden behind stylishly geeky glasses.

He approached her with his hand extended. "Are you Darby Kent?"

"Uh…" She was still taking in the change in his appearance, so his question, which seemed so ridiculous for someone she nearly married, rattled her again.

"Nice to meet you," he said, following through with the act, even though she'd fumbled. "I'm Sam Orlean, the potential donor from Dallas."

"Um, right. Hello." As she shook his hand, Savannah raised her head to see who her mother was greeting. *Uh-oh.* She hadn't briefed Savannah that they needed to pretend they didn't know Connor. Would her daughter recognize him despite the disguise?

"And this must be Savannah." He smiled at their daughter, who clung to Darby with a curious furrow in her brow.

"Why do you look like that?" Savannah asked, and Darby inwardly cringed. She glanced past Connor and saw just one other person in the waiting room. The front desk clerk watched them, as well. A small audience for their act, but according to Connor, no one, no matter how insignificant-seeming, could know who he really was.

Connor chuckled good-naturedly. "I think my beard makes me look handsome. Don't you?"

Savannah shrugged. "I guess."

"Uncle Connor is playing dress up," she whispered to Savannah, "like on Halloween. Can you play along and pretend he's someone you just met? Pretend his name is Sam Orlean and he is a new friend?"

Savannah looked skeptical, but she nodded. Darby decided distraction might be her best bet, and she searched the room for something to occupy Savannah. "Honey, do you want to play with the puzzles?"

Connor battled down the urge to pull both Darby and his daughter into his arms for a firm hug. The memory of the kiss he'd shared with Darby yesterday had kept him awake all night, filling him with foolish dreams of a happier ending than he knew was possible.

When he'd first spotted her across the office, his breath had backed up in his lungs. The sight of Darby still made his senses short-circuit, his body hum. Her beautiful face, vulnerable eyes and sunshine smile moved something in his soul every time he looked at her.

And the little girl in her arms, a heartbreaking reflection of her mother in so many ways, made his chest squeeze and emotions reel in ways he'd never known. His *daughter*...

Savannah glanced over at the stack of toys across the

room before giving Darby a look full of trepidation. "No poke today?"

Darby smoothed a hand over Savannah's thin wisps of hair and gave her a sad smile. "No, baby. No needles today. I promise. Dr. Reed wants to see how you're doing, but no needles."

A sudden, almost overwhelming wave of sympathy and concern for Savannah swept through him. His knees shook, and he dropped into the nearest chair before his legs could give out. His daughter had been relentlessly pricked and poked, injected with poisons to kill the diseased cells ravaging her tiny body. Cancer treatment was difficult enough for adults to endure. How much harder must it have been for a young child who didn't understand what was happening and why?

Savannah crossed the room and rummaged through the box of toys, while Darby signed in with the receptionist. When she'd finish checking in, Darby took a chair next to him. "The receptionist said we're next. It should only be a few—" She cut herself off midsentence and frowned at him. "Con—um, Sam, what's wrong? You're as white as a sheet."

He swiped a shaky hand over his mouth and whispered, "You've been dealing with Savannah's condition for months. I'm still taking in all the implications. It's a lot to process."

She sighed and sat back in her chair. "I may be past the initial shock, but I still have a hard time dealing with—" She bit her lip and didn't finish the thought.

He nodded his empathy. "Just now, thinking about the doctors using her as a pincushion, how scary this must be for her…" Connor's voice cracked, and he paused to clear his throat. Darby's expression softened.

"My reaction just caught me off guard. The grief and

sympathy…and anger—" He fisted his hands and clenched his jaw as that particular emotion swelled again. "Why did this happen to my—" He caught himself. "To such a small, innocent little girl," he said, switching to Sam Orlean mode. Connor forced himself to draw a slow, deep breath before continuing. He had to remember the role he was playing. He flashed a quick humorless smile at Darby. "It was a real kick in the teeth, ya know?"

"Tell me about it." Darby sent him a side glance and in a soft voice added, "But for her sake, save the meltdowns for your own time. She needs the adults around her to be strong and positive."

Connor lifted his chin and cocked an eyebrow. "Of course. It's just…I'm not used to feeling so…helpless."

Darby gave him a strange look, then twisted her lips in a wry grin. "That's right. Knowing you can't step in and take charge, manipulate the situation to suit yourself must be murder for a control freak like you."

He straightened in his seat. "I'm not—" He swallowed the denial. Not only did he want to avoid arguing with Darby, he had to admit he liked to be right. He needed order, predictability, direction, oversight…okay, yes, *control* over a situation. But he wasn't unreasonable. He wasn't the dictator or tyrant Darby made him out to be.

Savannah wandered back to her mother, carrying a naked Barbie with tangled hair. Clutching the doll in one hand, she climbed into Darby's lap and leaned back against her mother's chest. Connor felt a twinge in his chest. He wanted his daughter to feel as safe in his arms as she did in her mother's. He wanted to make up for the lost time together. He wanted to be the father he hadn't had the chance to be. He watched Savannah move the Barbie's long arms and legs into various anatomically impossible positions before tiring of the toy and tossing it aside.

"Ms. Kent?" a nurse in pink scrubs called from the door to the treatment area. "Dr. Reed will see you now."

"Savannah, will you draw one of your pretty pictures for me while your mommy talks to the doctor?" The nurse, Jillian according to her name tag, held her hand out, and Savannah hesitated only a moment before going to the woman.

"I'll be right back, sweetie." Darby kissed Savannah's cheek. "Be good for Ms. Jillian. Okay?"

Connor followed Darby into the doctor's office and closed the door. "Are we on the same page about what to tell the doctor about who I am?"

Darby took a seat on the couch across from the doctor's cluttered desk. "Like we agreed, she needs to know you're Savannah's father. Her nurse has seen your test results and knows I was upset yesterday, so she'll need the truth, too."

"And we need to impress upon them the urgency that they not tell anyone else. The fewer people who know about me, the safer you and Savannah will be." Connor fought the urge to straighten the papers on the desk and sat down beside Darby.

The office door opened, and an attractive middle-aged woman wearing a white lab coat and a casual pantsuit breezed in. Connor stood to greet the doctor, with whom he'd met yesterday.

"Sorry to keep you waiting, Darby," she said as she hung the lab coat on a coatrack. Before sitting down, the woman did a double take. Confusion flashed over the doctor's face as she studied Connor's appearance. "Mr. Orlean?"

"Yes...and no." Connor held out his hand to shake the doctor's. "I can explain the change in my appearance. And my real name is Connor Mansfield."

"Is there a problem I should know about?" Dr. Reed

asked, glancing from Connor to Darby and back. "Because my nurse tells me Darby was quite upset yesterday over your test results. If I'm going to treat Savannah, if we proceed with this BMT, I have to know exactly who and what I'm dealing with, both medically and logistically."

Connor firmed his mouth and met Darby's anxious and determined gaze. He jerked his head once in affirmation. "I *am* Savannah's father. But for almost five years, I've been living under the alias Sam Orlean as part of the U.S. Marshals Witness Security program. Darby didn't know this until yesterday."

Dr. Reed sank slowly to her chair, clearly absorbing the stunning news. "Witness protection? So that's the reason for your changed appearance?"

Connor nodded and explained his situation briefly.

Dr. Reed chewed the end of her pen as she mulled his revelations. "Should trouble arise, will you leave town again? I need a firm commitment from you. I have to know you won't disappear partway through the procedure."

"I will do everything in my power to complete the procedure. You have my word."

Savannah's doctor tapped a finger against her lips. Her expression clearly said she was analyzing the information and deciding how it might affect Savannah's treatment. "As long as everyone understands that Savannah's health is my primary concern, and I *must* have the final say in all matters regarding her arrangements, I don't see why we can't move forward and work through these circumstances. But I will *not* stand for any outside party interfering with Savannah's treatment or trying to supersede my authority in regard to her medical care in any manner."

Connor nodded. "Understood. I'll make sure the marshals know your terms."

"Of course, I'll do everything I can to cooperate with

the marshals for your protection, so long as it doesn't put Savannah's health at risk." Dr. Reed angled her head. "Where are these marshals now?"

"One is in an unmarked car in the parking lot," Connor said, "and one is in the hallway just outside the waiting room. More man power will be called in as the need is established."

Dr. Reed puffed out a breath and flipped open the file on her desk. "All right, then. Shall we get started? We have a lot to cover and only a few minutes to hit the highlights before I have to be in surgery." She sifted through the papers and met Connor's eyes. "We've completed the tests on the DNA sample you gave last week, and I'm satisfied with the numbers they sent."

Darby scooted forward, hovering on the edge of the sofa. Her eyes shone with eager anticipation. "Does that mean he's a match? Can Connor donate his marrow?"

The doctor smiled. "He's not a perfect match, but it would be rare, almost unheard of, for a parent to match all of the markers. However, he's close enough that we can move forward with the transplant."

Darby's face lit up, and happy tears filled her eyes. Connor's hopes lifted as well, loosening the pressure in his chest and allowing him to take an easier breath. His pulse was already revved when Darby reached for his knee and curled her fingers into the leg of his khaki pants. The gesture surprised him, and a side glance told him she might not have even realized what she'd done. Her attention was still focused fully on Dr. Reed, myriad questions in her eyes. But her touch, her unconscious quest for a connection between them, jolted through him. Quietly he wrapped his hand around hers and gave it a reassuring squeeze.

"I want you to know how rare it is to have a parental match. You're very lucky. That's the good news. Our detailed DNA tests analyzed the resolution for HLA-A, B, C and DRB1—"

"Whoa, whoa!" Connor shook his head and shot a hand up to stop Dr. Reed. "Enough of the alphabet soup. Layman terms, please, until I have a chance to do more reading on the procedure."

"HLA stands for *human leukocyte antigen.* They're proteins in your body's cells used to recognize which cells belong and which cells are invaders, such as viruses or bacteria that can make you sick. In a healthy human, the white blood cells, or leukocytes, can distinguish between the good cells and invaders and will destroy only the bad cells."

Connor nodded. "Right. I remember that from high school biology. And all blood cells are formed in the bone marrow."

Dr. Reed nodded. "Right. Savannah's leukemia means her white blood cells aren't developing properly, then dying off like they should. These 'bad,' or not properly developed, cells are crowding out the healthy blood cells— red, white and platelets— keeping them from functioning properly."

"So the point of a bone marrow transplant," Darby jumped in, clearly eager to get through the explanations that had to be old news for her by now, "is to replace the tissue that is creating abnormal cells with healthy marrow that will do the job properly."

"But…" Connor said, turning to Dr. Reed and lifting a palm to invite her to finish.

"But from person to person, there are numerous differences in white blood cells and the genetic codes that tell the cells what to destroy and what to leave alone. Even your matching antigens have what are called *microvariants,* which can be different and lead to tissue rejection."

With a grunt of frustration, Darby visibly wilted.

"If your bone marrow isn't similar enough to Savannah's, her body will think your cells are invaders and reject them." Dr. Reed closed the file in front of her. "That's why we have to be sure of as close of a match as possible."

"How soon can we start the transplant process?" Darby asked.

"Soon, I hope. Since Savannah just finished a round of chemo, this is an ideal time to do it."

"What happens next?" Connor asked.

"I won't go into the nitty-gritty now, but essentially, Savannah will be given a megadose of chemo to prepare her body for the new marrow. She'll be extremely vulnerable to germs at that point, so she'll have to stay in a sterile isolation room before, during and for a while after the procedure."

Connor frowned. "Isolation? Does that mean we can't be in the room with her?"

"We make allowances for short visits for parents as long as they are wearing proper sterile protective suits. Her room will have an observation window as well, where you can see her and she can see you. Otherwise, only authorized medical personnel in sterile gear will be allowed in with her."

"How long will she have to stay in the hospital?" Darby asked, voicing the question that was on the tip of Connor's tongue. They'd always been in sync, able to finish each other's sentences and read each other's thoughts. Knowing they still had some small part of that connection heartened Connor.

"Hard to say. Depending on how her body reacts to the transplant, she could stay in isolation anywhere from four to eight weeks."

Darby gasped. "So long?"

Dr. Reed gave them a comforting smile. "I know it seems like a long time, but not compared to the long years we hope to give you with her if the procedure works." Her expression sobered a bit. "Keep in mind, this is a very invasive process. We'll need to monitor her closely for as long as it takes for her little body to rebound. But…" Her smile returned. "I have faith that she will rebound, that she'll do well with the transplant. We wouldn't be moving forward if I didn't believe she was a good candidate."

Eight weeks? Connor swiped a hand along his chin as he mulled that news. Two months was a long time to be out of hiding, potentially exposed to the Gales' threat. He hated the idea of Darby and his family living under the stress of that danger for so long. And yet…the two-month prediction meant he'd have eight precious weeks with Darby and the people he loved most before he had to disappear again. Was eight weeks enough time to convince Darby to come with him into WitSec? And did he have a right to tear her away from her family, her home, her life here in Lagniappe?

Dr. Reed checked her watch. "I'm afraid I only have time for a couple more questions right now, but we'll get into specifics in future consultations."

He glanced next to him and found Darby watching him, her eyes reflecting the tangle of emotions expected for a mother facing such a risky procedure for her daughter.

"Do you have any more questions?" Darby asked him.

Yes, he thought. *How do I make you understand and forgive the choices I made? And how do I make you love me again?*

"No. Not now," he said instead.

Chapter 10

Sitting in the driver's seat of his Escalade, Victor Gale studied the blown-up photo of the health care workers who'd left Darby Kent's house that morning. The guy in question had kept his head down, a cap on, his face toward the house so that his cameras didn't get a clear shot. As if he knew cameras were capturing his every move and he'd hidden his face intentionally.

"What do ya think, Vic?" his right-hand man, Hollister, asked. "Is it Mansfield?"

"Can't be sure. But my instincts say it is." He dropped the picture on the seat beside him and drummed his fingers on the steering wheel.

"What do you want to do?" Hollister asked.

A deferral to his brother's judgment rushed to his tongue as it always did on matters that skirted the law, but he swallowed the words like a bitter pill. He hated always bowing to James's opinion, just because James was older and the CEO of the family company. Pop may have left James in charge of the business, but Victor knew more than James would ever know about the dark side of business, scores settled outside the boardroom.

And James had a weakness when it came to Connor Mansfield, because Mansfield had pulled James's son out of the swimming pool and revived him when Billy was a little tyke. In Victor's opinion, that favor had long ago expired, but James always hedged when it came to Mansfield. Until he'd turned traitor and testified against their father.

Still, Victor didn't trust James to do what had to be done regarding Connor Mansfield. James could be soft when it came to his kids.

Victor set his teeth and rocked his head from side to side, stretching the tendons in his neck. James would want proof before they took extreme measures, but in his heart, he knew the man who'd showed up at Darby Kent's was the man who'd betrayed his family and sent Pop to prison. Screw proof. This was his call to make.

"I know all I need to. I want Mansfield's head on a platter."

Hollister raised an eyebrow. "You got it, Salome."

Victor glared at Hollister for his dark humor, adding, "Not literally. No grandstanding. It has to look like an accident, a random act. And I want you to be sure it's Connor Mansfield you take out. A clean strike. Understood?"

Hollister hiked up his chin. "I got this."

Victor's gut rolled uneasily. "Be sure you do, or it's your head that'll be on the platter."

Darby stood when Connor entered the waiting room, a gauze pad taped to his arm where they'd drawn more blood for a new set of tests in preparation for the transplant. "Well?"

"All done for now," he said. "They'll be in touch once they get things set up with the hospital. She's sending us home to wait."

"On pins and needles," she added with a sigh. Rubbing her forehead where a tension headache was mounting, she glanced across the room where Savannah was coloring at a child-sized table. "Time to go, sweetie. You can bring your picture with you."

Savannah scurried up to them and shoved a crayon drawing at Connor. "I made this fow you. It's a pony."

Connor quickly wiped the worry from his expression and shifted his attention to their daughter. Darby's breath caught as he crouched beside Savannah, smiling, and took the picture. "And it's a wonderful pony! Thank you, Savannah."

Savannah touched the bandage on his arm and above the line of her mask, her nose crinkled. "You got a needle poke?"

"I did."

Savannah lifted her gaze to his, her eyes worried. "I don't like needle pokes. They hurt."

Connor stroke a crooked finger along her temple. "I don't like them, either, but sometimes the doctor has to use needle pokes so she can help you get well."

Savannah nodded, then her eyes grew wide. "Are you sick, too?"

He gave Savannah a warm smile. "No. The doctor wanted to check my blood to see if I could help you get well."

"Can you?" she asked, her voice brightening. The hope in her daughter's voice was heartbreaking. Not yet four years old, Savannah understood so little of what was happening to her.

A flicker of something akin to grief shone in his eyes for

an instant before he drew a breath and schooled his face. "Oh, I pray that I can, sweetie. I'm going to try."

"Did you cry when they poked you?"

Connor shook his head. "No."

Savannah glanced up at Darby, clearly impressed, before returning her gaze to Connor.

"Want to know what I did so I wouldn't cry when they poked me?" he asked.

Savannah nodded enthusiastically, and her small body canted toward him as if he were about to reveal the secret to the universe. Darby found herself holding her breath, too.

"When they poked me, I thought about the happiest thing I could, something that makes me smile all the way to my toes."

Savannah's eyes danced, and even with the mask in place, Darby knew her daughter was grinning. "What was it?"

Connor acted surprised by the question. "Why, *you,* of course!"

"Me?" Savannah blinked her wide gold eyes. A person would have to be blind not to see the similarities between the father and daughter. Darby's chest tightened.

Connor gave his daughter a light tug on the earlobe. "Yes, you, cutie-pie. Meeting you has made me very happy."

Eyes shining, Savannah turned her face toward Darby as if to ask, *Did you hear that?*

"I'm gonna make you another picture!" she said, turning to dart back to the table and crayons.

Darby caught her arm. "Hold up, Miss Priss. It's time to go home."

Connor pushed to his feet, squaring his shoulders. "I'll

see you in an hour or so. Jones will follow you home same
as he followed you here."

She blinked, startled. "Jones followed me here?"

"He did. Just the same, take precautions going home.
Stay alert, and call Jones if anything suspicious happens.
Anything." He narrowed his eyes, emphasizing that point.
"You still have his number?"

She nodded. "I entered it in my phone."

"Good. Be careful."

Darby watched him disappear down the corridor with
his warning ringing in her ears. Jones had followed them to
the doctor's office without her knowing. Could there also
be henchmen for the Gale family lurking nearby, unseen?
As long as they were in public, they were in danger. The
marshals had drilled that into her last night. A chill prickled her arms, considering the possibility, and she scooted
Savannah toward the elevator, eager to get home. Connor's return meant Savannah could get the bone marrow
she needed. But at what cost to all of their lives?

The trip to the doctor's office taxed Savannah's limited
strength, and even before she finished lunch, Darby could
see her daughter's eyelids droop. She tucked one of Savannah's few wisps of dark hair behind her ear and pushed her
plate away. "Are you ready for a little nap?"

"No!" her daughter whined like any child facing bedtime. "I wanna play with Uncle Connuh."

"You can later," Darby told her, scooping her into her
arms and heading down the hall. Connor appeared from
the bathroom where he'd been stripping off the morning's
disguise.

"Is she all right?" he asked, his focus on Savannah.

"Just tired. She wears out easily because of the chemo.
She takes several catnaps every day."

"Like Toby," Savannah said with a sleepy smile.

"Except you're cuter." He gave her a wink. "Can I help?"

Darby cocked her head in question. "Help?"

He waved one hand toward the bedroom. "Tuck her in... or whatever you do for her naps."

Darby tensed, ready to refuse his offer, when Savannah raised her head from her shoulder and held a hand out to Connor. "Will you wead me a stowy?"

The request clearly caught Connor by surprise, but his expression quickly softened, warmed. *Melted* would best describe it. "Of course, sweetie."

And Darby felt her heart go gooey in response. How many times had she fantasized about having Connor help tuck their daughter into bed? Of watching them play tickle or read books together? Of him carrying Savannah on his shoulders, the way her own father used to carry her...

She shut down the memory that caused a painful spike of resentment to pierce her chest.

"Cliffowd!" Savannah insisted, naming her favorite storybook character.

Darby saw the spark of life in her daughter's eyes and knew she couldn't disappoint Savannah, even if things were still unsettled between her and Connor. "Are you familiar with Clifford, the big red dog?"

Connor tugged his cheek up in a grin. "Absolutely. I had a Clifford book when I was a kid."

"And Dowa?" Savannah asked.

Connor's inquiring gaze drifted to Darby.

"Dora the Explorer," Darby clarified. "She's another favorite. Dora teaches us how to speak Spanish."

"Oh." Connor smiled at Savannah. *"Buena!"*

Savannah giggled. *"Buena!"*

The sound of her daughter's laugh fluttered in Darby's chest, a poignant reminder of the happy, active child Savannah had been before the chemo wore her down. Savannah had been a trooper through all the sickness and endless testing, but seeing Savannah's vibrancy fade day by day broke Darby's heart.

She'll be back. Once the chemo wears off and the cancer's in remission, the old Savannah will be back, Hunter had promised not two days ago. Darby clung to that hope.

Because the alternative was unthinkable.

Feeling tears rise in her sinuses, Darby cleared her throat, drew a cleansing breath and bustled into Savannah's room. She had to be brave for her daughter, couldn't let her emotions bog her down. That's how she'd survived her father's leaving, Connor's death. Shut it out, forge on. Don't let yourself feel too much.

Darby pointed across the room. "I think the Clifford book is on her dresser."

She settled Savannah on her bed, pulling Disney Princess sheets up to her chin and placing Benny beside her. "There you go. All comfy?"

Savannah shoved at her mother. "Move over. Uncle Connuh sit here. Like Hunter."

Darby shot Connor a wry grin. "You heard her. Hunter sits by her head and lets her turn the pages."

She moved out of the way, sweeping a hand toward the top of the frilly bed, then settled in the rocking chair where she'd nursed Savannah and lulled her to sleep every night for the first months of her daughter's life.

Connor took his place, sitting at an awkward angle until Savannah instructed him exactly how Hunter propped his feet on the bed, leaned against the headboard and held Savannah snuggled against his side.

"Like this?" Connor scooted into place, and Savannah nodded her satisfaction.

Pulling the book from his hands, she opened to the first page. "Show me the pictures."

Connor arched an eyebrow and sent Darby an amused grin. "Bossy little thing."

She returned a sassy smile. "She gets that from you. Apparently some traits are inherited rather than learned."

His eyes widened as if her comment startled him.

She arched an eyebrow. "Don't pretend you don't know what I'm talking about. Even your mother will tell people you bossed your brothers around your whole life."

He shrugged. "Maybe a little."

When Savannah shoved the book in his hands, he opened to the first page and bent to press a kiss to the top of Savannah's head.

The poignant gesture caught Darby off guard, and her heart clenched, stealing her breath.

Instead of feeling overjoyed, she was apprehensive, waiting for the disaster she sensed lurking. Connor might be back, but he'd brought danger with him. Needles of anxiety pricked the base of her neck, and she squeezed the armrest of the rocking chair. Men with connections to organized crime could have been watching her comings and goings for months. More important, they could have seen Connor since he returned and could even now be planning to strike. She stared blindly at the floor as her mind spun, and a chill crawled through her.

I left to protect you...not to save myself.

When the transplant was complete, he'd disappear again from their lives, go back to his new life, his new identity. A bitter ache filled her, churning in her stomach. Laughter—Savannah's tinkling and sweet, Connor's husky and deep—drifted to her from the bed, cutting into her fractious thoughts.

"Silly doggie!" Savannah said, her honey-brown eyes shining up at Connor.

"Clifford *is* silly," Connor said, beaming at his daughter. "Have you ever seen a dog wear a party hat like that?"

"No!" Savannah groaned comically.

Darby bit the inside of her cheek, fighting back tears. Her emotions were so tangled and all over the map. She didn't know whether to laugh or cry, have hope or rage. How was she supposed to sort out the competing feelings twisted inside her?

"I had a pawty."

Connor paused in his reading and met Savannah's eyes. "You had a party?"

She nodded. "A birthday pawty. We ate cake."

Her father smiled. "Mmm. I love cake."

Savannah's faced brightened. "You can come to my pawty. My new pawty. When I'm—" She struggled to hold up just four fingers on her hand. "Fouw yeaws old."

"Can I?" The bittersweet yearning in Connor's expression tugged at Darby's fragile composure.

"Mommy, can Uncle Connuh come to my birthday pawty?" Savannah's expectant eyes blinked at her, and Darby had to clear her throat before she could answer.

"Your birthday's not until July. That's still two months away."

"Can he come?" her stubborn daughter repeated.

"He can, if…if he's still in town then."

Clearly Connor heard the question in her answer. The censure. The years of hurt.

His brow creased, and an excruciating sorrow replaced the mirth he'd been sharing moments earlier with Savannah.

Their daughter, oblivious to the underlying tension in

the room, cheered and tugged at Connor's sleeve. "She said yes! You can come."

Pain slashed through Darby, hearing her daughter plan a birthday party Connor would likely never attend. A party that might never happen if Savannah's cancer—

Cutting the nightmarish thought off, Darby shoved to her feet, her stomach lurching. Her roller-coaster emotions were more than she could bear.

"Connor, don't," Darby interrupted, her voice little more than a rasp.

He looked over at her, his brow furrowed. "What?"

"We can have balloons!" Savannah said, patting Connor's cheek in an attempt to regain his full attention.

"Don't what?" His voice was tender, confused.

She paced to the door, agitated. "Don't give her false hope."

He plowed his free hand through his hair, leaving it sexily rumpled. Darby's thoughts jumped to lazy Saturday mornings in the past, when she and Connor would stay in bed past noon, making love and dreaming of the future. A bittersweet stab of grief sliced through her.

Connor's gaze darkened and arrowed into her. "Isn't hope, whether it's false or real, better than giving up?"

She bit the inside of her cheek, fighting tears. "Then don't disappoint her."

Chapter 11

By pulling strings and classifying Savannah's transplant as a priority surgery, Dr. Reed was able to work the transplant in the hospital calendar for early the following week. In preparation for the transplant, Savannah was admitted and placed in a sterile room to begin receiving the high-potency chemo. Every possible germ and defensive white cell in her body had to be killed, making her a blank canvass, ready to receive the new marrow from Connor.

The night before the chemo was to be administered, Darby watched through the observation window of the sterile room as Dr. Reed did a final check-in with Savannah. Connor stood beside her, his body as taut and vibrating with tension as her own. When Dr. Reed turned to exit Savannah's room, Connor slipped his hand in Darby's and squeezed. They met the doctor steps from the sterile room door, anxious for news.

"Well?" Darby asked.

"All her blood work and vital signs are on target. We'll get started in the morning." Dr. Reed shucked off the sterile gown she'd worn into Savannah's room. "Honestly, my best advice is for the two of you to go home and get a good night's sleep."

"Go home?" Darby asked, her tone as incredulous as if she'd suggested throwing Savannah into a volcano. "No. I need to be here with her."

Dr. Reed smiled. "I understand your desire to be here, but tomorrow will be a long, stressful day as we start the amped-up chemo. You'll want to be well rested."

"But—" she started, and Connor put a hand on her arm.

"She's right, Darby."

Hunter and Darby's sister Lilly joined them to hear what the doctor was saying.

"I've given Savannah a sedative, and she'll be asleep all night." Dr. Reed made a note on Savannah's chart, then handed the file off to a waiting nurse. "Your daughter will be better served by you going home and getting some sleep."

Darby searched the faces around her, looking for an ally. Surely someone understood her need to be near her daughter.

Lilly faced her and flashed an understanding smile. "I'll stay here for you, and I promise to call if there's the slightest change in her condition."

Hunter nodded. "I'll stay, too. She won't be alone. Besides, Mom texted me earlier to say she's at your house. She made lasagna."

Connor slid a hand under Darby's hair to cradle the nape of her neck. Tugging her closer, he kissed her forehead. "Come on, honey. You're about to drop."

With that he curled an arm around her shoulders and guided her toward the elevators. She resisted for all of two seconds before her tired body gave in to Connor's comforting touch. She followed him and Marshal Jones out to the waiting car. Even though she knew Hunter and Lilly were the next best thing to her being there for Savannah, Darby couldn't deny the hollow ache of anxiety that sat in her chest as she stared out the car window.

Marshal Jones drove them back to her house, leaving Raleigh at the hospital to guard Savannah, despite the security inherent to the well-monitored sterile room.

The scent of freshly baked lasagna and homemade garlic bread greeted them as they entered. Darby's stomach rumbled, and she discovered that despite her worry for Savannah, she was hungry.

Julia met them with a warm smile and hug. "Dinner is waiting. Come right to the table."

"Smells great, Mom." Connor kissed Julia's cheek.

She divided a worried look between them. "When was the last time you ate?"

Darby furrowed her brow as she thought back. "I had coffee for breakfast."

Julia scoffed and ushered Darby toward the dining room. "Darling, coffee is not breakfast. Sit. I'll fix you a plate. Marshal Jones, join us?"

Grant and his wife, Tracy, along with their two children, were already seated at the table, and they greeted Darby and Connor with supportive smiles. After Grant and Tracy married, they'd inherited the farm house, about thirty minutes from Lagniappe, where the Mansfield grandparents had raised Stan. But for the next couple days, Grant's family had moved into Stan and Julia's home, in order to be closer to the hospital and available to help as needed.

Connor pulled out a chair for Darby, and with a weary smile for his courtesy, Darby sat. Julia's sumptuous dinner was served, but despite her growling stomach, Darby found that she was too exhausted to eat more than a few bites. The past week's whirlwind of emotions, stress and sleepless nights taking care of Savannah caved in on her, and suddenly she barley had the strength to lift her fork.

When Julia got up to bring in the chocolate cake she'd made for dessert, Connor gave Darby a measured look. "Can we save our cake for breakfast, Mom? I think Darby's about to drop."

Though he spoke the truth, Darby stiffened her back. "I can decide for myself if I want cake or no—" A jaw-cracking yawn interrupted her tirade, and Connor's family chuckled.

"You were saying?" Grant teased.

She flashed Grant a playful scowl and turned to Julia. "Will you save me a piece of cake for tomorrow?"

Connor's mother covered her hand and squeezed. "Of course, darling. Sleep tight."

Connor was out of his seat and helping her pull back her chair before she could wipe her mouth and put her napkin on her plate. She remembered that about him. He was always the gentleman, always so in tune to her needs, always ready to assist her in little ways. Except when she'd needed him most.

When she'd believed he'd been killed in that hunting cabin, she'd needed his comfort, his support, his arms around her. When Savannah was born, she'd needed him beside her in the labor room. When the doctor had given her the results of Savannah's pathology tests in March, she'd needed his strength and encouragement.

A lingering bubble of resentment swelled inside her, and she pulled away from him when he tried to wrap an arm around her waist. She didn't miss his quiet sigh of frustration and disappointment, and some traitorous part of her soul wrenched in sympathy for his hurt. *But he's here now,* a little voice said.

Giving a nod to his family and Marshal Jones, he followed her back to her bedroom and started moving throw pillows from the bed. Toby, who'd been napping on the window seat, hopped down and stretched lazily before jumping onto the bed to demand Connor's attention.

As she stood at the dresser, taking off her earrings and kicking her shoes from her feet, she was blindsided by a wave of loneliness and despair. The cold sank to her bones, like a portent of some impending tragedy, and she shivered. "Connor?"

He looked up from scratching Toby behind the ears. "Yeah?"

"You don't have to sleep on the couch tonight."

He lifted Toby to the floor in order to fold back the sheets for her. "I thought I might sleep on Savannah's bed. That okay with you?"

Darby looked at him, then her king-size bed. She really didn't want to be alone tonight. But was she ready to have Connor sleeping beside her again? Her fingers trembled as she unhooked the clasp on her bracelet and set it on the dresser top. "I wasn't thinking of Savannah's bed."

He stilled, then raised a lopsided smile to her. "All right then," he said, clearly taking her comment as permission. "I'll be back as soon as I shower." Connor disappeared into the adjoining bathroom, and the sounds of his nightly ritual filtered out. Water running in the shower, the clink of his toothbrush against the sink, the rattle of his vitamin bottle as he shook out a supplement. Sounds she'd memorized years ago. A routine she'd thought would be part of her life every night until her old age. The familiarity of it twisted painfully. She'd missed everything about Connor, right down to the mundane tasks of his bedtime rituals.

Forcing her feet to move, she crossed the carpet to the bathroom and knocked. He pulled the door open, and she was greeted by a curl of steam, the scent of mint mouthwash…and Connor's bare chest. Darby's mouth dried. Because, really, there was no sexier chest in America. All sculpted muscle and smooth skin. Broad shoulders. Flat abs. A sprinkling of dark hair around his navel. Her hands itched to explore the expanse of warm flesh, relearning the texture and heat of him.

"Yeah?" He inclined his head slightly in query, completely comfortable standing before her in only his boxer briefs.

Darby swallowed hard, knowing she'd been caught staring. Gaping, in truth. "I, uh…need to brush my teeth."

"Oh, right." He stepped back to let her in, but in the confines of the narrow bathroom, she still brushed against him as she scooted past. The brief contact was enough to electrify her nerve endings and supercharge her senses.

He finished flossing his teeth, gathered his clothes from the floor and met her gaze in the mirror. "All yours."

Darby mechanically brushed her teeth and washed her face, hyperaware of the masculine scent of his soap that filled the bathroom, the slow drip in the shower where he'd just bathed. The implied intimacy of sharing a bathroom, a bed…intimacies that had once been real, not simply insinuated. A wave of nostalgia and longing swept through her, so powerful her knees buckled, and she had to grip the edge of the sink to stay on her feet. *He's back. You can reclaim what was lost.*

But did she dare? His leaving had hurt so deeply. How could she risk that much pain again?

With a hand on the wall for support, she walked to the bedroom and watched Connor for a moment as he sat on the side of the bed and checked the alarm clock setting.

When he glanced up, he gave her an automatic grin. But a dented brow and worried frown replaced the smile when she made no move to join him. Her own expression probably gave a clue to her tumbling, restless thoughts.

"What?" he asked, moving around the end of the bed toward her.

"I..." She stopped and cleared her throat, deciding honesty was best. "I'm scared."

He drew and released a deep breath before closing the distance between them. "Ah, sweetheart. She has the best doctors in the state taking care of her. We have to believe she'll come through this okay." He tugged her into an embrace, and his arms felt so safe, so warm and welcoming, she didn't resist. She didn't tell him he'd misunderstood what frightened her. "As scary as it is, we have to try to stay positive."

She nodded, burying her face in the curve of his throat, wrapping her arms around his wide chest. Clinging to him.

"Come on." He bent his knees, scooping her into his arms and carrying her the last few feet to the king-size bed. "Nothing like a good night's sleep for that shot of courage to face tomorrow."

Instinctively, she curled against him, savoring the contact. When, too soon, he set her on the crisp sheets, she reluctantly released him and snuggled under the covers. Her eyes closed, her body relaxed...but her mind buzzed with worry, with memories, with a bittersweet yearning too powerful to ignore.

Behind her, the mattress dipped as Connor crawled into bed and snapped off the lamp. "Good night, Darby."

She waited, half hoping, half dreading the feel of his body pressed against hers and his arm draped over her as he settled in for the night. They'd spooned that way so many nights in the past, it seemed natural that he'd hold her again. But he didn't. Something she dared not call disappointment speared her and, holding her breath, she rolled to face him.

Connor lay on his back, one arm raised and his hand under his head. He angled his head to meet her gaze in the dim light from the window. "Problem?"

"As tired as I am, I don't see how I'll ever get to sleep."

He curled up a corner of his mouth. "I know what you mean. Lots to think about." He paused, giving her a thoughtful look, then whispered, "Com'ere."

When he motioned for her to scoot closer to him, she balked and arched a skeptical eyebrow. Twisting his mouth, he grunted. "I'm not trying to put the moves on you. I just thought I could help you relax a bit, maybe even dose off. My shoulder massages used to help you."

This is a mistake, she told herself, even as she scooted against him, laying her hand on his warm chest and aligning her body with his.

"That's it," he murmured as his long fingers dug into her tense shoulders. "Now close your eyes and try to blank your mind."

She gave a snortlike laugh. "Yeah, right."

"Well, then try to focus on a happy memory or a quiet place."

His deep, slow massage continued, moving from her shoulders to her neck and hair. She tried to unwind, but her body had other ideas. Her scalp tingled, and her nerves sparked. Every inch of skin that touched his crackled with supersensitivity.

"Do you remember that covered bridge we found when we took a wrong turn in Georgia that time? It crossed over that big stream, and there were giant flat rocks around where people could sun, or fish, or just hang out."

Her heart clenched, then warmed from the memory.

"We had an impromptu picnic. Tuna sandwiches from the minute mart."

"Yeah." He chuckled, the sound a quiet rumble from his chest. "And that ugly stray dog smelled the tuna and came rambling up to beg for scraps."

She poked a finger in his ribs. "Which you gave him."

"He was hungry. And the sandwich had sweet pickles in it." He gave a little shudder. "I hate sweet pickles."

"And because you are a giant softie at heart." Tears filled her eyes as other memories flooded her mind, other acts of kindness and generosity Connor had shown through the years. Giving the last dollar in his wallet to a talented street performer. Giving up his day off to help build a wheelchair ramp for an elderly neighbor. Bringing her favorite almond M&Ms to her dorm when she had to study for finals.

And the way he'd doted on Peyton, his first niece. She'd known back then, watching him patiently play blocks on the floor with Peyton, that he'd be a loving, attentive father.

A sob welled in her throat so quickly, an anguished hiccupping sound escaped her before she could muffle it. She squeezed her eyes closed, trying to stop the burn of tears.

"Darby?" He levered back and put a hand under her chin to tip her head toward him. "Are you crying?"

She pinched the bridge of her nose, not bothering to give the obvious answer. He'd missed so much of Savannah's life. First smiles, first steps, hundreds of bedtime stories and games of blocks...

"Darby, what? I didn't mean to upset you. That was a happy memory for me, and I thought—"

"It was happy. *We* were happy. At least I thought we were. I know I loved you. But then you left. So maybe I didn't make you happy enough."

Connor flinched. "That's crazy talk. Of course you

made me happy. I didn't want to leave! Surely you know that."

She sighed heavily, her minty breath fanning his cheek. "I thought I did. But I thought my father loved me, too. And he left and never looked back."

"Darby, you know this isn't the same. I've told you why I had to go without you." The reassurance rolled easily from his tongue since there was truth behind it. But an uneasy niggling nipped his conscience. He'd had another reason for not asking her to go with him. One he could barely admit to himself. Because it shamed him, haunted him. And he still hadn't found a way around the obstacle, which was even bigger and more threatening since his return.

"I know the reasons you've said, and I guess they make sense, but…" Her voice cracked, and bitter pain and rejection in her voice lanced his heart. "I thought you loved me as much as I love and needed you. But if you had, how—"

"Darby, don't…" He pulled her closer, squeezing her against his chest and burying his face in her hair. "Don't second-guess what we had. It was real. It was deep and true, and I wish to God I'd never had to give you up. I did what I did, made the choices I did, *because* I loved you. I had to protect you the best way I knew how."

Darby stilled, grew quiet for several seconds, then asked, "What if we left with you? What if Savannah and I joined WitSec? Would they let us?"

The tremor of fragile hope in her voice broke his heart. "Jones and Raleigh think it'd be too risky, that it'd be too easy for the Gales' men to find us through her medical records. Her illness means there'd be a paper trail. Too many computer files that could be hacked and too many health care workers who could say the wrong thing to the wrong person. They won't even discuss that option."

"So we're back to square one."

"We never left square one." He closed his eyes, feeling the burden of his choice like a boulder crushing his soul. "Because I still love you enough to want you safe. I want you and Savannah to be safe more than I want my next breath. More than my own happiness. More than anything else. For that to happen, I have to leave."

"Then your mind's made up?" He felt the moisture of her tears drip onto his skin. "When the transplant is over, you're going to disappear again?"

"I don't see any other way this can end."

Darby made a small noise, full of hurt, as she pulled away and turned her back to him. "That you don't...tells me everything I need to know."

Chapter 12

Darby woke the next morning with a sore throat and a sinus headache. The symptoms were not unusual, given her allergies and the abundance of pollen in Louisiana, but she cursed the rotten timing. She took a vitamin C supplement and two acetaminophen tablets before she left for the hospital with Connor and Marshal Jones.

As part of Marshals Jones and Raleigh's plan to keep Connor safe, Jones took a different route to the hospital that morning. Darby saw Jones check the rearview mirror frequently as he navigated the back streets of Lagniappe. The plan was to continue to change routes throughout the transplant process so no definitive pattern was set that the Gales could manipulate to set an ambush. Connor would rotate disguises, as well, and today he was clean shaven and wearing Hunter's clothes, favorite Saints cap and Ray-Bans.

Connor squeezed her hand and flashed a confident

smile as they rode the elevator up. "We got this. Our girl is strong. If she has even a fraction of your fight, I know she'll be racing around the yard with her cousins before you know it."

His encouragement stirred a warmth in the center of her chest. His smile calmed her nervous jitters enough that she managed a deep breath before they stepped off the elevator. Holding his hand, she twitched a cheek in the nearest facsimile of a smile she could muster. "Thanks."

Savannah's doctor was waiting for them outside her room when they arrived.

"Are we late?" Darby asked, standing on her tiptoes to peer past Dr. Reed through the observation window to the sterile room.

"No." Dr. Reed tucked a clipboard under her arm and greeted them with a smile. "Her numbers are still right where they should be. Everything is a go. The nurse is starting the IV drip now."

The doctor launched into an explanation of the procedure, much of it a repeat of what they'd already been told. Darby couldn't help fidgeting as she listened to Dr. Reed. As much as she appreciated the woman's candor, knowing how vulnerable Savannah would be to germs and infection, knowing that the chemo was poisoning her daughter's body to prepare it for the transplant made her uneasy.

"How long—" she started, then paused to clear her throat. "How long will it take to administer the chemo?"

Rather than answer her question, Dr. Reed frowned at Darby. "Are you feeling all right today?"

"Uh, well…" she stammered, caught off guard by the question. "I'm nervous about the procedure, naturally. Why?"

Now Connor was eyeing her with concern, as well.

"Your cheeks are flushed, and I noticed you've cleared

Chapter 13

Darby screamed as the door frame by her head splintered. She spun out to the hall, cringing as a second shot pocked her bedroom wall.

Marshal Jones was there in no time, his weapon drawn. "Get out of the house!"

Her legs wobbled, rubbery, as shock and fear coursed through her. Staggering back down the hall, she fumbled her front door open. The echo of more gunfire followed her outside.

She raced back to the marshal's car and climbed in the backseat. Reaching for the auto lock button on the driver's door, she locked herself in and huddled on the floor. Her breath stuttered from her as she fought to calm her panic.

Was the man in her house one of the Gales' thugs, or had she stumbled across a common burglar? A neighborhood addict looking for cash or items he could pawn for drug money? She shivered despite the summer heat.

Over the thudding of her heartbeat in her ears and the uneven rasp of her breathing, she listened for signs of what was happening inside. Closing her eyes, she replayed the seconds that felt like an eternity. The intruder raising his weapon. The sting of splintering wood hitting her cheek. The desperate scramble to get out of the line of fire.

What would she have done if Savannah had been with her? Or Connor? He was, after all, the target of the Gale family.

With a sickening clarity, she remembered arriving at the hunting cabin almost five years ago and getting the crushing news that Connor was gone, stolen from her. How much more horrifying would it be to *see* him shot? Or know he died taking a bullet to save her? Because that is what Connor would have done, she had no doubt. Her stomach rolled. If she hadn't come home early, would the shooter have been lying in wait to ambush Connor?

A whimperlike moan formed in her throat. As mad as she was at Connor for his deception, his unilateral decision making and the pain she suffered without him, the thought of losing him again, mourning him again, sent a chill to her heart. And wasn't that why she was keeping him at arm's length? The agony of loving him, then losing him again? Because he had said he saw no other choice but to leave again when Savannah's transplant was over. Fresh pain slashed through her, remembering his stubborn mind-set last night. He still refused to even *ask* her to join him in WitSec.

She forced enough spit into her mouth to swallow and shoved thoughts of what would happen down the road out of her mind. Right now she had a more immediate crisis to handle. She strained to listen but heard nothing from the house. The quiet was almost as unsettling as gunfire. What did she do if Marshal Jones had been shot?

your throat and pinched the bridge of your nose several times since you arrived," Dr. Reed said, setting the clipboard aside.

"Well, I woke up with a little sinus headache, but I'll be fine."

"Hmm." The doctor stepped up to Darby and ran her fingers along the sides of Darby's neck. "Is your throat hurting?"

"Um, a little. But I'm sure it's just allergies. Sinus stuff, you know?"

"Your skin is overwarm. I think you have a fever."

Darby's shoulders drooped. If they delayed the procedure because of her stupid sinuses, she'd scream. "Of course my skin's warm. It's ninety-three degrees outside." She scoffed. "I'm fine."

Dr. Reed shook her head. "We can't chance it. Savannah will be extremely vulnerable to illness. What might be a little cold for you could make her quite sick."

"You want to delay the treatment?" Connor divided a worried look between Darby and Dr. Reed.

"No. Savannah has been prepped and is already receiving the drugs." The doctor's brow furrowed sternly. "But you need to go home. I can't have you around Savannah and risk passing her your germs."

"But..." Darby goggled at Dr. Reed. "I have to be here! I can't let her go through something so difficult alone!"

Dr. Reed shook her head. "I'm sorry, Darby. I know you're worried about her, but Savannah won't be alone. My staff will take good care of her."

"And I'll be here. And my family, your sister..." Connor added.

She shot him a dirty look. He knew how important being with Savannah was to her. How could he be siding with the doctor?

"I won't go in her room. I promise. I'll stay out here and watch through the window. But I want her to be able to see me, at least. She'll be scared—"

"No, Darby. I have to insist." Dr. Reed looked as stern as Darby had ever seen her. "You can't be here and risk passing anything on to her or my staff who work with her. You can come back when you've been symptom free for twenty-four hours."

Connor signaled Marshal Jones, who stood off to the side by the vending machine. "Will you take Darby home? She's got a little cold or something—"

"It's just allergies! I swear," she pleaded, her heart sinking.

"—and the doctor thinks she should go home. Just in case."

Now her head *really* pounded. They couldn't honestly be thinking of pumping poison into her child without her there! Leaving Savannah overnight was difficult enough, but during the procedure itself? Impossible.

"Connor…" She faced him with pleading in her eyes.

"I'm sorry, Darby. But think about it. You don't want to risk giving Savannah anything, risk her getting sick if it's not allergies."

She drew a breath to argue, but couldn't. Of course she didn't want to risk getting her daughter sick. She wet her lips. "What if I just wait for news in the cafeteria or the waiting room?"

Connor framed her cheeks with his palms. "If you are coming down with a cold or sinus infection, then your immunity will be low, too. The last place you need to be is a hospital, around other germs."

Dr. Reed aimed a finger at her. "Doctor's orders. Go home and rest."

Darby snorted. "Rest? Not likely."

She looked from one stubborn, concerned face to another and realized she was outnumbered. *Damn it.* She sighed in defeat. If her staying put Savannah in even the remotest danger of complications, then how could she take the chance? She couldn't.

After waving to Savannah from the observation window and blowing her kisses, Darby followed Marshal Jones back out to the car and rode home. She stared silently out the window on the drive back to the house. She fumed with frustration, and her body hummed with anxiety over the harsh procedure her baby had to endure. Without her there.

When she huffed a sighed for about the hundredth time, Marshall Jones sent her a commiserative glance.

"I've got kids of my own. I understand how hard this must be for you."

"It's just allergies," she complained as if he had any say in her banishment from the hospital.

Darby had the passenger door open almost before Marshal Jones had the engine turned off. She stormed to the front door, knowing she was being petulant and not caring. She didn't want to be sitting idly at home. She wanted to be beside Savannah. Or in lieu of that, if she couldn't be in the room with her, she wanted to be doing *something* useful. Something that helped her daughter recover faster. Something to make the burden of the procedure easier for her family. Something to ensure the transplant of Connor's tissue was a success.

"Help yourself to anything you want from the fridge," she told the marshal as he entered the kitchen behind her and stooped to give Toby a pat.

She tossed her purse on the counter and headed back to her bedroom. She was in no mood to make friendly chatter with Marshal Jones. As she walked down the hall, she toed off her sandals. Grunting her frustration, she plowed through the door to her room and threw her shoes toward the closet.

Rest, the doctor had said. As if she could relax knowing—

A movement across the room snagged her attention, and she glanced up.

A large man stepped out of her bathroom, swung up a gun. And fired.

form of the man who'd fired at her. A long, hideous streak of blood smeared the wall behind where the gunman had stood. Acid collected in her gut as she crept into the room and found that a red puddle was soaking into her carpet beneath the dead man's head. She gasped and choked back the surge of bile that rose in her throat.

Spinning to face her, Marshal Jones scowled. "What are you doing in here? I told you to get out of the house."

"I did get out. But…I came back," she said numbly, stating the obvious.

"Let me call you back. Meanwhile, work on getting a team out here." Jones disconnected his call and narrowed his eyes on her. "You shouldn't be in here." He stalked toward her, taking her arm and steering her out to the hall.

"It's my house," she said inanely, simply because she was getting sick of being ordered about, literally pushed around. "Was that the police you were talking to?"

"No. It was the marshals' office in Shreveport." He hustled her into the kitchen and pulled a chair out from the table. "I don't want the cops here yet."

She pulled her arm free of his grip and refused to sit. "Why not?"

"I want our people to view the scene and start working on an ID of the guy before some rookie local uniform contaminates the scene."

"You don't think very highly of the Lagniappe PD."

Jones gave a small shrug. "Nothing against your locals, per se. Let's just say I've seen it happen before. Too often." He gave her a considering glance. "I don't care whether you sit or not, but stay out of the bedroom. It's a crime scene." He pulled his phone back out and divided his attention between her and dialing. "I need to let Raleigh know what happened and have him get Sam out of—"

"No!" She grabbed his wrist when he would have lifted the phone to his ear.

"Pardon?" He arched an ebony eyebrow.

"Connor needs to stay with Savannah. If the doctor won't let me be there, she needs him with her."

He gave her an impatient sigh and twisted his mouth as if to say she was being ridiculous. "She has other members of your family. Not to mention the staff at the hospital."

"But..." She knew what he'd said was true, but somehow pulling Connor away from the hospital when Savannah was undergoing the radical chemo seemed wrong. Frightening. "What purpose does it serve to pull Connor away from the hospital?"

Jones opened his mouth to answer, then closed it with a sigh, even as Raleigh's voice came on the line through his phone. Though turning his attention to the call, Jones kept his gaze on Darby. He explained to Raleigh what had transpired, then listened a minute and said, "No. Don't tell him yet. She's unharmed, and he doesn't need to be worried about this mess while his little girl's in treatment."

Darby released the breath she'd been holding and sank onto the chair Jones had pulled out earlier, suddenly too tired to stand.

"I'll arrange for more men to be sent to the hospital to back you up. As a precaution." Jones rubbed the back of his neck as he listened to Raleigh. "I agree. I'll ask the Shreveport office to start working on it." He disconnected without further comment and shot a glance at her. "Happy?"

"Hardly. A man just shot at me, and my daughter is in the hospital." She pulled her shoulders back. "But I do appreciate your concessions so that Connor can stay at the hospital and not be distracted by this mess until later."

"Raleigh and I want to move Sam—"

"Connor," she corrected.

"To a safe house," he continued, ignoring her. "Until our people find a suitable property, be prepared for changes around here. More safety measures."

She gritted her back teeth. As much as she appreciated the protection the marshals were providing—Jones probably saved her life today—the thought of more changes, more disruption to her life, more being told what to do, chafed.

Jones's phone trilled, and he took the call as he headed out of the kitchen. Darby stared at the table, stewing for several minutes before getting up to fix herself a glass of iced tea. She needed something to calm her nerves and soothe her throat, and it was too early in the day for liquor. Especially if she wanted to put her own plan into action. She only debated her options for a minute or two. The need to find some resolution to the danger hanging over her family compelled her to act. The need to take charge of her life, to be proactive rather than a pawn, sharpened her focus to a fine point. She had to be the one calling the shots in some area of her life, take back some control.

Ever since her father left her family, she'd felt pushed aside, overlooked, ignored. Learning that Connor had chosen WitSec without consulting her had only deepened that sense. Shoving down the twinge of fear and doubt that tickled her brain, Darby channeled the determination to take the initiative, be on offense rather than reacting to life as it swung at her.

Pulling her smartphone from her purse, she did a search for the address of the prison where William Gale was serving his sentence. She put the address in a GPS mapping application and had driving directions within seconds. William Gale was sitting in a cell only ninety minutes from Lagniappe. She could be there and back before dinner time.

While Jones stood over the intruder's body and talked to his office, Darby slipped out to her car and headed south.

Less than two hours later, Darby pulled through the main gates at the federal prison and received her visitor's pass. Signs directed her to the front desk, where she passed through security checks and signed in on the guest log. The guard at the front desk made a call to have William Gale brought up to the visitors' room and buzzed open the door to the back halls.

"This way," the uniformed man said, motioning to her. "Visiting hours are almost over. You'll have about twenty minutes."

She nodded, praying that would be enough time to convince William Gale to call off his goons. Pressing a hand to her swirling stomach, Darby followed the prison guard to the visitors' room, trying to project the confidence and courage that had brought her here. While meeting with the head of the crime family with a bounty on Connor's head, she knew showing her fear would be the kiss of death. Maybe coming to see William Gale was a mistake. Should she turn around now and forget her plan? Was she just poking a hornet's nest by being here?

Darby swallowed the doubts. She had to do this. She had to take the initiative if she wanted to turn her life around. She refused to be pushed aside, victimized or have her life dictated to her again. She wanted the power to decide her fate, to make her life what she wanted.

"Over there," the guard said. He pointed to an empty metal chair in a row of seats facing a thick, transparent partition. Thin privacy walls separated the long table into visiting stations without truly affording privacy to the inmates or their guests.

Darby took a seat, clutching her purse in her lap and tugging on her blouse to adjust her collar while she waited.

She sat straighter in the hard chair when, with a metallic clang, the door to the cell block opened and a guard ushered an older man in a bright orange jumpsuit into the room. The guard motioned to the station where she sat, and William Gale furrowed his brow in confusion. He said something to the attendant, and the guard nodded. Shrugging, William Gale sauntered over and sat in the chair opposite Darby.

Lifting her chin, Darby flashed a smile, even as her gut roiled with a greasy disgust for the man responsible for trying to kill Connor. "Hello, Mr. Gale."

He jerked a suspicious nod. "Have we met? I'd like to think I'd remember a pretty gal like you, but I'm afraid I can't place you."

"No, sir," she said almost choking on the courtesy title. But the man was old enough to be her father, and some habits were ingrained. "We haven't met. My name is Darby Kent." She took a deep breath for courage. "Five years ago, when you were convicted, I was engaged to Connor Mansfield."

She knew the instant the name registered, because William's eyes grew flinty and his mouth firmed. Just as quickly, though, he schooled his features. His expression became almost placid, but a tiny tic in his jaw told Darby he was calculating, sizing her up, mentally reviewing his grievances against Connor. When he spoke, his words startled her.

"I understand Connor Mansfield was killed in an unfortunate accident soon after my trial ended." He inclined his head slightly. "My condolences, Ms. Kent. While I don't grieve the lost of Mr. Mansfield, seeing as he was largely responsible for putting me here—" he raised a hand to in-dicate the prison "—I'm not unsympathetic to your pain."

Darby blinked, startled as much by the man's condo-lences as by the notion that William Gale could be unaware that Connor was still alive. Had his sons not informed him of Connor's return from the dead? Was it possible the Gale brothers didn't know Connor was back in town? Unlikely, considering the dead man in her bedroom. She worked hard to school her face, not give away anything before she decided how to proceed. "Thank you."

William leaned back in his chair, folding his arms over his chest. His eyes were a cool gray, his gaze keen and cun-ning. "So what brings you here today, Ms. Kent? I can't imagine this is a social call."

For the briefest moment, Darby considered lying, tell-ing him she was there about some bogus legal matter. A little warning bell inside her stanched that impulse like a cigarette under a boot heel. If William Gale was playing her, testing her to see if she'd confess that Connor was alive, her honesty might win points with him. If he didn't know the truth, perhaps her candor would still give her credence with the man. Either way, being caught in a lie wouldn't go over well down the road, she felt sure. She'd come to negotiate a cease-fire, and that's what she would do. *Be bold. Be proactive. Take your life back.*

"Mr. Gale, the thing is…" She filled her lungs, squared her shoulders and bolstered her bravado. "Connor is still alive."

One graying eyebrow lifted, but he showed no other reaction to the news.

"I only learned the truth in the past several days myself. I truly believed my fiancé was dead." She held her breath for a moment, watching him, but he remained still, stoic. "Connor faked his death because he believed your sons had a contract out on him. Whether by your authority or not, I don't know."

She hesitated, her heartbeat thundering so loudly in her ears, she could barely hear herself speaking. Surreptitiously, she wiped her hands on the legs of her pants. "He left WitSec and came back to town because...we have a daughter together. A daughter he only recently learned of."

He nodded once. "Savannah."

A chill rippled through her, and she could do nothing to hide her shock and dismay. "Y-you know about her... know her name?"

He flashed an indulgent smile. "You're surprised? Ms. Kent, in my business, it's prudent to know all you can about your enemies."

"Enemies." She swallowed hard as bile rose in her throat. "Isn't that term a bit harsh?"

Again he arched his eyebrow. "What term would you use for a man who turns his back on seven years of gainful employment to disclose confidential company files and send you to prison?"

His calm demeanor, his pale-eyed stare were somehow more menacing to her than if he'd been ranting in her face and frothing at the mouth. She sat on her hands to stop them from shaking. "Connor did what he felt was right. He would have been complicit if he said nothing. It wasn't personal."

William sat forward now, a bitter smile twisting his mouth. "And yet it felt so very personal to me, seeing as how his testimony stabbed me in the back and sent me here."

"I...I only meant—"

"Why are you here, Ms. Kent?" Though a certain amicability had returned to his tone, she knew better than to be fooled into believing he was being polite for more than the benefit of the guards watching them.

"Are you aware that my daughter—Connor's daughter—is ill?"

The older man's forehead creased as if this were news to him.

"Connor came back," she continued, "despite knowing your family wanted him dead, hoping to save our daughter's life. He'll be donating his bone marrow soon for a transplant that we hope will put Savannah's cancer in remission."

"And you're telling me this because…?"

"Mr. Gale, Connor has already missed out on almost four years of Savannah's life and has been away from his family even longer."

"As have I, Ms. Kent. I have a family as well, and because of Mr. Mansfield's testimony, I will miss many more years of birthdays, Christmases and new babies. What is your point?"

She sighed. "Could you please lift the contract on Connor? Call off your men, and let Connor stay in Lagniappe with his daughter without fear of being gunned down or run off the road by one of your hit men?"

An amused smile lit William Gale's face without reaching his eyes. "Call off my men?"

Darby inhaled and released a tremulous breath. "Yes, sir. I'm not above begging, if that's what it takes."

"Ms. Kent, does Mr. Mansfield know you are here? Did he send you?"

She sat straighter. "No."

"What do you think he'd say if he knew you were here, talking to me?"

Darby sighed. "He wouldn't like it. I'm sure he'll be furious when he finds out. But I felt I had to do something.

I had to at least try to convince you to cancel the contract on his life."

He gave her a long, silent stare for several unnerving seconds. "I'm unaware of any threat to Mr. Mansfield's life, especially one from my family. Despite what Connor Mansfield led the jury to believe with his lies, my family and I are not criminals. Mr. Mansfield has nothing to worry about from me or my sons."

She opened her mouth to counter his assertions, but snapped it shut again. Did she really think he'd own up to the contract with guards in earshot? With security cameras recording their visit?

She hesitated, deciding how to approach the issue. "Okay, let's put it this way—will you promise me no harm will come to Connor if he stays in town with his family?"

William Gale spread his hands and gave her a sly grin. "I'm not God, Ms. Kent. I can't stop bad things from happening to Mr. Mansfield, even if I wanted to."

She wet her lips, noticing that the guards were sending other inmates back to lock up. Her time was almost up. "Mr. Gale, you're still the head of your family. Surely you have the power, the influence with your sons to do this?" When he continued to stare at her coolly, she added, "If not for my sake or Connor's, would you do it for Savannah's sake? She's just a sick little girl. She needs her father. Please, don't take Connor from Savannah."

William shifted his gaze to the barred window where the Louisiana sun beat down, baking the earth without mercy, then faced her again. "That was a very moving speech, Ms. Kent. But I'm afraid you've wasted your time and breath coming here. I have no knowledge of any contract out on Mr. Mansfield, and I have no control over whatever fate has in store for him."

She curled her fingernails into her palms in frustration. "But if you'd just speak to your family about—"

He stood, and the guard stepped over to him. "Goodbye, Ms. Kent. I'll say a prayer for your daughter tonight if you'd like."

"I..." His offer rattled her, just as she was sure it was meant to.

He flashed a smug grin as the guard led him away, toward the cell block.

"Mr. Gale, please! If you'd just—"

The door slammed shut with an ominous clang, signaling a close to her best chance of saving Connor from the Gales' threat. As she collected her purse and headed out of the prison, she couldn't help wondering if, instead of helping, her candor with the Gale patriarch had opened a Pandora's box of new trouble for her family.

"You did *what?*" Connor shouted, aghast at Darby's confession. When Marshal Jones reported that she'd disappeared for long hours that afternoon, he'd been out of his mind with worry. But had he known where she was, what she'd been up to, Connor would have been apoplectic. Especially given the dead man in her bedroom and the mounting evidence the guy had worked for the Gales.

"I thought it was worth a try," she returned, meeting his fury with an unapologetic calm and confidence. "I couldn't sit back and do nothing when I had strangers invading my house and trying to shoot me and the people I love."

If she'd been confronting anyone other than a member of the Gale family, Connor would be proud of her gumption and moxie. But she'd gone to see William freaking Gale himself. He could only pray she hadn't woken a sleeping giant.

"Darby, the Gales are my problem. They want me. This isn't your battle to fight—"

"The hell it isn't! It sure felt like my battle when that creep was shooting at me!" she volleyed.

As it had the first time he'd heard about the shooting, Connor's stomach fell to his toes, leaving a cold pit of fear inside him.

Darby huffed a sigh. "In hindsight, maybe it wasn't the smartest move—"

"Ya think?"

She glared at him and continued. "But at least I did *something* to try to put an end to this mess. I wanted to confront the situation, have some say in my life, not meekly let life trample me like it has for the past several years. My choice. My call. Maybe it was a bad decision, but it was *mine!* I had to take some authority back in my life. Why can't you understand that?"

He had no answer for Darby, so he turned to Jones and the deputies who'd arrived that afternoon to investigate the intruder, and he vented at them. "And where were you? Why didn't you stop her? You're supposed to be protecting her!"

A muscle in Jones's jaw twitched, and he cleared his throat. "No, we're here to protect *you*. Ms. Kent is only our responsibility insofar as she directly affects our job of protecting you. She left while I was handling the little matter of a finding out who the dead guy in her bedroom was." Jones's expression matched his sarcastic tone.

"Are you kidding me?" Connor raked his hand through his hair. "You don't care that she went to see the very man I put in prison? The reason you're protecting me in the first place?"

"Obviously we aren't happy about it," Raleigh said. "But

she is a private citizen and, as such, she's free to do whatever or go wherever she wishes."

Connor gaped at the marshal. "No, she can't!"

"Excuse me?" Darby crossed her arms over her chest and cocked her head, full of attitude.

He sighed and held his hands up, hoping to placate her before another fight started. "Darby, before you blow up, think about who we are talking about. Do you have any idea how dangerous the Gales are?"

She twisted her mouth as if in thought. "Oh, I'd say dangerous enough to send a hit man to my house to ambush and shoot at me."

Connor waved a hand in frustration. "Exactly! And knowing that, you still drove down to the prison to rattle daddy's cage? Are you crazy?"

"Maybe I am," she tossed back with a humorless laugh. "And maybe nothing will come of my appeal to Mr. Gale. But I didn't see how asking for a truce could make matters any *worse.* How can things be worse than having members of organized crime gunning for you?"

"It could be worse if they *succeeded.* We don't want to make things easy for them!"

She glanced away, and when she met his gaze again, Darby's tone was calmer and pleading. "I wasn't in danger, Connor. I had a thick sheet of glass between us and guards all around. Please understand. I had to do *something.* I hate the idea of constantly looking over my shoulder, of being passive instead of proactive."

He crossed the room and placed a hand on each of her shoulders. "And I hate that my return from the dead has put you and every other person I love in jeopardy." His chest seized, making it hard to breathe. He ducked his head, mumbling. "The sooner I leave again, the better for everyone."

If not for Savannah and his scheduled marrow donation, he'd leave town that night.

Beneath his hands, Darby trembled, and when she spoke
again, the tears in her voice brought his head up, his gaze
latching on to her. "You don't get it, do you?"

"Get what?" He couldn't hide the frustration in his tone.

"I don't want you to leave again! I'm trying to find a
way that you can stay! Your family needs you. They love
you. Savannah deserves a father in her life. I was *trying*
to make that happen rather than accepting defeat without
a fight!" A tear broke free of her bottom lashes, and seeing it track down her cheek kicked him in the gut. And
gave him hope.

"And you?" The muscles in her shoulders tensed, but
he continued. "Do you still love me? Can you forgive me
for leaving?"

"If I did forgive you, would it really make a difference?
Aren't you still planning to leave again?"

Defeat weighted his shoulders, and he sighed as he
pinched the bridge of his nose. "Darby, try to understand—"

She wrenched free of his grip, her face a mask of hurt
and disappointment. "That's what I thought."

"Daddy!"

James Gale scooped his five-year-old daughter into his
arms as she bounded across the foyer to greet him. "Hello,
princess. Have you been a good girl today?"

Melinda nodded vigorously. "I helped Angela make our
dinner. She let me stir the gravy!"

He kissed her cheek. "Fabulous! I can't wait." He set his
squirming daughter back on the floor and glanced down
the empty hall. "Where's your mom?"

"In there." She pointed to the closed door of his study.
"Uncle Victor is here. He brought me bubble gum. See?"

She opened her mouth and showed him a wad of pinkish goo.

"Yeah," he answered, distracted by the news that Victor had felt it necessary to see him at home rather than the office. "Tell Angela I'm home. We'll eat after I talk to Uncle Victor."

Loosening his tie and unbuttoning the top button of his dress shirt, James entered his study and divided a glance between his wife and brother, who sat in chairs opposite each other in the conversation nook by the empty fireplace.

They both stood when he came in, his wife crossing to him to kiss his cheek. "Look who stopped by. I asked him to stay for dinner, but he declined."

"Victor, what brings you by?" James closed the door behind him.

"Family business. I had an interesting call today." Victor paused and sent James's wife, Heather, a meaningful glance.

She pulled a face and turned the doorknob. "I'll give you two privacy."

When she'd gone, James propped against his desk and crossed his arms. "Go on. Who called?"

"Pop." Victor shuffled to a seat by James's desk and sat down.

"Pop? What'd he say?"

"He had a visitor."

"And?" James waved a hand, egging him on. "Get to the point. My dinner's getting cold."

Victor scowled. James knew he resented being bossed around by his older sibling, but he had little patience with Victor's petty beefs. "Connor Mansfield's girlfriend went to see Pop. He said she wanted us to call off our contract on Mansfield."

James grinned. "You don't say? Takes balls to come

right out and confront Pop like that." Sobering, he eyed his brother sternly. "Wait a minute. Was the man seen going into her house last week confirmed to be Mansfield?"

Victor cleared his throat, hesitated. "Yes and no."

"Victor…" James growled.

His brother sighed. "The photos weren't conclusive, but my gut said—"

James grumbled a curse. "Your gut? Damn it, Vic, what did you do?"

Victor surged to his feet, his face suffusing with color. "I did exactly what you'd have done. Don't get all high mighty, *Jimmy.*"

James tensed hearing the nickname he despised. He wasn't a five-year-old and hadn't used the childish name since he was in first grade. "What. Did. You. Do?"

Victor opened, then balled his fists as he regained his composure. "I told Hollister to take Mansfield out. To make it look like an accident."

"I take it he failed."

"He broke into Darby Kent's house when no one was home. We believe Mansfield has been staying there the past couple of days. Darby came home, Hollister shot at her. She had a cop with her, a bodyguard or something."

Groaning, James stroked a hand down his face, knowing where this was going before his buffoon of a brother confirmed, "Hollister's dead."

"And his connection to you leads the cops right to our door." James gave Victor a snarl of disgust. "Brilliant, Victor." He paced over to the picture window looking out on his back terrace.

"So following this home invasion, Darby goes scurrying down to visit Pop in prison to beg a cease-fire." He shot his brother a glance. "What'd Pop tell her?"

Jerking a shrug, Victor scoffed. "That he had no knowledge of any contract or other threat from our family, of course."

"Of course." Pop was no fool. "Did she buy it?"

"I doubt it. She rephrased her plea, kept harping on him for a promise we'd leave Mansfield alone. Pop gave her nothing." Victor narrowed his gaze, his expression smug. "She confirmed what we suspected, though. Mansfield faked his death. He came back 'cause their little girl has cancer. He's the kid's donor for some kind of transplant."

James grunted, mulling the information, and glanced at a photo of his children on his desk. "That'd be enough to bring me out of hiding. When's the operation?"

Victor shrugged. "Don't know. But if we're gonna get him, we need to act fast. Once he's made his donation, he could disappear again."

James watched a robin hop across his lawn in the fading daylight. Once again, it was up to him to fix one of his brother's screwups. Facing Victor, he took his time answering. "Your premature action has Mansfield and his bodyguards on the alert. It will be difficult to get to him."

"But not impossible." Victor leaned forward, moving to the edge of the chair, his eyes narrowing. "Seeing as Ms. Kent has seen fit to insert herself into the equation, I think she might be our best way forward."

James gritted his back teeth. "No."

"She made herself relevant to the situation when she confronted Pop."

"No."

"Think about it, James. It would hurt Mansfield more than anything else. Killing him draws a line under the whole affair too easily. But by eliminating Ms. Kent, Mansfield suffers a bit first. He has time to consider the pain he caused our family by locking Pop away."

James slammed a hand on his desk. "I said no! Leave his family out of this, Victor."

Victor lunged to his feet and braced his arms on James's desk. "It's not your call to make! Pop wants Mansfield to suffer, and I say taking out Kent or his kid is the least he has coming!"

James stood slowly, squaring off with his brother. "Darby and the little girl are off-limits. Do you hear me? I owe Connor that much."

"Because he pulled Billy out of the pool *seven years ago?*" Victor shouted, his tone incredulous. "That's ancient history!"

"Yes! Because he saved my son's life." James stalked around his desk and stuck his face in Victor's. "You might be able to write that off as old news, but I will *never* forget that Billy is alive today because of Mansfield." James's body hummed with tension and intensity as the horror of that night replayed in his mind like a bad dream. "I cannot allow you to hurt his family. Not when he gave me back my boy."

Victor's mouth twisted in an ugly sneer, and he poked James in the chest. "You're pathetic. Avenging Pop should be your priority. The strength of the Gale family has always been in our unity. But you've let your kids and some crazy idea of nobility turn you soft."

James balled his hands, resisting the urge to smash a fist in his younger brother's smug face. "Mansfield will get what's coming to him for betraying Pop. I haven't changed my mind on that. But you will leave his family alone."

Victor stared at him, a muscle in his jaw working. With a scoff, his brother shook his head. "No. Darby Kent and the rest of the Mansfields are fair game. I'll do whatever it takes to bring Mansfield down, even if that means collateral damage."

With that, he turned and stalked toward the office door.

"Victor—" James said, his gaze falling on the photo of his children. His brother paused at the door, sending James a dark glare. "I'm warning you. You may be my brother, but I will not let your mistakes sink my family."

Victor yanked open the door, scowling. "My only mistake was ever thinking you had the balls to head this family and make the hard calls. I have no trouble avenging Pop, whatever it takes."

Chapter 14

With Darby's bedroom now a crime scene, the U.S. Marshals decided to move Connor, Darby and Toby the cat to his parents' house until a better safe house could be secured. Additional deputy marshals from Shreveport arrived to assist, and new protocols regarding transportation back and forth to the hospital and guarding the Mansfields' house were put in place. In addition to taking alternate routes, the marshals would use different cars, including those of the family members, different passenger groupings and transportation schedules to keep the Gales guessing. Connor would never travel with fewer than two marshals, one driving him, one armed and ready to take defensive measures.

Out of concern over Darby's possible germs, Dr. Reed ordered Connor to stay clear of Darby and anyone else with even a hint of illness. He had to stay as healthy as possible in preparation for his donation. While at the hospital keeping vigil over Savannah, he wore a surgical mask and stayed out of public areas. At his parents' house, he slept in his old bedroom, longing to hold Darby, who slept in the guest room down the hall.

On the third night of their stay with his parents, a light knock roused him as he restlessly searched for sleep. "Yeah?"

The door creaked open, and Darby stood silhouetted by the dim light from the hall. "You awake?"

"Yeah. What's wrong?" He propped up on his elbows and squinted through the darkness, trying to read her face.

"Nothing really. I just…" She shifted her bare feet and glanced away for a moment. "Have I thanked you properly for what you're doing? Because I don't want you to leave again without knowing I'm eternally grateful for the risk you've taken coming back and for your willingness to donate your marrow to our daughter."

Our daughter. His pulse quickened hearing her use the plural possessive. He cleared the emotion from his throat and said, "It's my honor. I only wish I could do more to ensure her recovery."

"Me, too," she rasped.

She hovered in the doorway, silent and pensive. After a moment, Connor asked, "So…how are you feeling? Any fever? Sore throat?"

"No. I'm fine. I told you it was allergies." She straightened her shoulders resolutely. "I'm going to the hospital tomorrow, and God help anyone who tries to stop me."

"In that case…c'mere." He patted the side of the bed and waved her over. "I'm calling an end to this quarantine."

She hesitated only a few seconds before crossing to him and cuddling next to him on his old twin bed. He held her close in the shadow of his high school tennis and baseball trophies, Saints pennant and dusty collection of CDs. He found he needed the reassurance and strength he gained from holding her as much as she needed his support.

"How is she, Connor?" she asked, breaking the silence. "The truth. Don't spare my feelings or whitewash it. How is Savannah? Really?"

Connor pictured the listless, pale little girl he'd left at the hospital that evening, and his gut tightened. He'd wanted to shield Darby from the harsh reality of the toll the preparatory chemo was taking on Savannah, but he wouldn't lie to her. "The treatment's been hard on her. She's weak and nauseated most of the time. She sleeps a lot and has no appetite. The rest of her hair has fallen out, and her skin is even more sallow than before."

She raised a hand to her mouth, muffling a sob. "Oh, God."

"But…" He sat all the way up and fixed a hard stare on her. "Look at me, Darby."

Her head came up, and she met his gaze with anxious eyes.

"Everything she's going through is within the parameters of what the doctor expected. It's normal, considering the treatment. Our girl's a fighter. She's going to be fine." She didn't answer, and he added, "I know you're scared for her, but this…this is the darkness before the dawn. She's going to be okay."

Darby bit her bottom lip when it quivered. "Promise?"

He pulled her close, cradled her head against his chest and kissed her hair. He wished he had the power to guarantee their daughter would survive, would grow up and live a full life. But if he had that kind of magic in him, he'd never have been separated from Darby to begin with. All he could do was hope, pray and use every resource available to him to protect his daughter and Darby from the men who wanted him dead.

* * *

The next morning, Connor woke, alone, to the sound of voices and laughter from the front rooms of his parents' house. He tossed back the sheet, stretched the kinks from his back and stumbled to the guest room door to peer in. Darby was still asleep in the double bed, clearly having left him at some point after he fell asleep with her snuggled against him. Toby was curled in the crook of Darby's legs, a tight ball of sleeping fur.

As if sensing his presence, Darby rolled to her back, disturbing the cat, and blinked sleepily at him. "What time is it?" she asked with a yawn.

He flipped his wrist and checked his watch. "Seven-eighteen."

She groaned and closed her eyes. "What's all the racket?"

Connor tipped his head, listening. "Well, Mom's up, for sure. And I think I hear Jones. And—"

A baby's wail drifted down the hall, followed by a deep voice calling, "Tracy! Your daughter wants you."

Connor grinned. "Grant's family."

Toby arched his back, then stretched his lithe body as he hopped off the bed and sauntered over to rub against Connor's legs. Darby smiled as she stretched like the cat and slid her feet to the floor, her hair tousled and sexy. "Dang, they must have been up at oh-dark-thirty if they're here already."

Connor battled down a spurt of morning lust as Darby raked hair back from her face and fixed the strap of her pajamas, which had slipped off her shoulder. She caught his stare and grimaced as she jammed her arms in a summer bathrobe. "Don't laugh. I know I look scary in the morning."

He strolled into the room and wrapped her in a hug.

"Honey, *scary* is not the word I was thinking. Quite the opposite."

"Wow," she deadpanned as she wiggled free. "You men will say anything for sex."

He barked a laugh and headed down the hall to the kitchen, which was a beehive of activity. His mother was at the stove cooking breakfast, and the scent of bacon and biscuits filled the air. His father was thumbing through the newspaper. Tracy was trying to feed her fussy baby a bottle. Grant had his blond-haired daughter climbing on him while he tried to pour a mug of coffee. Toby had made his way down the hall and sat in the middle of the floor, tail twitching, ready to trip someone if they didn't feed him. *Now.*

Marshals Jones and Raleigh sat at the kitchen table with steaming mugs, clearly trying to stay on the periphery of the family chaos.

Tracy spotted Connor first and sent him a cheerful smile. "There's the sleepyhead. Good morning, Connor." Her grin turned wry. "We didn't wake you, did we?"

He chuckled as he stepped into the fray. "Naw! Why would you think that?" He tugged on the blond girl's ponytail. "Good morning, little monkey."

His niece glanced up at him with wide, startled eyes. It stung to realize his brother's child didn't remember him. But why would she? She'd been a toddler when he left.

Peyton sidled behind her father and gave Connor a wary peek. Crouching to his daughter's level, Grant stroked her back and said, "Peyton, can you say good morning to Uncle Connor?"

She gave a timid wave and whispered, "Hi."

Grant stood again and flashed a lopsided grin. "Give her five minutes, and she'll be talking your ear off."

Connor winked at his niece. "I look forward to it."

Then to Grant, "You're here awfully early. Did I miss the memo?"

His oldest brother shrugged. "We were up with Kaylee by five, so we figured we'd come on into town. Mom said she'd help me with the kids today so that Tracy could go to the hospital for a while."

Connor nodded and clapped his brother on the shoulder as he moved past him to pour himself and Darby mugs of coffee.

When Darby appeared a few minutes later she was already dressed, and her wet hair said she'd grabbed a quick shower. She sent the room full of people a half smile. "Looks like the party started without me."

Julia stepped over to her and gave her a hug. "We didn't want to wake you, sweetheart. You needed your rest."

Darby gave his mom a peck on the cheek. "I got a little sleep last night. Thanks." She turned to the marshals, adding, "I'm completely well again, so I'll be going to the hospital today."

Marshal Jones raised his mug in acknowledgment. "We've already been working on a plan for the day."

Connor stumbled over Toby as he headed back across the kitchen to hand Darby her coffee. "Forget the Gales. I think Toby's got a secret plan to kill me."

Darby scooped the cat into her arms and kissed Toby's furry face. "Baloney. Toby doesn't have a mean bone in his body. Right, sweet boy?"

Over the next half hour, Julia fed the family a huge Southern breakfast, complete with veggie omelets, cheese grits, bacon, biscuits and fruit salad. Darby gave Toby his breakfast, and the marshals briefed everyone on the protocol for the day.

When it was time to head to the hospital, Raleigh whistled for quiet, and Connor's family gathered around. "All right, I'll take Tracy and Darby in to see Savannah now in Darby's car. Connor, you wait here with Jones. He'll drive you over in a couple of hours."

Jones nodded to Connor's mother. "Thank you for breakfast. That was the best omelet I think I've ever had."

Julia beamed. "Old family recipe. I could tell you the secret ingredient, but then…"

"You'd have to kill me," Jones finished for her, his grin saying he'd heard that line many times.

"Something like that."

Tracy gave Grant a kiss as she gathered her purse. "You sure you don't mind watching the kids?"

"I'm sure. Tell Savannah hi for me."

Tracy nodded. "Keep a close eye on Peyton. She's getting more adventurous and doesn't know her limits."

"Will do," Grant said, balancing the baby on his hip.

Connor followed Darby to the front door. Even though he knew he'd see her again in a few hours, parting ways with her still caused a hitch in his chest. The memory of telling her goodbye four and a half years ago, believing he'd never see her again, scraped through him like sandpaper, because he knew all too soon he'd need to tell her goodbye again. Permanently. Unless he could convince her they belonged together, that being a family was worth all she'd have to give up. And did he even have the right to ask so much of her? Would she even consider giving everything up for him?

The support and love of his extended family through the past several days, facing Savannah's transplant surgery and all the extra security measures his presence required, made him appreciate his parents, his brothers all the more. How could he give them up a second time? How could he ask Darby to give up all the people she loved to be with him? She'd said she couldn't let herself love him again, but last night her eyes had said something quite different.

He pulled her close, brushed the hair back from her cheek and simply stared into her eyes for long seconds, memorizing their color.

She tipped her head. "What is it, Connor?"

He sighed. "Just…savoring this moment. You."

"I have to go now. Raleigh is waiting for me." She canted forward and gave him a quick kiss. "See you soon."

He let her slip out of his arms and watched her hurry to the car. Tracy was already in the backseat, and seeing Darby approach, Raleigh finished a conversation with Jones on the sidewalk and climbed behind the steering wheel to drive. When Darby reached the passenger door of her Honda, she paused to give Connor another smile and wave.

His chest clenched painfully, and without thinking about what he was doing, Connor bolted through the front door and jogged across the lawn to the car.

Darby blinked her surprise when he appeared at the side of the car. "Connor?"

He leaned in to give her a long resounding kiss. "I love you."

Sadness filled her gaze, even though she flashed him a smile. Knowing he'd put that sadness in her eyes was a bitter pill to swallow. Realizing she hadn't responded to his admission stung. He bit the inside of his cheek, vowing not to pressure her. He needed to give her more time.

"You need to get inside." Raleigh sent him a warning glare as he turned the key in the ignition. The engine didn't catch, but a metallic click came from the undercarriage.

Raleigh growled a harsh curse, his expression sheer panic.

A tingle of premonition raised the hair at Connor's nape.

Even as Connor recognized the threat, Raleigh was shouldering his door open. "Get out!"

Connor had already grabbed Darby's arm. He yanked hard as he instantly stumbled back from the car.

The Honda exploded in a searing fireball, and the powerful concussion threw him to the ground. He clung to Darby's arm, pulling her with him as he crashed to the lawn. When she landed on him, he quickly rolled on top of her, shielding her from the secondary blast of the gas tank going up.

For a few stunned seconds, he simply lay on his parents' front yard, ears buzzing from the volume of the blast, and he held Darby against him. Safe. Darby was safe.

But the numb moments of shock and relief quickly shattered as Grant burst through the front door of the house, screaming, "Tracy!"

With a nauseating dread, Connor glanced at the burning shell of the Honda. Horror slammed his gut. Tracy hadn't made it out of the car. His sister-in-law was dead.

Chapter 15

Through a numb veil of surrealism, Connor processed the nightmarish scene. Grant charged toward the burning car, screaming for his wife. Marshal Jones stopped him, virtually tackling Grant to keep him back from the conflagration. Marshal Raleigh staggered into view from the far side of the car, clutching his arm and clearly suffering significant burns to much of his body.

Beneath him, Darby moved, a strangled sob racking her body. "Oh, my God...Tracy!"

Connor shook himself from his shock. He searched Darby's face and arms with a frantic gaze and searching hands. "Are you hurt?"

She lifted wide eyes to his, her expression reflecting the same anguish and disbelief that gripped him. "I...I don't think so." Her attention shifted to the front door, and she gasped. "Oh, no, no, no! She can't see this!"

Darby pushed on his chest as he turned stiffly to see

what Darby had seen. Peyton stood behind the glass storm door, straining to see what had caused the commotion. Connor's heart seized. Peyton, whose mother had just died. Because of him. Because he'd returned from WitSec. Acid pooled in his gut, and bile climbed up his throat.

Darby shoved to her feet, staggered to the front door and swept Peyton into her arms as she disappeared in the house with the little girl.

"Call 911!" Jones yelled as Stan raced out the front door. "Raleigh needs an ambulance!"

Connor struggled for a breath, grief and guilt crushing him. A keening moan reached him, raising the hair on the back of his neck. The agony and despair of the sound sent chills through him. Slowly he turned, knowing the source of the cry and hating himself all the more.

Grant strained against Jones's grip, still trying to reach his wife. Swallowing hard against the bitter taste filling his throat, he staggered over to his brother.

"Grant," he rasped.

His brother's wild eyes darted to him, desperate, pleading. "T-Tracy."

Jones moved aside, rushing to help Raleigh, as Connor pulled his brother into a firm hug. "I'm so sorry."

Grant swayed and dropped to his knees, but Connor clung to him. His brother's voice was choked with tears as he repeated, "Why? Why?"

Connor knew why Tracy had died. Knew her blood was on his hands. Knew he could never make amends to his brother for the pain he'd caused.

All he could do at that moment was hold his brother, cry with him. Then get the hell out of town and disappear again before anyone else he loved got hurt.

* * *

"I have to get to the hospital," Darby said to no one in particular.

Grant sat across the living room from her, his expression shell-shocked, devastated. He held Peyton on his lap, his daughter crying softly and burying her face in his chest, while he stared blankly into near space. Connor's parents were taking turns with Kaylee, who seemed to sense the grief of her family and fussed inconsolably.

Raleigh had been taken to the hospital by ambulance with serious burns on the right side of his body. The local police and fire crew were still on the scene, but Marshal Jones was dealing with the situation and managing things outside. Darby had given her brief statement, for what it was worth. No one had seen the perpetrator plant the bomb, but everyone in the Mansfields' living room knew who was responsible. Finding proof would fall to law enforcement.

Darby's thoughts spun in a hundred directions. She was as shocked by what happened, as full of anguish as everyone else. But in light of the morning's tragedy, one need separated itself from the confusion in her mind. An overwhelming urgency to be with Savannah. In the wake of the horror of the car bomb, her maternal instincts screamed that she needed to be near her daughter.

Savannah was still waiting for them at the hospital. Her baby was in an isolated room, receiving high doses of poison to ready her tiny body for the transplant. Even if the hospital staff wouldn't let her in the room, wouldn't let her touch her baby, she wanted to see her child and assure herself Savannah was safe.

Connor sat beside her on his parents' couch, holding her hand, deep in his own troubled thoughts if his dark frown was any indication. She tugged on his arm to get his attention. "If the Gales did this, who's to say they haven't tried to hurt Savannah?" A chilling dread spun through her as she raised a panicked look to him.

"Hunter is with her. He'd have called if—"

Her grip tightened. "*I* need to be with my baby."

He blinked once, slowly, then jerked a nod. "Wait here. I'll talk to Jones."

Squeezing her fingers, Connor rose from the couch and craned his neck to look out through the front window at the assembly of firemen and police in the yard. The scrape of a kitchen chair drew his attention to the breakfast nook, and he headed that direction, disappearing from her view.

Darby shivered as the sights, sounds and scents of the bomb blast replayed in her head. If Connor hadn't pulled her out of the car a split second before the explosion, she'd be dead. Like Tracy.

Another wave of agonizing sadness and disbelief swamped her, making it difficult to breathe. How could Tracy, one of the kindest, gentlest souls she'd ever known, have been stolen from them this way? She was an innocent bystander. Her death was unfair on so many levels.

"Don't you think I know that?" Connor's raised voice pulled her attention to the kitchen.

Snippets of Jones's tense reply followed. "If you…our orders…never…"

"…doing your job, this never… Why didn't…"

"Damn it, my partner is…hospital because…"

The volume and verve of the argument grew, drawing the attention of Connor's parents and Grant, as well.

"…know that! My brother's wife…" Connor shouted. "What do you want me…"

"…do things the right…or get the hell out of here…"

Darby's pulse, already jangling thanks to the morning's trauma, ratcheted higher. She wiped her hands on her pants and gritted her back teeth as she listened to the fighting and watched the flood of emotions that filled Grant's face.

"…going anywhere…my daughter still needs…"

"…screwing around with people's lives…I have a family, too, and I…"

Clenching her hands into fists, Darby shoved off the sofa and marched into the kitchen.

"You want to leave?" Connor yelled as she stormed into the breakfast nook. His face was tense, and he'd pulled his shoulders back in challenge.

"I want you to take a hard look at what happened today, and think about it the next time you—"

"Stop it!" Darby shouted, adding her voice to the din. "Stop this fighting, right now!"

Jones and Connor both turned startled looks toward her.

"Do you two really think this shouting is helping anything?" She huffed angrily and divided a glare between them. "Stop yelling at each other and figure out how to keep it from happening again!" She aimed a finger at Jones. "Do your job and protect this family or get the hell out of this house! But don't you *dare* try to take Connor out of town before he donates his marrow.

"My baby is lying in that hospital, *completely* vulnerable. Her body's defenses have been reduced to *nothing* in preparation for the transplant. If she doesn't get his bone marrow now, she doesn't have the strength or the immunity to recover. She will almost certainly die." Her voice cracked, and she paused to catch her breath.

"Darby…" Connor took a step toward her, and she shot a hand up to stop him.

She pinned a hard stare on Jones. "My daughter is waiting for me at the hospital. Are you going to take me or should I drive myself?"

* * *

By the end of the day, a new team of U.S. Marshals, Marshals Morris and Ramsey, had been assigned to help Jones protect Connor and the rest of the family.

Darby and Connor divided their time between the hospital and his parents' house, where they helped Grant, who remained withdrawn and shaken to his core by his loss, take care of his children. Darby helped Julia make arrangements for Tracy's funeral, and Connor prayed it was the only one the family had to plan for years to come. The sooner he gave his marrow and got out of town, the better.

Dr. Reed scheduled the transplant surgery for the day after the funeral so that Connor could attend the service with his family. As the family gathered at the cemetery, the sun shone with almost mocking glee, in harsh contrast to the mood of the crowd saying goodbye to a mother and wife taken far too early.

On the plot next to Tracy's, Connor noticed the headstone that read, Connor Morgan Mansfield, Beloved Son and Brother. A chill slithered through him, imagining a service like this one held for him a few years ago, how Darby had felt burying him. He glanced at Grant's devastated face, considered how he'd feel if it were Darby in the casket, and shuddered. How in the world did he ever make up for the pain he'd caused his family, the heartbreak he'd put Darby through, no matter how noble his intentions of protecting them?

While the minister and funeral director spoke off to the side, waiting for mourners to assemble, Darby, who held two-month-old Kaylee, turned to Connor. Her eyes were hidden behind sunglasses, and her cheeks were damp with tears. "Connor," she said softly, "if you're alive, who did we bury?"

He jolted and jerked his gaze back to the headstone with his name. "I...I don't know."

He hadn't questioned the marshals about the details of the plan when he'd entered WitSec. He'd assumed they'd told his family there wasn't a body left to bury after the explosion and fire.

"Friends and family," the minister began, "today we gather to say goodbye to Tracy Mansfield, a loving and joyful wife and mother..."

Connor stared at the flower-draped coffin without really hearing what the minister said, words meant to comfort and encourage. But how could he find any comfort knowing he was to blame for his brother's deep grief? His return was the reason two sweet little girls had no mother.

Beside him, Darby held Kaylee on her lap, cradled in one arm, but she slipped her other hand onto his knee and squeezed. The gesture startled him from his morose train of thought. He lifted his eyes to meet hers. Pushing her sunglasses up, Darby wiped her eyes, then gave him a look that said what words couldn't. The kind of silent communication they'd had before he disappeared. Her expression said she knew his heart, shared his sorrow.

Taking her hand in his, he savored the connection to her. He raised her fingers to his lips, thanking her for her silent support and giving his in return. Was this evidence that they still shared that soul-deep unity, a sign that he might still have a chance of winning back her heart?

His lungs seized, and regret climbed his throat. What right did he have to repair and rekindle Darby's affection for him if all he could give her was more heartache when he returned to WitSec?

Behind the affection and sympathy that shone in her emerald gaze, shadows still lurked. Scars he'd left on her heart when he'd vanished from her life. Knowing the lasting pain he'd caused her drilled his chest with a fresh dose of bitter guilt. As long as he was in danger from the Gales, they had no future together. He simply refused to put her or his family in the line of fire any more than he had to in order to save Savannah. Losing Tracy was already too high of a price.

As he turned his attention back to the minister, a movement in his peripheral vision drew his eye. He glanced beyond the crowd of mourners to the line of cars on the cemetery drive. A dark blue sedan joined the others parked on the shoulder of the road, and a tall man in a dark suit emerged. Connor squinted at the late arrival, trying to discern who'd come so late. When the man removed his sunglasses, a chill snaked up Connor's spine. Followed by a blaze of fury.

James Gale.

"The bastard," he muttered.

Darby frowned her curiosity.

Dropping her hand, he whispered in her ear, "Stay here."

As he moved out of the circle of family surrounding the casket, Jones grabbed his arm. The marshal's eyes were locked on the new arrival, and his grim face said he understood Connor's intent. "Don't."

Connor jerked his arm free of Jones's grasp, ignoring his keeper's order. Jones's hiss of frustration followed Connor as he stalked across the cemetery grounds to intercept Gale. His body hummed, a thirst for vengeance writhing inside him. He stopped, muscles taut, directly in front of the man responsible for his brother's suffering.

"What the *hell* are you doing here?" he grated through clenched teeth.

"Connor Mansfield," James said coolly. "So the rumors are true. You've returned from the grave."

"Can't you give my family peace long enough to bury

an innocent woman?" Connor stuck his face in James's, blatantly challenging him by invading his personal space.

Without backing down, James met Connor's glare. "I have no desire to disrupt your gathering. I came to express my condolences."

The gall and hypocrisy of his assertion stoked Connor's anger. "You son of a bitch! Tracy is dead because of *you*."

James tipped his head, a false dent of confusion puckering his brow. "I had nothing to do with it."

"Don't insult me with your denials," Connor snarled. "Tracy was an innocent. A wife and mother whose blood is on *your* hands."

"I have never condoned the killing of innocent women and children," James said calmly. "You have nothing to connect me to the woman's death."

Connor jabbed James in the chest with a finger. "Believe me, we will get proof. And you will rot in prison for this."

"Mansfield," Marshal Jones said in a low, warning tone behind him.

James angled his head to glance past Connor. "Aren't you going to introduce me to your friend?"

"No."

James chuckled. "Easy, fella. I'm not here to rumble." He glanced behind him. "As you see, I came alone. Well, except for my driver, but I fear he'd be no help in a brawl."

Connor sincerely doubted that. Even now Gale's driver probably had a bead on him with a high-powered weapon. He gritted his teeth and narrowed his eyes on James. "Listen to me, Gale. Your beef is with me, not my family. You want me? Come after me. But leave my family the hell alone. Got it?"

"I intend to." James leaned closer and pitched his voice low, for Connor's ears only. "You're the one who betrayed my father, and you're the one who must pay. But I haven't forgotten that you saved my son's life, and in return, I will spare your family. Consider it a courtesy in light of your heroism on my son's behalf. My brother, I'm afraid, doesn't share the same mind-set. Victor is out for your blood, and he doesn't care who else's gets spilled in the process."

As James straightened, stepping back from Connor, Grant appeared at Connor's side, his red-rimmed eyes locked on James. "Connor, what's going on? Who is he?"

Connor raised an arm to push Grant back from James and shook his head. "Never mind. Leave this to me."

"Are you the widower?" James asked, turning toward Grant.

Grant stiffened. "Who's asking?"

"James Gale." He extended a hand to Grant. "I'm sorry for your loss."

"Gale?" Grant repeated, and Connor saw the shudder that shook his brother.

Facing Grant, Connor stepped between his brother and James. He put a hand on Grant's chest, trying to stop what he knew was coming. "Go back with the others. I'll—"

Shoving past Connor, his mouth tightening to a grim line, Grant lunged at James Gale. He swung a hard, quick punch to the man's jaw, and as James stumbled back, stunned by the blow, Grant tackled him. "You killed her!" he shouted, his voice full of venom. "You did this!"

Adrenaline surged in Connor's blood. He rushed forward, Jones on his heels, and grappled to restrain his brother. Seizing one of Grant's arms while Jones grabbed the other, they peeled him off James. Within seconds, Hunter arrived, helping restrain Grant and casting a dark glare toward James.

Grant continued to struggle, snarling and crying at the same time. "Let me go! I'm gonna kill him!"

Connor noticed Gale's driver had left the car and was almost upon them, his hand on the bulge under his coat. Jones clearly noticed, too, and drew his weapon. James raised a hand, waving off his thug as he approached, then dabbed with his fingers at the leak of blood from his split lip.

"Get out of here," Connor said, his voice taut with rage. "Your fake sympathy is an insult."

James straightened his suit coat and squared his shoulders. "I'm sorry you feel that way. It was given in good faith." He glanced toward Grant, who'd stopped struggling but still glared daggers at Gale. "I won't bring charges against your brother for assault. I understand his grief. If anyone hurt a member of my family, I'd want a pound of flesh, as well." He paused, his eyes earnest. "But as I said, I had nothing to do with her death."

Connor gritted his teeth. "Leave. Now."

James wiped the blood from his fingers onto a handkerchief and held Connor's glare. "I hope the transplant goes well, for your daughter's sake. But when it's over, you'll be hearing from me again."

"So there's a division between the Gale brothers about who's fair game in their vendetta against you and who's not?" Darby asked as she paced the Mansfields' living room after the funeral guests had left.

"That's the impression I got from what James said." Connor sat on the edge of the couch, his arms resting on his thighs and his fingers steepled. "He claims he has no intention of hurting my family, but Victor has no qualms about collateral damage."

"So Victor is the one the cops should look at for the car bomb?" She rubbed her temple, trying to make sense of the bizarre and horrifying events of the past couple of days. She glanced at Marshal Jones, who stood to the side with his arms folded over his chest. Marshal Morris, a trim dark-haired man who reminded her of a clean-cut college frat boy, and Marshal Ramsey, a dirty-blond who was easily twenty years older and thirty pounds heavier than his partner, flanked Jones. The marshals from Shreveport were opposites in their style of clothing and appearance but equally grim faced.

Connor barked a humorless laugh. "Good luck finding anything that will stick to either of the Gales. They hire professionals to do their dirty work, men who know better than to leave fingerprints or serial numbers that can be traced."

"They may be smart," Morris said, "but so are the men who do our forensics. We'll find something."

"I overheard Gale mention something about his son, something you did for him?" Jones said. "What's that about?"

Connor nodded and flopped back on the couch. "It happened about seven years ago. His son was three, I think."

Startled, Darby stopped her pacing and looked toward Connor. Seven years ago was before she'd started dating Connor, and she'd never heard anything about an incident with James's son. She held her breath as he elaborated.

"I was at James's house, along with a lot of other employees at Gale Industries, for a Fourth of July barbecue. It started raining a little after we ate, so we'd all moved inside for dessert and drinks. I happened to be near a window at one point, and when I glanced out to see if it was still raining, I noticed Billy, Gale's son, was out by their swimming pool. I didn't see anyone else with him, so naturally, I got concerned."

Darby bit her lip, seeing where this was going. "He fell in the pool."

Connor glanced up at her. "Yeah. In all the noise and

confusion of moving the party inside, Billy managed to slip outside. When I saw him out there, I went to bring him inside, looking around for James's wife as I went. I didn't find her, and by the time I got out to the pool, Billy had fallen in and was sinking to the bottom."

"Damn," Jones mumbled.

"I yelled for help, went in after him. When I pulled him out, he wasn't breathing. James and his wife got there about the time I started CPR on the boy."

Darby's eyes watered, and pride swelled in her chest. "You brought him back. You saved that boy's life."

Connor shrugged. "I did what anyone in my position would do. I was in the right place at the right time."

"And even after you saved his kid, James still wants to kill you." Jones grunted and shook his head. "There's gratitude for you."

"For saving his son, he says my family is safe. From him. But he believes I betrayed his father and that I have to pay for that sin." Connor sighed. "And then there's Victor, the hothead of the family."

Darby's shoulders drooped as she sank onto a stuffed chair. "So what do we do? How do we stop Victor from killing anyone else?"

"*You* don't." Morris strolled deeper into the room and sat on the arm of the sofa. "That's our job. You'll need to take precautions, sure, but catching Victor, guarding your family is a police matter. You concentrate on taking care of your daughter."

"You'll have your donation procedure tomorrow as planned," Jones added, looking at Connor. "And when you're discharged from the hospital, you will go by our rules. No more sidetracks from SOP. You want our protection, you follow our orders."

Sitting straighter, Connor met Jones's challenging gaze

with one of his own. If the circumstances hadn't been so dire, Darby might have laughed. Connor, the king of control, being bossed around the way he bossed others.

A muscle in Connor's jaw twitched, and he faced Marshal Jones. "And what does SOP say will happen when I'm discharged?"

"You disappear," Jones said flatly, and Darby felt the words like a punch in the gut. "No more staying with the family. Clearly the disguises weren't enough to keep the truth from leaking out somehow."

Darby doubled over, dropping her head to her hands and curling her fingers into her hair. She'd known it was coming, but hearing Jones spell it out so plainly left her sick to her stomach and panicky inside. She just buried a dear friend, a woman she considered family. The idea of losing Connor again, so soon, raked through her with merciless claws. Yet she'd known all along he'd leave again. Why did talk of his departure fill her with so much anxiety and pain?

Despite every intention and caution not to, had she fallen in love with him again? Had she ever really fallen *out* of love? The ache in her chest was answer enough.

And wasn't that why her father's abandonment hurt so much? Because she'd loved and trusted him and he'd tossed her aside like yesterday's trash. Now Connor was preparing to leave her for the second time. How stupid was she to allow herself to love a man who'd do just what her father had done? Even with his track record, having already left her once, she still had feelings for Connor. She truly was a glutton for punishment. For her own sanity, she had to find a way to break the hold Connor had on her. She had to protect herself from the pain of another desertion.

A shadow fell over her, and a warm hand cradled the back of her head. "Darby?"

She glanced up at Connor, and the concern in his eyes made her heart catch. "Are you all right?"

She inhaled a stuttering breath. "Do I have a choice? Seems to me things are going to happen the way they're going to happen, whether I'm okay with it or not."

His eyes full of misery, Connor opened his mouth as if to counter her claim, but closed it again without speaking. Because he couldn't argue with the truth.

She lifted her cheek in a humorless smile as she shoved to her feet, pulling away from Connor's touch. "That's how it has been for months. Years even. I had no choice when you 'died' four plus years ago, and I don't get a say in your leaving again now. I have no control over Savannah's illness, no power to heal her or ease her pain. You tell me that because our daughter's sick, we can't go with you into WitSec. I've had assassins gunning for me, and U.S. Marshals living in my home. And I've had no choice in any of it."

She stalked out of the room, determined not to cry again. She'd already shed too many tears, and they'd gotten her nowhere. As she retreated to the guest room, she couldn't help wondering what she'd do if she *were* given the option of joining Connor in WitSec, if Savannah's illness didn't make the question a moot point. Could she give up everything she knew and everyone she loved to be with Connor?

A few days ago she would have said an emphatic *no*. But since then she'd seen how much his decision haunted Connor. She'd glimpsed the family they could be when Savannah got well—because Savannah's recovery was the only future she dared to consider. And she'd felt the stir of old emotions, familiar longings, a trusted connection waking inside her, pushing back against the doubts and fears and pain of her losses.

If Savannah weren't sick, if she were given the chance, if Connor were to ask her to enter WitSec with him, her answer today might be much different. She scoffed at herself and muttered one of her mother's favorite sayings: "If *ifs* and *buts* were candy and nuts, we'd all have a merry Christmas."

And maybe she and Connor could find their elusive happy ending.

Darby looked up from her daughter's pale face to the observation window when she heard a knock on the glass. Hunter signaled for her to come out of Savannah's sterile room, and she nodded.

"I'll be right back, honey. I promise," she told Savannah, squeezing her small hand gently. Her daughter was heavily sedated, being prepped to go into surgery, and she couldn't be sure Savannah even knew her mother was there.

Darby exited through the antechamber of the isolation room, removing the sterile clothing and mask that were required when visiting Savannah, then stepped out in the waiting area where Hunter met her.

"They're about to take Connor into the procedure room. I thought you'd want to know."

She flexed her fingers and wiped nervous perspiration on her pants. "Yeah, thanks."

She'd been dividing her time between Connor's room and Savannah's since arriving with the rest of the family at 5:00 a.m. that morning. With one more anxious glance into Savannah's room, Darby followed Hunter down the hall. They spotted the transplant team wheeling Connor's gurney into surgery, and she jogged a few steps to catch up.

Seeing her approach, Connor said something to the orderly, who stopped the gurney and glanced back at Darby. Connor smiled at her, his expression full of confidence and hope as he held a hand out to her. "It's all good, beautiful. This is gonna work. Everything's going to be fine. Have faith."

Her heart tugged. How like Connor to be encouraging her, even when he was the one about to be put under anesthesia.

She took his hand and bent to give him a quick kiss. "Thank you."

His brow dipped. "How's our girl?"

"They're prepping her now. She's so weak, so limp. If this doesn't work—"

He squeezed her hand, cutting her off. "It will." He twitched a grin. "My marrow's like gold. Good stuff. She'll be turning cartwheels and playing dress-up in no time."

She smiled, despite the swarm of angry bees buzzing inside her.

His eyes grew more serious, and he held her gaze. "Before she goes in for the procedure, will you…tell her I love her?"

Darby's pulse tripped, and the tears she'd been battling to hold at bay filled her vision. "Of course." She sniffed and wiped her eyes. "I'll be there when you wake up."

His expression warmed again. "That's the best news I've had all day."

Darby gave him a little wave as they rolled the gurney into the surgical suite, and she sent up a prayer for him. When she turned to go back to Savannah's room, Hunter was waiting a few steps away. He opened his arms, and she walked into his hug. "And now we wait."

"Come on," he said. "I'll buy you a cup of coffee."

Two hours later, Darby stood by Connor's hospital bed and rubbed his arm, coaxing him awake. His mother stood on the opposite side of the bed while his father and Hunter hovered close by. When he opened his eyes groggily and blinked at the light, she gave him a bright smile. "Welcome back. You're all done. Donation complete."

His hand moved to his hip, where the surgeon had removed marrow from Connor's pelvic bone with a large hollow needle. He grunted tiredly. "Good."

"Hi, darling," Julia said, patting his cheek. "How do you feel?"

"I'm fine, Mom."

A nurse moved up beside Darby and checked his IV bag. "Hey there. Can you tell me your name?"

Another grunt. "Which one?"

When the nurse scowled, he quickly said, "Connor Mansfield."

She pulled out a gadget that scanned his hospital ID band on his wrist. "Can you rate your pain for me from one to ten?"

He rubbed his hip again, his face creasing in a grimace. "Eight."

Darby bit her lip, concerned for him.

"Doctor says you can have a painkiller if you want it. Shall I get it?" the nurse asked.

He closed his eyes again and breathed deeply. "Naw. I'll be all right."

"Connor…" Julia groaned.

The nurse chuckled. "You know, you don't get any medals for unnecessary suffering. And since I'm the one on duty tonight, I'd rather you were comfortable and able to rest."

He met Darby's eyes and asked softly, "How's Savannah?"

Darby fidgeted, straightening his sheets. "Not out of surgery yet, but the update we got a few minutes ago was she's doing fine."

He glanced past her toward the door. "And the marshals…?"

"Marshal Ramsey is posted at your door. Morris will be outside Savannah's room, and Jones will be roaming, keeping a general watch." She stroked the side of his face. "You've earned a rest. Take the painkiller."

He glanced from Darby to the nurse and tugged up a grin. "Fine. Give me the drugs."

"Got it. I'll be right back. If you need anything tonight, my name is Anna. Just push the blue button on that cord." Anna disappeared into the hall but was back moments later with a hypodermic needle and a handful of supplies.

Darby couldn't help but grin seeing the wary way Connor eyed the needle.

"What's your name and date of birth?" Anna asked.

"Really?" Connor said. "Didn't you just ask me that?"

"Hospital protocol. Just play along."

He answered, and with a nod, Anna checked and scanned his ID band again, swabbed his IV port with antiseptic and injected the medicine through the port. As Anna was finishing, Dr. Reed stepped into the room, still in her surgical scrubs.

She tugged down her mask and smiled at them all. "I thought I'd find everyone in here."

Darby sat straighter, her heart thundering. "Is the transplant finished? Is she okay?"

"She's fine. They have her in recovery, and all her vital signs look good. She's a trooper, your daughter. You can see her when they get her back in the isolation room in about thirty minutes."

Relief, sweet and strong, poured through Darby, and she sank back in the chair by Connor's bed, shaking. "Thank God. And thank you, Dr. Reed."

The doctor acknowledged her with a small nod. "Savor

passing this hurdle. It's huge and important and deserves celebrating. But be aware she still has a tough road ahead. We'll be watching her for signs of tissue rejection, infection and other complications. If her body accepts the marrow donation, she'll still need to stay in isolation for several weeks while her body regenerates its immunity and builds a healthy blood supply."

Darby noticed what went unsaid. "And if she rejects the donated marrow?"

Dr. Reed hesitated, clearly choosing her words. "We'll cross that bridge only if we need to. Stay positive. Okay?"

Darby's stomach rolled, and she tried to push down the worry that came with what-if.

"Okay," she croaked.

Connor reached over and laced his fingers with hers. "Breathe, sweetheart. My marrow is gold, remember? We got this."

Dr. Reed excused herself, promising to keep them updated, and when she'd left, Stan pushed away from the wall where he'd been leaning. "Julia, now that you've seen that your boy's okay and know that his baby is in recovery, what do you say we get some lunch? I'm starved."

Julia pulled a face. "You're always hungry."

"True, but let's give Darby some private time with Connor." Stan took his wife's elbow and nudged her toward the door. "We'll see you in a little while, son."

Hunter fired a finger and thumb gun at his brother and winked at Darby. "I'm gonna head, too, and let you rest. You done good, bro."

Darby scooted her chair closer to the bed once his family left. As eager as she was to be at her daughter's side, Darby found that being with Connor gave her comfort and strength. His optimism buoyed her spirits, and she needed that now, more than ever. She'd missed his good-natured teasing, his glass-half-full mentality and his unflagging belief in her.

"Can I get you anything?" She rubbed the back of his hand, his fingers still laced with hers.

"How about a kiss?" His lips twisted in a wickedly seductive grin that made her skin tingle.

"Well…" She glanced toward the door, her own teasing smile burgeoning. "I can see if Anna will kiss you. She did say call if you need anything. Or maybe the dietary lady when she brings you dinner—"

He laughed and tugged on her hand. "C'mere."

Her smile brightened as she canted toward him and gave him a quick, soft kiss.

He threaded his fingers through her hair, then cupped the side of her face. Connor's eyes looked drowsy, and his words had become slower and less distinct. "You're the only one I want to kiss, lady. The mother of my child." He paused, an odd look on his face. "Mother of my child. Do you have any idea how sexy that is?"

She lifted an eyebrow. "Sexy?" she scoffed. "I think that's the painkiller talking."

"Uh-uh. I've always thought you were beautiful. From the day I met you." He sank back in his pillow, and his eyes drifted closed. "I was so damn jealous of Hunter when he brought you home. I thought you two were a couple. I spent all of dinner that night eating my heart out and wondering how the hell my baby brother got so lucky."

The memory of the night she'd first met Connor washed through her with the sweetness of a summer breeze. "As I recall, you spent most of dinner staring at me."

"Did not," he mumbled and frowned at her.

"Oh, yeah. You made me very self-conscious. I was sure I had spinach in my teeth or a stain on my blouse or a booger hanging out of my nose."

He laughed and squeezed her hand again. Turning his face toward her, he opened his eyes and gave a sleepy sigh. "Nah. I just couldn't get enough of the prettiest auburn hair and green eyes this side of the Mississippi. And you're still the best-looking woman in all of creation."

She chuckled. "Now I *know* the drugs have kicked in. Maybe I should let you sleep."

He rocked his head side to side and tightened his grip on her hand. "No. Stay."

She stroked his cheek and nodded. "I will. For a few more minutes. But I'll need to go when Savannah leaves recovery."

"Savannah." He closed his eyes and smiled. "Such a pretty name. Savannah Mansfield."

Darby cleared her throat. "Actually, it's Kent. Savannah Morgan Kent."

A mix of emotions passed over his face. "Morgan. You gave her my middle name."

She sent him a sad smile. "Yeah. Seemed fitting." Glancing to her purse, she asked, "Want to see pictures of her as a baby?"

His eyes found hers, lit with warmth. "You have to ask?"

Sliding her cell phone out of her pocketbook, she brought up her saved photos of Savannah and scrolled to the earliest pictures of their daughter as a newborn with pink cheeks and a dusting of dark hair.

Connor sucked in a sharp breath and exhaled a stuttering sigh. "Oh, my God. She was beautiful. The prettiest baby ever."

Darby bit her lip and chuckled. "Naturally."

She continued to scroll through photos of Savannah's infancy, first steps and first birthday party. When she reached an image of Savannah with icing coating her face, she hiccupped a laugh. "Get a load of this." She showed Connor the picture, and he smiled tiredly. "First birthday cake. She was so sleepy at the family birthday dinner, but I was determined we would have her cake before she went to bed for the night. We'd barely gotten the candle blown out and removed before she fell asleep and did a face-plant right in her mess cake." Darby laughed at the memory. "She woke up, of course, as soon as she tried to breathe through the icing and couldn't. Then, confused by finding herself coated in goo, she started crying."

Connor's forehead dented. "Poor baby."

"Soon enough she discovered the goo was sweet and delicious, so she and Hunter spent the next several minutes swiping icing from her cheeks and eating it."

A crooked smile tugged Connor's cheek. "That sounds like Hunter."

Darby brushed her finger across the screen to scroll to a more recent picture, Savannah at age three in her Easter dress. "This is another of my favorites."

He studied the photo for a moment, and his grin faded. Connor's eyebrows drew together in consternation. "She should have my last name."

Darby looked down at her lap as tangled feelings resurfaced. "Yeah, well, you died before we could marry. Remember?"

Connor gripped her hand almost to the point of pain, and she glanced up sharply. The intensity of the gold stare she met sent a tremor through her.

"So marry me now. I want you and Savannah both to have my name."

Darby's heart lurched. "What?"

"It's what we'd planned before I went into WitSec. We can get a justice of the peace or the hospital chaplain to come—"

"Connor, stop." She wrenched her hand from his and shook it to get the blood circulating again. "Think about what you're saying!"

"I don't need to think about it. It feels right. It *is* right." Determination and conviction set his jaw and shone in his gaze.

Her pulse raced so hard her head spun. At one time, marrying Connor and growing old with him had been her heart's desire, a dream within her reach. Now he was offering her another chance at the dream that had been snatched from her. She should be grabbing on with both hands. But she couldn't. How could she marry a man she knew planned to leave her in a few days?

She wilted in the chair and gaped at him. "Right for you maybe. But what happens afterward? Your plan is to leave. Would you walk out again, go back into WitSec, leaving behind a wife and child?"

He hesitated, blinking hard, clearly struggling to think while the painkiller coursed through him. "So you'd go with me. Families can join WitSec."

"Connor, Savannah is sick! She's not going anywhere for weeks. You heard the doctor. And Marshals Jones and Raleigh told you how difficult it is to hide a sick child because of medical records and all the personnel in doctors' offices who might talk to the wrong person."

He scrubbed a hand on his face and groaned. "I want her to have my name. I want her to know I'm her father."

"No. You can't give her a gift like that and then rip it away from her the next day!" Darby's hands were shaking, and she fisted them to try to still the tremors. But nothing could calm the trembling in her soul. "How do you think she'd feel knowing she had a father who left her?"

Connor gave her a pained look. "I'm not your father."

A sharp pain stabbed her under her ribs. "I know that."

"I'm not leaving because I want to." His tone matched the fierce look that blazed in his gaze. "If I knew any other way to keep you safe—"

She shoved abruptly to her feet. "I can't have this conversation. Not now. Not today."

"Darby…"

She stalked toward the door.

"Yeah, who's running away now?"

She stopped and took a slow breath to rein in her temper before turning. "It's almost time for them to bring Savannah out of recovery. I promised her I'd be there when they take her to her room."

With effort, Connor sat up in the bed. His expression reflected remorse and a bone-deep weariness. "I'm sorry. I shouldn't have said that. I'm just so…" He paused and lifted a heartbreaking gaze. She saw longing, love and broken dreams etched in the lines of his face. "Give her my love. I'll try to visit her later if the doctor will let me."

She nodded. "All right."

He wobbled as if dizzy and flopped back on the bed. "I think you're right about the painkiller. I should probably sleep now."

Darby started for the door again, but she hesitated and returned to the bed. Bending at the waist, she brushed a hand along the side of Connor's face and pressed a kiss to his lips. "Sleep well. I'll check in on you in a couple hours."

Late that night, Connor lay in his hospital room, not quite awake but too keyed up to get fully to sleep, either. A night nurse bustled into the room, turned on a small light and approached the side of his bed. He blinked away his grogginess, noting that he had a male nurse now. Odd. He'd thought what's-her-name?—he fumbled muzzily for the nurse's name…oh, yeah, *Anna*—had said she'd be on duty through the night.

Knowing the routine, he dutifully stuck out his wrist, so the nurse could scan his ID bracelet. Before it was asked, he answered the question that had been the first from every other nurse who had been in to check on him today. "The pain's manageable. I don't need anything for it."

Ignoring Connor's ID bracelet, the guy in ill-fitting scrubs glanced at him and jerked a nod. "Good."

"What's that?" Connor asked, nodding to the syringe the guy pulled out of his pocket.

"This will help you sleep." The nurse gripped Connor's arm and turned it so the IV port was accessible.

"I didn't ask for help getting to sleep." A prickle started at the base of Connor's neck. A warning. Connor tugged his arm back when the nurse moved the syringe near the port.

The male nurse tightened his grip and tugged Connor's arm close again. "Doctor's orders."

More alarms sounded when the nurse jabbed the syringe needle in Connor's IV port without wiping the port first with an alcohol swab. The break from routine and careless disregard of sanitary procedure irritated him. Just that morning, his doctor had explained how important sanitation would be since his marrow donation left his immunity compromised for several days as he recovered. In a heartbeat, he reviewed the other lapses the male nurse had made just since entering Connor's room.

He hadn't washed his hands. He hadn't consulted the chart detailing Connor's most recent vital signs. Hadn't verified Connor's name and birth date.

Warning sirens now blared in his head. Adrenaline shot through him. Connor grabbed the syringe, even as the nurse started to squeeze the plunger. "No!"

The intruder—because Connor was now certain the man was not a nurse—fought back, battling to get the amber liquid from the syringe injected into Connor's body.

"Ramsey!" Connor shouted, feeling a funny haziness creeping over him. Desperate to keep any more of the suspicious injection from getting into his system, Connor ripped the IV needle from his arm.

With the port and IV tubes dangling free, his attacker jerked the syringe from the port and swung the needle toward Connor's neck.

Rolling away, Connor dodged the strike. He tossed back the bed covers and kicked them, mindful that his head was growing fuzzier by the second.

"Ramsey!" he called again, but the name sounded slurred to his own ears.

Connor swung his legs to the floor, but when he tried to roll out of bed, to get away from his attacker, the man's arm snaked around his throat. His viselike grip squeezed Connor's windpipe.

He couldn't die. Not now. Not when he'd just found Savannah. Not when he had his first real hope that Darby would forgive him.

With his rapidly fading strength, Connor fought. He jabbed an elbow into the man's gut. He threw his head backward and heard a satisfying pop and howl of pain as his skull busted the man's nose.

His brain registered a shout from the door. Air rushed to his lungs when the intruder released him abruptly. The sounds of a scuffle…and a gunshot.

Blurry vision. Fuzzy head. Gasp for breath…

Connor collapsed. Then blackness.

Chapter 16

"Are you married, Marshal Morris?" Darby asked the clean-cut man sitting beside her outside Savannah's sterile room.

He raised an eyebrow, obviously surprised by her attempt at small talk after a long evening of silence as she wrestled with the bombshell Connor had dropped. Her own circular thoughts were making her stir-crazy, and she hoped pleasant conversation with the marshal could provide a much-needed distraction.

Morris gave a tight nod. "Six years."

A small grin of acknowledgment flickered over her mouth. "Kids?"

His face brightened. "Two. Boy, four, and a girl, almost two."

She gave him a bigger smile, then fell silent, imagining the handsome man in pressed khakis playing with two small children, going home at the end of an assignment to a pretty wife. Maybe a dog. A golden retriever. He looked like the retriever type.

"Isn't it hard, being away from your family for assignments like this?"

"Sure. Harder on my wife, I think. She's the one managing two willful little kids by herself while I'm gone."

Darby smiled politely again. "I bet." She paused, while fidgeting with the hem of her blouse. "What do you do when—"

"You don't really want to talk about me, do you?" He pivoted on the vinyl hospital couch to face her.

"I…was just making small talk."

"I may be a man, Ms. Kent, but I'm not completely clueless about women. Something upset you earlier, and since, by all indications, the transplant went smoothly, I have to assume that something has to do with Connor Mansfield."

She chuckled wryly. "Wow. Give you a gold star."

"I can't promise I'll have any answers for you, but my wife has trained me to listen, if you want to talk about whatever Mansfield did to upset you."

"Your wife *trained* you? That's quite the admission coming from a U.S. Marshal."

His grin was cocky. "A *smart* U.S. Marshal. Smart enough to figure out how to keep my wife happy and avoid fights. If letting her think she's *trained* me will keep the peace, then I'm happy to let her believe it."

Darby snorted and folded her arms over her chest.

"But I meant what I said about listening, if there's something you want to get off your chest."

Darby eyed him skeptically and shook her head. "Thanks, but…"

He flipped a hand up. "Whatever."

They sat in silence for another minute before she blurted, "He asked me to marry him."

Morris's eyebrows lifted, and he shifted on the seat to face her again.

"Well. Not so much asked as…demanded. Not 'Will you marry me?' but 'Marry me. I want Savannah to have my name.'"

Morris hummed and nodded. "What'd you tell him?"

"I said no."

Morris looked genuinely surprised. "No? Because women hate commitment from the father of their children?"

She glared at him. "Really?"

Raising a hand toward her, he looked contrite. "Sorry. I'll drop the sarcasm."

"Thank you." She pushed to her feet, restless and needing to expend energy. "How can I marry him knowing he's leaving for WitSec again in a few days?"

"You know we can put wives and children in the program. We're not in the business of busting families unnecessarily."

She chewed a fingernail. "Yeah, I know that."

"So…do you love him?"

She started to answer, then hesitated. "Is this confidential?"

Morris arched an eyebrow. "Uh, sure. If you want it to be."

"I do," she said, then for clarification added, "want it to be confidential." She paused. "And…love him." She took a deep breath and hurried on. "But that doesn't make a difference in our situation. It doesn't decide anything, it only complicates things. It muddies what has to be clear and decisive. I can't marry a man who's just going to leave us again in a matter of days."

"Then you wouldn't consider going into WitSec with him?"

She frowned at him in disbelief, then swung an arm toward the door to Savannah's isolation room, sending him a look that said, "Helllooo?"

"Oh, right." He dragged a hand over his mouth, clearly embarrassed for his forgetfulness. "That does make things messy."

"Messy?" She stopped pacing to give Morris a scowl of frustration. "Jones says a sick child makes it nearly impossible to ensure security. In other words, Savannah and I *can't* go with Connor without jeopardizing his safety. All of our safety, if the Gales really are willing to hurt anyone in their path to killing Conner."

"Hmm," Morris grunted and settled back on the couch with a frown and a dent in his brow.

Darby stared at him, waiting, she supposed, for him to deny Jones's assertions about Savannah's medical needs complicating their chances for protection. Or offer a workaround option. "Well?"

He glanced at her, a puzzled furrow in his brow. "Well what?"

She gave him an exasperated sigh. "You don't have some advice or an opinion on all of this?"

"My opinion is your situation sucks. No advice." When she rolled her eyes and growled her frustration, he added, "If you'll recall, I said I was a good listener, but generally had no answers."

Darby twisted her mouth in a wry smile. "You did say that. My bad." Raking the hair off her forehead, she returned to the couch and sank down beside him.

"Look, I can't imagine how hard it must be having your kid in the hospital, being separated from the guy you love, knowing there are people out there—" he waved a hand in the general direction of the hospital exit "—who want to kill Connor and don't mind hurting you in the process, but…" He sighed heavily and scrubbed a hand on his cheek. "If it were me, if I really loved someone and had a child with that someone…I wouldn't quit looking for ways to be with him, to make it work."

"Don't you think I'm trying? Our circumstances don't leave many choices. If—"

"Morris!" A breathless voice crackled over the marshal's two-way radio.

The tension in the voice sent a jolt of alarm streaking through Darby.

Marshal Morris raised his radio to his lips. "Morris here. Go ahead."

"I need backup!" the voice on the other end of the transmission shouted. "Third floor. Shots fired!"

Shots fired? The breath whooshed from her lungs. Connor! She scrambled to follow the marshal as he darted toward the stairs.

He glanced over his shoulder as he took the steps two at a time. "Stay here! Alert security!"

His warning stopped her cold. Alert the hospital security guard who patrolled that floor…to protect Savannah. She gasped and glanced back toward Savannah's room, torn between guarding her daughter and her worry over Connor. *Shots fired. Oh, God, please let Connor be all right!*

She stumbled back down the stairs and located Savannah's nurse. "Something's happened downstairs. An attack of some sort. Shots were fired. The marshal stationed at Savannah's door had to leave to assist." When the nurse's face paled, Darby seized her arm. "You need to find the security guard. Send him to my daughter's room to stand watch."

The nurse scurried off to do as Darby asked, and Darby rushed back to Savannah's door. Hunter and Lilly had left the hospital together close to an hour earlier. She called Hunter now, wanting her own version of backup in place so she could leave Savannah long enough to check on Connor. Who may have been shot.

Her knees buckled, and dropping her phone, she braced a hand on the wall to keep from crumpling. Even if Connor wasn't hurt, she'd be heartsick if one of the marshals had been injured—or killed—protecting Connor.

Her mind flashed to the fireball that had consumed her car just days ago. Tracy's charred body.

She pressed a hand to her mouth and swallowed hard when she felt her gorge rise. There'd already been too much tragedy and suffering. Damn the Gales and their petty vengeance!

"Hello? Darby, you there?" Hunter's voice called her attention to the phone that had slipped from her hand and lay on the floor at her feet.

Shaking all over, she bent carefully to pick up the cell phone. "Hunter, I…come back. Something's happened. I need you to…" She paused, gulping oxygen and trying to hold herself together.

"Darby? What? What's happened?"

"Gunshots… I don't… Can you come?" she rasped.

"I'm on my way." Hunter disconnected, and Darby staggered back to the waiting area outside Savannah's room. Drawing slow, lung-expanding breaths, she gathered her composure as best she could. She needed her wits about her, needed to be alert. If one of the Gales showed up, she needed to be prepared to defend her daughter.

A light pierced the darkness. A jarring, unsettling brightness. He groaned, and the light flashed away quickly.

"Pupils are responsive," a male voice said.

A male voice…a male nurse…intruder! Connor fought

the weight of whatever drug made him so sleepy, so sluggish.

Savannah! Darby! If the Gales' man had gotten to him, his family was at risk. He had to warn them!

He clawed with every fiber of his physical and mental strength to climb out of the drug-induced morass that held him. He tried to speak, but his tongue felt thick, dry, useless. He managed to make another guttural noise in his throat. A moan.

Someone near him gasped, and he felt a cool hand on his face. "Connor? Can you hear me?"

Darby! Darby was there. With him. Safe. Relief washed through him, leaving his heavy limbs tingling.

But if Darby was here…Adrenaline kick-started a scampering heart rate. Who was guarding—?

"Sssa-nna?" he mumbled, struggling to open his eyes. Fuzzy images swam before him.

"Doctor, he's waking up!" Darby cried, her voice thick with emotion.

Connor tried to focus the surge of adrenaline, use it to sharpen his mind, form the words he had to. He heard the doctor move back to the other side of the bed opposite Darby.

"Connor? It's Dr. Moore. Can you hear us? Can you wiggle your fingers or toes?"

"Sa-van-nah…" he rasped. With effort he turned his head, peered through his lashes at Darby. He groped with his hand until he found her arm, and he gripped her wrist with all his strength. "S'-van-nah."

Darby covered his hand with hers and clutched his arm to her chest. Leaning close, she kissed his cheek. "Savannah's with Hunter and Marshal Morris. She's safe."

Mollified, Connor allowed his muscles to relax, his eyes

to close, but his brain kept ticking, analyzing. Remembering. "Intruder…"

Darby drew a deep breath and released it. "Marshal Ramsey stopped him."

A loud *bang* rang in his memory. "Gun…shot."

Darby squeezed his hand. "Yeah. He shot him. The guy's dead."

He forced his eyes open and met Darby's worried gaze. "Good."

"Connor, I want to check your blood pressure again." Connor felt the hospitalist jostle his right arm as he wrapped a blood pressure cuff around his biceps. "Your attacker managed to get a small amount of toxin into you. We've given you an antidote, but we need to monitor your heart for damage."

He let his eyes close again. Weak with relief, he sank back in the pillow behind him. He clung to Darby's hand, savoring the connection.

Savannah and Darby were safe. For now.

But the transplant was complete. He'd done what he'd intended when he came back to Lagniappe and defied the U.S Marshals' WitSec rules. He done all he could to save Savannah. His presence now was nothing but a liability to Darby and his family. Tracy's death and this attack proved the extent of the danger.

He needed to disappear again, taking the threat with him. As soon as he was strong enough to travel.

"Connor?" Darby whispered, leaning close enough to his ear that her warm breath fanned his cheek.

He squeezed her fingers. "Hi, beautiful."

"When they said there'd been shots fired…and then that you were unresponsive…" She laid her cheek on his shoulder. "I was so scared…so afraid I'd lost you."

"No," he managed to murmur, "You'll always have me. You're the…only one for me."

He heard her sniffle, and she curled the fingers of her free hand in his hair. "Oh, Connor…"

After a moment, he roused again, finding the strength to ask, "You're sure S'vannah's okay?"

Darby lifted her head and stroked his cheek. "I'm sure. Dr. Reed came back in to check her, just in case. And the nurses and marshals have redoubled their efforts to check everything that enters her room and verify the credentials of any hospital staff who tends to her."

He nodded weakly. "That's all…that matters."

She jostled his shoulder slightly. "Don't talk that way. You matter, too. Not just to me and your family. To Savannah. Maybe she can't have you in her life now, but down the road, years from now, there may come a time when she can have you in her life."

He forced his eyes to focus on the soft lines of Darby's face. The warmth and affection in her green eyes arrowed straight to his core. Even if she was reluctant to say the words, he knew she cared for him. Maybe even forgave him…or loved him. It wasn't the declaration of feelings he wanted, the promise of a future together, but he treasured the glimpse of her heart that shone from her eyes.

"I have to leave." He heard the dejection in his own voice. "You see that now, don't you? I'm a liability." He swallowed hard. "I have to go, as soon as possible. To keep you and our daughter safe. My family…everyone…" He stopped, needing to fight for a breath. Emotion sat on his chest, compressing his lungs. Whatever substance had been injected still pulled at him, weakening him.

Darby bit her bottom lip as tears puddled in her eyes, and she nodded slowly. "I know."

* * *

Over the following three days, Connor recovered fully from the small amount of toxin injected by the intruder. By that time, he'd already stayed two days longer than he'd originally been scheduled to stay from the donation procedure. Darby spent those three days dividing her time between her daughter's room and Connor's. As worried as she was for Savannah, she knew the clock was running on the time she had left with Savannah's father.

She fervently wished Connor had the luxury of staying around until Savannah was more alert, more able to communicate and make memories of her father before Connor disappeared from their lives. But the repeated attacks by the Gales' henchmen proved that wasn't wise.

On the day of Connor's release from the hospital, Marshals Jones and Ramsey developed an elaborate plan to get Connor away from the hospital undetected. He would make a brief stop at his parents' house, giving him the opportunity to say a private goodbye to his family. The detour to the Mansfields' home was a major concession on Connor's behalf, but one Darby was grateful for.

She'd never had the opportunity to tell her father goodbye when he took off for greener pastures, and she'd always felt that lack of closure like a seeping wound, in addition to the bitterness of betrayal and heartache of abandonment.

She was with Savannah the morning Connor was released, instructed firmly to stay away from Connor's room during his release. Instead, she spent the fifteen minutes she was allowed at her daughter's bedside holding Savannah's hand and singing all of her daughter's favorite songs, as much to distract herself from the heavy pall of the day as to cheer Savannah. Hooked to tubes and wires like the object of a mad scientist's experiment, Savannah managed a weak smile of recognition but was still frighteningly weak and lethargic.

Darby remained frustrated by Savannah's slow progress following the transplant, even though Dr. Reed assured her all of her test results and vital signs were on target.

When her allotted visitation was over, Darby stripped off the sterile garb and mask required while in with Savannah and exited the isolation room's antechamber to the waiting room.

"All done here?" Marshal Morris rose to his feet, his hands in his pockets, jingling his keys.

Darby bit her lip and glanced back through the large observation window. "For now, I suppose."

He hitched his head toward the elevator. "Let me take you back to the house then. He's waiting for you to tell you goodbye."

Darby's throat tightened. How in the world was she supposed to say goodbye to Connor? A profound ache surged through her, followed by cold anger that the Gales had forced this circumstance on them. "This isn't right," she gritted under her breath, then louder. "It not fair! The Gales have no right to destroy Connor's life, my life and Savannah's this way!"

Morris gave her a commiserative look. "I don't think the Gales particularly care about what's fair, or even what's legal."

She stepped closer to Morris, her shoulders taut and her mouth pressed in a firm line. "Catch them. Find the link between these attacks and the Gales and take them down! Put them behind bars, away from their families. You can't let them get away with what they've done! Tracy deserves justice!"

"You're right. She does." His eyes held a glint of determination and passion. "I didn't get into this business to see the guilty walk. I'll do everything I can to see the Gales brought to justice."

Her shoulders dropped a little, and she rubbed her temples. "I know you will. I just hate…" Her voice trailed off as she gathered her purse, slinging the strap over her shoulder.

Hunter, who'd said his goodbyes to Connor earlier, was draped over one of the lounge chairs, asleep. He'd come straight to the hospital after work and hadn't even had a chance to shower and change clothes. Hunter's dedication to Savannah touched Darby. He'd spent the past week working his job as construction foreman for the family business and keeping watch outside Savannah's room with only brief visits to his apartment for sleep and showers. Darby stepped over to tap Hunter lightly on the arm.

He roused from his nap, and when he saw Darby, worry flashed over his face. "What? Did something happen?"

She shook her head. "No. Go back to sleep. I just wanted to tell you that Marshal Morris is taking me to your parents' house now."

The cloud that passed over Hunter's face said he understood the purpose of the trip. He nodded. "Tell him I said…" He paused. Sighed. "Tell him…"

Darby nodded sadly. "I'll give him your love."

"Tell him I respect his choice. And that I'll look out for you and Savannah."

She bit her bottom lip and nodded. She wanted to tell Hunter that intentions and justifiable choices were no substitute for the presence of a father in a child's life. She'd never know her father's reasons for leaving his family. She hadn't cared. As a young girl, nothing could justify her father's abandonment. Just like nothing could ease the sting of Connor's leaving now. "I'll probably grab a shower before I come back up here. So maybe two hours. Call my cell if there's any—"

Hunter's expression said, *Really, Darby? Don't you think that's understood?*

She chuckled at herself and lifted a hand in a wave as she left. "Right, right. Okay, bye."

"You're lucky to have such a large extended family that loves you and takes care of you." Morris pushed the elevator button and angled his gaze to watch the lighted numbers over the door mark the cage's ascent.

"I am lucky. My family means the world to me." She glanced back at the waiting room, thinking how much she'd have to give up if she were to go into WitSec with Connor. If Savannah weren't sick. She'd miss Hunter's unflagging friendship, her sisters' love and support, Grant and his precious girls, who were as dear to her as Savannah. Connor's parents. How could she ever get along without them? The logistical help, love and encouragement they'd showed her, especially during Savannah's illness and hospitalization, were exactly why the idea of leaving them behind seemed so impossible.

And that was exactly why Connor hadn't asked her to come with him the first time. He knew her too well, knew what her father's desertion had done to her family and how she felt about the relationships she cherished. He really had been put in an impossible situation. Maybe his leaving had hurt her, but he hadn't made his choice lightly. He'd left her behind because he'd thought it was what was best for her. She got that now. Really understood it. But it still chafed that he'd made the decision without her. Hadn't trusted her with the plan to fake his death. Knowing he was still alive and safely ensconced in a new town with a new identity would have made losing him so much easier.

Or would it have? Darby frowned, considering what

life would be like in the coming years, wondering what Connor was doing in his new life. Worrying if he was still safe or if the Gales had found him. Wishing she could hear from him, if only an anonymous postcard. Wondering if he'd found someone else to take her place, to marry, to make love to.

A prick of uneasiness sawed in her gut. Would Connor move on with another woman? Her heartbeat sped up, and a sick feeling knotted her stomach.

You'll always have me. You're the only one for me. Connor's vow just three days ago reverberated in her mind. Her heart somersaulted, somewhat mollified, and yet it wasn't fair to Connor to expect him to live the rest of his life with no one beside him, no one to share life with, make a family with. Maybe it couldn't be her, but she had to convince him to move on, to give love with someone else a chance.

Even if she knew she never could.

"Hey, earth to Darby. You coming?" Morris's voice nudged her from her disturbing line of thought. He stood in the elevator, holding the door open with his arm.

"Oh. Yeah." She shook off the unnerving idea of Connor replacing her with someone new in his life, in his bed, in his heart and stepped into the elevator.

"Should I ask where you were just then? 'Cause you sure weren't here." Morris pushed the button for the parking garage and sent her a side glance.

She gave a little grunt of despair. "Nowhere good. Letting my imagination run in directions that hurt to consider."

"Mmm. Well, save the woolgathering for the shower. When you're in public, especially when we're moving between locations, you need to stay alert. Be aware of your environment."

"Right. Sorry."

"That's good advice for a woman anytime they're in public. Not just for you in your circumstance. Thieves target women who aren't paying attention, people they can get a jump on."

She nodded. "Keys ready, head up, walk with purpose. I know the drill. I'm usually much more careful."

The elevator dinged as it arrived at the parking garage in the basement and the doors slid open. She let Morris step off first and sweep his gaze around the garage.

"All right."

She followed him a few steps away from the elevators before he held his hand up, his head turning left and right as he checked the area. "Wait here while I check the car out. Don't move from this spot. I'll be right back."

She nodded, doing her own visual sweep as he hurried down the line of parked cars. The garage was quiet except for the soft thud of Morris's shoes on the concrete floor and a black cricket chirping by the trash can in the corner of the elevator lobby. She leaned to the side to see between cars, ducked her head to look for men hiding under vehicles, raised her gaze to the garage rafters…and noticed a black plastic sack had been put over the security camera for that section of the parking lot.

She frowned. That was odd. And more than a little worrisome. Someone should report it to the hospital security. In fact, why hadn't security already noticed the bag and done something about—

Without warning, a heavy cloth bag swished over her head.

Chapter 17

Before she could even scream, a muscled arm snaked around her chest, squeezing the wind from her lungs. Her attacker lifted her from her feet, and her world upended as she was tossed over his shoulder. Still struggling to regain her breath, she gasped to call out to Morris. But the cry was too weak to be heard beyond a few feet.

She fought her captor as he jostled her, making his escape. She heard a car engine, the squeal of brakes being applied hard, the click of a door being opened.

No!

Several thoughts fired in her brain in seconds. The Gales! If she let them put her in the car, she was as good as dead. *Fight!* She thought of Savannah, of her sisters… of Connor. If she died, Savannah would lose both parents today.

She kicked her legs, twisted her torso, thrashed her head—anything she thought might help wrest her free of the kidnapper's grip. Finally she drew enough air into her lungs to yell, "Marshal!"

The next second, she was tossed onto a padded seat, presumably into a car. With her arms now free, she battled to regain her balance. Her wrists were seized, pulled behind her and cuffed. "No! Let me go. Don't do this. Please!"

She fought harder, lunging in the direction of the door. Her exit was blocked by a large wall of man. He pushed her backward, climbed in beside her and slammed the door shut.

"No! Please, don't do this!" She thought of Savannah, her precious little girl, upstairs battling for her life. Savannah needed her. She couldn't die. And Connor—a pang of sorrow and regret choked her. "Please, let me go," she said, tears rushing to her eyes. "My daughter needs me."

"Darby?" Connor's voice. He sounded stunned. Worried.

She stiffened. "Connor?"

Her query was answered with a string of curses. She turned the direction of Connor's voice as he railed, "What the hell are you doing? Why is Darby here? Let her go!"

No one answered him as the car drove away, bouncing over the curb then turning sedately onto the street. No roaring engine or speeding vehicle to draw attention. But surely Marshal Morris had heard her scream, seen the vehicle, gotten a tag number or other information to track her. Even now, she prayed, he was jumping into her replacement car and pursuing the kidnappers, calling for backup.

"You bastards! Darby is not a part of this. You're terrorizing her! Let her go!" Connor continued to argue on her behalf. Though she appreciated Connor's efforts, she doubted the Gales' henchmen had any sympathy for his demands.

For her part, she could try to gather as much information as possible, assess her situation, just in case she got a freak chance to call for help. Just in case she and Connor found an opportunity to attempt an escape. Just in case she found a weakness in the kidnappers' execution to exploit. *Execution.* She shivered. Poor word choice. She didn't want to even think about what would happen if she and Connor didn't get away.

Steadying her ragged composure with a slow breath, Darby scooted closer to Connor and took stock of her situation, her environment. *Be smart. Think. Plan.*

A beefy goon sat to her right, but could they get away out the other side of the car? She wiggled slowly, trying not to draw attention with her slight shifts. An inch at a time, she moved farther to the left, closer to Connor.

"It's all right, Darby. I'll straighten this out. I won't let them do this to you."

She answered by leaning into him and whispering, "I trust you, Connor."

But she wouldn't leave their safety, the possibility of escape, entirely up to Connor. She continued working through what information she could sense. She knew of at least two henchmen in the car, including the driver. She sighed her frustration and recognized the new car smell that filled her nose. So it was a recent model vehicle. She filed that tidbit away. What else could she detect? After initially taking various turns that tumbled her left or right, the car had been traveling mostly straight ahead for the past few minutes. Based on the engine and road sounds, they were traveling at a pretty high speed. Okay, so they were off the city streets and on a highway of some sort.

Her stomach sank. Were they headed to a remote bayou out of town where she could be shot and her body tossed in the water for the alligators? The thought had her hyperventilating. Given the smothering hood over her head, that meant she was using oxygen too quickly. She felt her head spin. *Calm down. Think clearly.*

"Taking Darby was not part of the bargain! You jerks, someone answer me! What are you doing?"

The bargain? Had Connor negotiated some kind of truce with the Gales, giving himself up in order to end the vendetta and save his family? Her heart slowed as she considered what might be happening. The other men in the car remained eerily quiet. Maybe if she could get them to talk to her, she could deduce more pieces of information she might use to her advantage. "What do you want from me? Where are you taking me?"

Silence.

"Look, I have a little girl. She's very ill, and she needs me. Please, let me go back to the hospital. Don't leave my baby without her mother!" Her voice broke, even though she fought to suppress the tears in her voice.

Beside her, the man to her right sighed heavily. "Calm down, Ms. Kent. You're not in danger."

The voice was deep and suspiciously familiar. She keyed in on that man. Could he help her? "Who's there? What's going on?"

"Darby, you're safe," Connor said, frustration thick in his voice. "But these a-holes aren't when I get my hands on them."

She frowned. "You know them?"

Connor blew out a huff of disgust. "Yeah. And so do you. That's Ramsey beside you, and Jones is behind the wheel."

Shock flowed through her. "*The marshals?* But…" She gritted her teeth. "Were all these cloak-and-dagger dramatics really necessary? Morris was taking me to your parents' house to say goodbye."

"We're not headed to the Manfields'," Jones said, his voice filtering back from the front seat.

"Then where—" She fisted her hands, still cuffed behind her, and took a breath for composure. Confusion, anger and unspent adrenaline had her shaking all over. "Why am I in cuffs and blindfolded?"

"So you don't hurt yourself or one of us before we get to our destination. We knew you wouldn't come willingly. The hood is so you don't see where we're going. An attempt to keep you from trying to leave or giving our location away to anyone accidentally."

She scowled and felt a bead of sweat roll off her forehead. Beneath the heavy hood they'd put on her, it was hot and stuffy. "I…I don't understand. All of this just so I can tell Connor goodbye? Isn't this overkill?"

"We're taking you with us to a safe house." Ramsey's voice.

"What?" Shock shuddered through her. "No! You can't do that! I can't—"

"The protection detail decided it was for the best. We determined you were at risk, and we could best protect you if you were at the safe house with Mansfield."

"*You* decided?" Connor barked. "Without even mentioning this to me?"

"We knew you'd fight us. But this way is for the best—"

Connor bit out an earthy obscenity.

Panic squeezed Darby's lungs. "But I can't…Savannah needs me! You can't do this. Take me home!"

"I'm sorry, Ms. Kent. We can't allow that. Yet." Jones sounded contrite, but his refusal still gnawed at her.

The air under the hood was growing increasingly hard to breathe. Between the cuffs and the hood over her head, she was at a distinct disadvantage. Of course, that was the marshals' objective. She wondered where Morris was. Was he in on this kidnapping? She had no reason to think not. The sting of betrayal bit her. She'd trusted Morris, confided in him. She'd trusted all of the marshals. Connor and his family had put their faith, their lives in these men's hands.

"So that's it? No discussion? No questions? Just bam, I'm your hostage?"

"*Hostage* is a harsh word." Ramsey again.

"You think?" She pivoted on the seat toward him, even though she couldn't see him. "And yet I'm handcuffed, hooded and being taken somewhere against my will. What would you call it?"

"I'd call it a crock," Connor grumbled. "As Raleigh would say, FUBAR."

"This is all for your safety, your protection," Marshal Ramsey said, his voice rife with irritation. "We're doing our job, the best way we know."

Darby worked to tamp down the frustration and worry spiking her pulse. Freaking out was not going to advance her argument at this point, but *it was* making it harder to breathe under the hood. Keeping an even tone, she said, "Look, it's hard to breathe under here. Can you at least pull the hood up a bit, allow more fresh air in?"

The muscular arm next to her tensed. After a brief hesitation, Ramsey shifted her head cover, letting in more air. She drew the fresh oxygen deep into her lungs. And caught a scent that made her heart skip a beat. It was subtle, but— she inhaled again, held the air in her lungs.

She could smell Connor's masculine scent, and she relished the comfort in the familiar aroma tinged with cedar. Her pulse leaped into overdrive. She'd slept beside him, made love to him, snuggled with him, kissed him, hugged him, lived with him long enough to memorize the scent of his skin, the unique body chemistry that was his. The clean male scent that never failed to make her body sing and her heart race.

If there was a silver lining to be found in this ordeal, at least she was with Connor. While she hated, *loathed* to the point of nausea, the idea of being sequestered away from Savannah when she was so weak and vulnerable, she knew Connor had her back. She knew Connor would understand her need to get back to their daughter. And until they could convince the marshals of that urgency, she could store up a few more treasured moments with the man who would always own her heart.

Chapter 18

Blindfolded for the trip to the safe house, Connor was dwelling on the marshals' subterfuge, his back teeth grinding together, when he felt Darby scoot closer to him on the backseat. She snuggled against him, her body strung tight and trembling. The press of her hip against his, her thigh along his leg, her breast brushing his arm was a sweet torture. In the years he'd been without her, he'd savored memories of how perfectly her body fit with his, how the simple touch of her hand in his or a kiss from her could pull him from a bad mood. She'd spoiled him for any other woman.

As Sam Orlean, he'd had opportunities to sleep with other women, but he'd turned them down. Even believing he'd never see Darby again, he'd felt in his bones that being with anyone else equated to cheating on the woman he loved. And now, thanks to the marshals' bringing her with them, he had days, maybe weeks ahead of him, secluded with Darby, endless, empty hours to talk. To reconnect. To rediscover the magic they'd shared. A new hope blossomed in him that somehow, he and Darby could come up with a way to stay together and also keep them all safe.

Connor clenched his jaw, hating the guerrilla tactics the marshals had employed to whisk Darby into hiding. Obviously, Darby would never have left Savannah willingly, but the strong-arm tactics the marshals had used would only make Darby more defensive.

The car Jones had acquired for their operation bounced over a rut as they turned onto a dirt driveway. Darby didn't miss the significance of the change in direction and road quality. She gasped, and her body tensed.

"We're there," Ramsey said, and Connor felt his blindfold get tugged off.

Blinking in the sudden daylight, Connor took in their surroundings, miles from town, in the middle of acres of forest. Beside him, Darby had been unblindfolded as well, and she eyed the scenery with a wide, wary gaze. As they bumped down a rutted dirt road, they passed a pasture with cows grazing and a dilapidated house with a rusted truck in the side yard. Some things were a cliché for a reason, and this part of Louisiana certainly contributed to the popular image of the rural South.

When Jones pulled to a stop outside a wood-frame house in desperate need of a new coat of paint, Ramsey opened his door and took Darby by the arm, guiding her out of the car.

"You have no right to keep me here," Darby said, her voice quaking. "Just let me go home, and I'll forget all about your horrid kidnapping tactics."

Jones said nothing as he stepped out of the car.

Darby glanced from one marshal to another, clearly looking for an ally, a weak link. "Please! We have a little girl who needs us. You can't keep us both away from her!"

As he climbed awkwardly from the backseat, his hands still cuffed behind him, Connor's hip gave a throb of protest. Though he'd recovered from the small injection of poison to his system, he still had a dull ache in his hip from the marrow extraction. He considered it a good pain, though. He thought of his little girl, his marrow at work in her body, and prayed it was healing her, building her strength and defenses. *Please, God.*

The hum of an engine and rumble of tires crawling over parched ground drew his glance down the long drive. A nondescript sedan, much like the one that had brought them out to the safe house, pulled in behind where Jones had parked. Marshal Morris was behind the wheel, and another man sat in the passenger seat.

Darby sucked in a sharp breath, and Connor saw hurt flash in her eyes. When Morris cut the engine and joined them by Jones's vehicle, Darby narrowed her eyes at the younger marshal. "*Et tu,* Morris?" He opened his mouth to respond, and with a shake of her head, she quickly added, "Save it. I know the company line."

Morris set his jaw and pulled his shoulders back. "I know our method of getting you here was extreme, but honestly, would you have come with us voluntarily?"

"She shouldn't be here at all. This was never part of the plan!" Connor shot an angry look at Morris.

Jones shrugged. "The plan changed. From here on out, we do things our way. Bending the rules for you got your sister-in-law blown up, Raleigh burned and you nearly killed."

Ramsey pulled a key out of his pocket and unlocked Darby's handcuffs.

"But Savannah—"

"Will be fine," Jones cut Connor off. "She has your family, the hospital staff and two more marshals sharing protection detail and reporting in to us. If there is any significant change in her condition, we're close enough to the hospital to get you there within the hour."

"An hour! That's sixty minutes too long." Darby rubbed her wrists and sent an encompassing glance around them. "Where the hell are we, anyway?"

"Far enough from Lagniappe that you should be safe if you follow our rules, but close enough to town that we can get back soon enough if anything changes with Savannah," Jones said. "That's all you need to know. Morris, car key."

Marshal Morris tossed Jones the key in his hand, and Jones slipped both cars' keys into his pocket. "Just in case you get any ideas of trying to steal a car and leave, the keys will be kept in a safe. We'll also be locking up your cell phone, which is not secure—" he nodded toward Ramsey, who held her purse in one hand and pulled her phone from a pocket "—and the one secure line cell phone we arranged for official business."

Connor frowned. "Can't a cell phone be traced even if it's turned off?"

"Turned off, yes," Ramsey said, "but I had her battery and SIM card out of her phone before we were two blocks from the hospital." He dropped Darby's cell back in his pants pocket, then pulled out the tiny data chip and cell battery.

"Each of us—" Jones's gaze encompassed the other three marshals "—is, of course, armed, but extra weapons and ammo will also be stored in the safe."

Darby gaped at Jones, horrified at what she was learning. "You can't do this! Holding me against my will is illegal."

"Are you saying you no longer want the protection of the U.S. Marshals for you and your daughter?" Jones asked, arching an eyebrow.

"I—" Darby scowled at Jones. "Of course I want my daughter protected, but this…" She huffed her disgust with Jones. "If something happens to my daughter, I need to be *with* her. Immediately! You need to take me back to Lagniappe. Now!"

The marshals only stared back at her, their expressions neutral. Unmoved.

Connor balled his fists, sharing Darby's frustration and fury and itching to hit something.

Jones pointed to the red-haired man who'd arrived with Morris. "This is Marshal Hargrove. He's also from the Dallas office. You have him to thank for finding this property and getting the place set up and supplied. We'll be divvying up our protection detail out here in rotating shifts. Now, how about we check out your new digs?"

Darby angled a look of disbelief to Connor, and he stepped closer to pull her into a hug. "I'm sorry I got you into this."

She wilted against him, curling her fingers into his shirt. "You're not to blame. None of this would be necessary if not for the Gales. I blame them."

James Gale glared across the dining room table at his brother and struggled to hold his temper. "So not only did your man screw up the hit on Mansfield, he was shot in the process? Do you realize that every time one of your buffoons gets caught, the police have one more opportunity to link the attempts on Mansfield's life to us?"

Victor, who'd showed up at the house just as James's family was finishing dinner, gave a nonchalant shrug. "Then I guess it's a good thing Bolton was killed. That way, he can't talk."

James slammed a hand down on the table, rattling the dishes. "Don't blow this off like it's some video game you lost! Real people are dying. Real felonies are being committed by people with real connections to this family."

"I know that," Victor growled. "At least *I'm* doing something to avenge Pop."

"Yet Mansfield is still alive." James leaned forward, lowering his voice and narrowing his gaze on his brother. "Word is he and Darby Kent have disappeared. And we're no closer to giving Pop the justice he deserves."

Victor mirrored his combative position. "Maybe that's because you're sitting here in your white bread castle, refusing to get your hands dirty!"

"I have a family to think about and a company to run. I don't hear you complaining when you cash your dividend checks every month." Grinding his back teeth, he glanced out the back window to the patio where his wife and daughter were enjoying the swimming pool. He couldn't look at the cool, clear water without thinking of Billy's limp body and Connor Mansfield breathing life back into his boy. Acid gnawed his gut, and he shoved aside the conflict warring inside him. "Do you have anyone *competent* left on your payroll to finish the job? If Mansfield goes back into hiding, we may never get another chance to take him out."

"I have people I can call. But I'm tired of relying on other men. I have a new plan of attack—a plan Pop suggested and I intend to handle myself."

An uneasy feeling tickled James's neck. "What plans?"

"Mansfield and the woman may have disappeared, but there's a surefire way to draw them outta hiding."

James stiffened. *"No."*

"The kid is just lying there in the hospital. Too weak to fight back."

"I said *no.* Don't. Touch. The. Girl."

Victor flipped a palm up. "It'd bring them running

out of the shadows. Might not even have to kill her." He twitched his mouth in callous dismissal. "We'll see."

James lunged to his feet and jabbed a finger toward his brother. "Stay away from that little girl! Mansfield's family is *off-limits!*"

"For you maybe. I ain't got no problem using whatever means needed to finish this once and for all, and neither does Pop." Victor pulled out his cell phone and set it on the table. "Call him yourself if you need confirmation." He frowned and snapped his fingers as if remembering something. "Oh, wait. You can't call Pop anymore. Mansfield got him locked up."

Melinda burst through the back door and scampered into the dining room, dripping water on the hardwood floor. Her eyes were bright with excitement, and she bounced on her toes, waving for him to follow her. "Daddy! Daddy! Come watch. I know how to dive now!"

He schooled his face and sent his daughter a proud smile. "That's great, princess. I'll be right there."

"Hurry!" Melinda chirped and ran back outside.

Victor pushed his chair back and stood. "Go on. We're done here."

James sighed, still edgy about Victor's intentions. "Don't do anything without my approval, Victor. We don't need any more screwups."

Victor shoved his hands in his pockets and tipped his head as if in deep thought. "Uh, no." He started for the door. "I'll handle Mansfield my way."

A chilling premonition of disaster snaked through James. "Victor!"

His brother stopped and sent an impatient glare over his shoulder.

James set his jaw and leveled a hard stare on him. "I'm warning you. Don't go near Mansfield's daughter. I would just as soon let Pop go unavenged as hurt that innocent child."

Victor grunted. "Well, that's where you and I differ. And I don't answer to you. My loyalty is to Pop."

Chapter 19

That evening, after a dinner of turkey sandwiches and restlessly pacing the floor while Marshals Ramsey and Jones played Texas hold 'em with Connor, Darby retired to one of the two bedrooms in the old but comfortable safe house. Hargrove had done an admirable job of supplying the house with beds and linens, a small amount of furniture, a stocked pantry and refrigerator, a TV and DVDs, books…and all the add-ons the marshals needed to keep the place secure and hold Darby hostage. Dead bolts had been put on all the doors, wired alarms and locks secured the windows, and the safe with a combination lock sat in the living room for the storage of a secure cell phone, keys to the cars and extra weapons.

Hargrove had even brought Toby out to the safe house at Julia's suggestion, to make the place feel more homey and to relieve Stan's cat allergies, which had flared up since having Darby's cat living with them. It irritated her a bit that Julia had known the marshals' plan and had said nothing. But she knew Julia saw the move as being in Darby's best interest. Especially in light of Tracy's death.

When Darby had questioned Hargrove about the expense and effort of purchasing and furnishing the short-term safe house, he'd given her a mysterious smile. "WitSec is always going to have someone needing a new place to live and make a new life."

Now, with the late May sun sinking behind the loblolly pines out the bedroom window, Darby dropped on the edge of the queen-size bed and stroked Toby's soft fur. Toby had settled into his new digs obligingly after roaming the entire house, sniffing everything. He slept soundly, curled up on the bed Darby had claimed for herself and Connor, and purred as she idly patted him. She squeezed her eyes shut, and immediately, an image of Savannah, tethered to her hospital bed by IV lines, oxygen tubes and monitor wires, hovered in her mind's eye.

"Dwelling on Savannah's condition will only make you crazy, you know."

Darby opened her eyes to find Connor standing just inside the room. Seeing his broad shoulders filling the doorway still sent a surreal tremor through her, even after spending the past eleven days with him. He'd shed his earlier disguises and looked more like the Connor she remembered, but her brain still balked as if she were seeing a ghost. Albeit a sexy, golden-eyed ghost with a heart-melting smile. "How do you know I was thinking about Savannah? Maybe I was trying to think of a way to escape the marshals."

"Because I know you. I know your looks. And because our daughter has been just a thought away in my own mind all day." He walked into the connecting master bathroom, and she heard him tear off a few sheets of toilet tissue. As he came out of the bathroom with the tissues in his hand, he stopped and studied the bathroom door. "Huh."

"What?"

"This door was installed backward, the hinges on the outside. It opens into the bedroom." He moved the door, demonstrating.

She hesitated, confused. "So?"

"So nothing. Just an observation. And proof that you can take the man out of the construction business, but you can't take the construction business out of the man."

She sent him a weak smile, and he crossed the room to hand her the tissues. As she wiped her eyes and nose, he sat beside her, ruffling Toby's fur before he put his arm around Darby's shoulders. When she relaxed in his comforting embrace, he nudged her head down on his shoulder. "For your own sake, try to find something else to think about, to distract yourself from worrying about Savannah."

She shook her head and murmured, "Impossible. It's a mother's job to worry. I don't see how I can think of anything else."

"In that case…" He shifted on the mattress, pulling her down to lie beside him in the fading light from the window.

She noticed that he was careful not to kick Toby, still snoozing at the foot of the bed, in the process, and his consideration of her sleeping cat touched her. But that was Connor. He'd always been kindhearted, thoughtful. A good man to the core.

"Tell me about our little girl," he said. "Let's focus on your happy memories instead of on worry. I want to hear more stories like her birthday cake face-plant."

Darby gave a short, sad laugh and laid her head on Connor's chest. She could feel the strong, steady thump of his heartbeat under her ear, and the even rhythm was calming. "Where do I begin?"

"At the beginning." He stroked a hand up and down her arm, and she curled more snugly against him. "Was it a good pregnancy? What was it like to feel her kick? Did you find out she was a girl before she was born?"

She smiled as fond memories flowed through her. "Yes, other than morning sickness. Amazing. And yes."

Connor jostled her. "Not good enough. I want details. Spill."

She did. For the next couple of hours, until long after the sun had set and the only light in the room came from the moon's glow through the blinds, she filled in the blanks of Savannah's birth and early days, laughing at times and shedding an occasional tear. Milestones, funny quotes, favorite foods, habits, injuries, imaginary friends. Some of her stories started into territory she thought would bore him, minutia about Savannah's first tooth or her favorite T-shirt that sported a picture of an alligator saying, Later 'Gator.

"She thought the expression was riotously funny." Darby shook her head and waved a dismissive hand. "Oh, well. That's probably more than you wanted to know."

"Wrong." He brushed the hair off her forehead and kissed her cheek. "That's exactly what I want to know. That's the good stuff—the kind of things a parent knows and no one else cares about except with their own kids."

She angled her head to meet his gaze, and a jolt ricocheted through her when she found moisture in his eyes. She rolled to her side and cupped his face in her hands. "Connor, what—?"

"I can't stand the idea that I'm going to continue to miss all these moments with her when I leave. I may never see her again." He drew a ragged breath. "And I hate that she might think I wasn't there because I didn't love her. I'm leaving *because* I love both of you more than anything else."

Darby's chest seized, and her throat knotted. "No. I won't let that happen. I'll tell her every day what a wonderful and loving man you are. I'll make sure she knows you love her. I promise."

His fingers tightened on her arm. "Thank you." He closed his eyes for a moment, clearly struggling with his emotions before locking a gaze on her that penetrated to her marrow. "Remember that for yourself, too. I love you, Darby Kent. Every day. Always."

His profession arrowed through her, and a bittersweet ache exploded beneath her ribs with a strength that left her winded and raw. She tried to pull away, unwilling to hash through their untenable circumstances and heartbreaking sacrifices again.

But Connor looped an arm around her waist and hauled her back, rolled on top of her. "No. No running away."

His fingers plowed into her hair and dug lightly into her scalp as he held her head immobile and captured her lips with a searing kiss. Longing rushed through her like water from a broken dam, a powerful wave that swallowed everything in its path. All of Darby's defenses crumbled. A five-year-old desire surged from the corner of her heart where she'd suppressed it for long months. She wrapped her arms around Connor, her fingers clinging to his back, then threading through his hair. She pulled him closer, angling her head to deepen the kiss. His lips molded hers, his tongue sweeping inside to tangle with hers, and heat built in her, tingling under her skin and coiling at her core.

Connor's hands skimmed down her sides and sensuously traced the curve of her breasts, the dip of her waist and swell of her hips before traveling up again to find the hem of her shirt. He slipped his fingers under the blouse, and his warm palms stroked the bare flesh over her ribs. His thumbs nudged aside her bra, and a gasp of pleasure escaped her when he cupped her breasts, grazing her tight nipples.

He broke their kiss long enough to shove her shirt and bra off over her head in one smooth motion. In turn, she peeled his shirt from him and drank in the sight of his broad chest in the pale moonlight from the window. Raising her gaze to his chiseled cheeks and square jaw, her pulse jolted. *Connor.*

He was here. With her. Holding her again. Making love to her again. The fulfillment of a dream that had seemed so unlikely just weeks before, that she'd not dared to acknowledge it. And now it was real. She had this moment, even if it was all she'd ever have with him again.

He was staring at her with the same awestruck wonder and heartbreaking emotion that made her eyes fill with moisture. "I want to memorize this. Every detail. To hold on to on long, lonely nights ahead."

He nodded his agreement, then his brow dented in consternation. "We don't have protection."

Darby bit her lip, weighing that truth, but didn't need more than a few seconds to make up her mind. "Doesn't matter. If I get pregnant, so be it. I consider Savannah one of your greatest gifts to me, and I'd love her sibling just as much."

Connor remained serious, brooding. "I'm going to arrange with the marshals some way to send you child support, including back payments."

She blinked hard, stunned by his change of topic. "I…I don't need you to send money."

His gaze hardened. "I have a responsibility to you and Savannah that I won't ignore."

She clapped her hand over his mouth. "We will *not* talk

about this now." He tried to say something, his lips tickling her palm as they moved, but she shook her head. "No. No more talk. Kiss me, Connor. Hold me. Make love to me."

She felt his lips curve into a smile, saw the spark of light and love that lit his eyes, and her heart swelled. Sliding her fingers from his mouth, she stroked his jaw and tangled her fingers in his hair. She traced the shell of his ear with her thumb, then dragged his head closer to kiss him.

A sensual growl rumbled from his chest, and he rolled, pulling her on top of him. His kiss moved from lips to her ear, her neck, the sensitive dip between her collarbones, while his hands explored, massaged and aroused.

Soon they'd shed their remaining clothes, and their bare limbs twined together. Her passion-dampened body strained to press closer to his. Her hands roamed restlessly, eager to relearn everything about the texture of his skin and the taut shape of his muscles and sinew. She moved through their lovemaking without conscious thought, as if muscle memory took over, her body at home with Connor. She relaxed her mind to the heady sensations, the incredible joy and sweet release as he made them one.

Darby hooked her legs around his, clung to his shoulders and arched into him, riding a climax that shook her to the marrow while Connor murmured her name and pledged his undying love. His whispers dissolved in a primal moan when he peaked, his arms tightening around her as he thrust deeper, harder. Then he collapsed on top of her, clutching her head to his heart. After a moment of silence, the two of them listening to the serenade of tree frogs outside and their own ragged breathing, Connor whispered hoarsely, "This is where you belong. With me."

A knot of emotion clogged her throat as she gave a small nod, but her heart asked, *Then why haven't you asked me to go with you into WitSec?*

* * *

The next morning, Darby's first thought, as it was every morning lately, was of Savannah. Her heart lurched when she pictured her baby in the hospital bed, fighting for her life without her mother at her side. Connor's admonition about dwelling on Savannah's condition and making herself sick with worry resounded in her head. He was right, of course, but as she'd told him, it was impossible for her not to fret over her daughter's health and well-being. Just the same, she drew a cleansing breath and battled down the grief and frustration that surged in her throat.

She rolled to face the other half of the bed, but it was empty. Connor's pillow still bore the dent from his head and the faint scent of cedar…and sex. Her pulse leaped when she remembered their lovemaking last night. His ardor balanced with tenderness. The weight of him pressing her into the bedding, his body flush with hers. The sensual feel of his hands and lips exploring her skin.

The indescribable intimacy of their bodies joined, their souls reconnected. Their hearts reunited. She squeezed a fistful of the sheet and bit back the sound of despair that rose in her throat. Despite her best effort to keep her heart safe, to not open herself to the pain of losing him a second time, her love for Connor refused to be shunted away or repressed, regardless of the cost. Maybe her fight to protect herself from heartache had been a losing battle from the start. Connor was too deeply rooted in her soul, too visibly evident in their daughter's genes, too much a part of who she was and what she wanted from life to ever be denied.

She heaved a resigned sigh, knowing the inevitable bleak days of yearning and loneliness that lay ahead for her.

Dragging herself out of bed, she dressed in clothes Hargrove had brought to the safe house from her home. The idea of Hargrove packing her panties and bras gave her the heebie-geebies, but she was glad to have clean underclothes given the circumstances. She pulled on a pair of athletic shorts, jogging shoes and her old track club T-shirt from high school before following the scent of fresh coffee to the kitchen. When she entered the front room, Connor was at the stove with a spatula in his hand, and Jones was comfortably kicked back in a chair at the table, sipping from a large mug.

"Hey, whatcha cooking?" She crossed to Connor, gave him a chaste kiss on the cheek. His face still bore the stubble of the day before, and the rough texture of his unshaven skin was tantalizing against her lips. Quashing the stir of lust at her core, she peered into the frying pan.

"I made you soft scrambled eggs with diced ham and cheese, just the way you like 'em." Connor grinned, clearly proud of himself for remembering her preferred breakfast.

"Oh." Darby caught a whiff of the cooking eggs, and her stomach turned. "Connor, that's sweet of you, but…" She winced and backed away from the pan, covering her nose.

"What?" His brow furrowed.

"It's just that, when I was pregnant with Savannah, I was hypersensitive to certain smells. Things I used to be fine with, even like, suddenly made me nauseated."

He glanced at the omelet he was making, then back at her, his expression crestfallen. "Let me guess. Eggs?"

She shot him an apologetic look. "Especially eggs. I still can't eat them. I know it's just a lingering association with the persistent morning sickness I had during my pregnancy, but…" She looked into the pan again and shuddered.

"Same thing happened to my wife when she was pregnant with our son," Jones said. "Except for her, it was the smell of vinegar. Anything with vinegar in it—pickles, ketchup, salad dressing—made her sick as a dog. I ate a lot of plain hot dogs and lettuce those nine months."

Connor turned the heat off under the pan. "You're sure you can't eat some of this? I made a ton. It'd be a shame to waste it."

"Feed it to Toby." She nodded toward the brown tabby winding himself through Connor's legs and clearly hoping for a treat. "He'll be thrilled to have eggs for breakfast."

"Feed it to Jones," the marshal said, a wry exasperation in his tone. "Jones would like to have eggs for breakfast."

Connor waved a hand to the pan. "Help yourself."

Before Jones could take them away, Darby snagged a bite of egg and blew on it to cool it. Crouching, she held it out to Toby, who gulped it down and licked her fingers. "That's my boy. You've been so good through all the moves and upheaval." She scratched him behind the ear, then lifted his front paws off the floor to kiss the top of his head.

After pouring herself a cup of coffee, Darby walked to the window and stared out at the dappled sun streaming through the trees. Even in May it didn't take long for the Louisiana sun to turn the day miserably hot. She faced Jones, who was at the stove heaping scrambled eggs onto a plate. "What are the chances you'll let me go out for a run? I'll go stir-crazy if I have to stay inside, and I think a brisk jog before the day gets too hot will help me unwind."

The marshal's gaze took in her attire, and he scowled. "Not a good idea."

She groaned, her shoulders drooping. "Really? There's nothing out there for miles but trees and an occasional farm house. Even if the farmers in those houses did happen to look out their window at the exact moment I jogged by, I can't believe they'd have enough interest in a runner on the street to give me anything more than a glance. If this cabin is isolated enough to be safe, the deserted roads within a couple miles of the cabin have got to be safe, too."

Jones set his plate on the table and licked cheese from his finger. "Still no. Hargrove is asleep, and I have to stay here with him." He jerked his head toward Connor, who pulled a disgusted face that expressed his opinion of being babysat by the marshal.

Darby took a sip of coffee, then squeezed the mug with frustration. "I'll stay close to the house. I just need twenty, thirty minutes to work off some stress."

"Sorry," Jones said and shoveled in a bite of omelet.

"What if I go with her?" Connor turned a chair backward and straddled it. "Now that my hip's feeling better, I wouldn't mind loosening up my muscles with a run myself."

Jones glanced up from his breakfast and chuckled wryly. "What part of protective custody don't you understand?"

The rumble of an engine outside caught their attention, and Jones rose quickly to peer out the window, standing to the side and squinting through the tiniest of gaps cut from blinds.

His obvious agitation over the arriving vehicle made Darby tense. She took a step closer to Connor and watched Jones reach for his weapon.

The marshal's brow puckered. "What the…? It's Morris." Though he visibly relaxed and moved his hand from his gun, Jones was obviously still bothered by Morris's unexpected arrival.

Savannah! Darby's stomach pitched. Was Morris here because something had happened to Savannah? Could she have taken a turn for the worse?

She rushed to the door on Jones's heels, anxiety beating its wings inside her.

"What are you doing here?" Jones asked gruffly as Morris trekked in, lugging a large bag with him. "What's all that?"

Morris looked past Jones to Darby, then to Connor. "It's some stuff I was asked to pick up." He stepped past Darby and handed the bulging bag to Connor. "I couldn't find some of the stuff on your list. I hope this will do."

Connor took the sack and looked inside. "Thanks. I guess it's for her to decide if it'll do." He, in turn, handed the large bag to Darby. "For you."

She gave him a puzzled look and reached for the bag. When she peeked inside, her heart gave a hard thump, and tears sprang to her eyes.

Art supplies. She saw at least two blank canvases, a large pad of high-quality drawing paper, charcoals, paints, pencils...more tools of her craft than she even had at home. Of course, she'd had to set aside her art in recent years to concentrate on raising Savannah and earning a living, so she'd allowed her supplies to dwindle on purpose. Her art had to take a backseat to the demands of a young child, the need for health insurance and the practicality and convenience of working for the Mansfields' family business.

She blinked back the moisture—darn it all, the stress and losses of the past few weeks had turned her into a leaky faucet—and raised a wide smile to Connor. "I...I don't know what to say."

Connor pulled her into his arms. "Say that you'll paint something I can take with me when I have to leave town."

She nodded. "Of course." After setting the bag on the floor, she hugged him tightly. "Thank you. This is so sweet of you." She glanced to Morris over Connor's shoulder. "And thank you."

He acknowledged her with a grin. "No signing your

work, though, if he's going to take it with him. Even that'd be a link to his past if someone saw it."

Morris's warning cast a cloud over her happy moment and reminded her of one of the reasons Connor said he'd left her behind four and a half years ago. He hadn't wanted to put her in the position of giving up her art, her passion. And yet, Connor had given up everything he loved—people, hobbies, career and home—to protect her and his family. The generosity of his sacrifice hit her anew, and a tremor rolled through her. She squeezed him tighter, not wanting to let go, knowing if not for Savannah's illness, she'd gladly give up her art to be with Connor. If given the choice of her past or a future with Connor, she'd choose Connor.

But he hadn't asked. And the fact that he hadn't given her that choice, that he hadn't asked her to join him, cut her deeply.

Morris stayed at the safe house that morning, joining Hargrove and allowing Jones a respite he seemed grateful to receive. Morris informed them he'd checked at the hospital and had a "no news is good news" report from Ramsey and a message from Hunter that Savannah continued to make baby steps forward in her recovery.

And so it went, day after day. The men watched TV or played cards while Darby sketched and dabbled at painting. And worried about Savannah.

She glommed onto every scrap of information she got from the marshals about Savannah's condition, her appearance, every minuscule event they could report. She wanted to hear about her daughter's every request for juice, for her stuffed bunny…and for her mommy. Her heart broke knowing her daughter wanted her and she wasn't there. Hunter had told Savannah Darby was taking care of important business and was still there in spirit, but she knew that excuse rang hollow. No business was more important than her daughter. She'd vowed to herself the day Savannah was born that she'd never abandon her little girl the way her father had abandoned his family. Yet the marshals' actions, bringing her to this safe house in the Louisiana woods, meant Savannah felt deserted by her mother when she needed her mommy the most.

Darby would never forgive the agents for the heartache they'd forced on her daughter—even if she understood the need. Every day, she battled not to break down and exert the choice Jones had given her to leave their protection. But then an image of her incinerated car or of Tracy's casket would flash in her mind, and she'd stay put, determined to keep the Gales' danger away from Savannah if at all possible.

By night, she lay in Connor's arms, cherishing every moment with him, making love to him and sleeping with her head resting over the drumming of his heart, while losing another tiny piece of hers to him each day.

Later that week, Darby convinced Morris to allow her and Connor to go for a walk in the woods behind the safe house—with Morris tailing them as their protection. She took a large tote bag full of the art supplies, genuinely excited by the prospect of finding a tranquil nature scene to sketch, the opportunity to stretch her legs and breathe fresh air.

As they trekked through the shaded woods, the scent of pine and honeysuckle redolent in the air, Darby cut Morris a side glance. "I'm curious, Marshal. Earlier this month, when I went to see William Gale at the prison, Marshal Jones told Connor that guarding me, restricting my movement, wasn't part of his assignment. His official job was only protecting Connor as the WitSec client. Even after the bomb blew up my car, his family and I were only under your protection in that Connor was living in the same house with us. What changed? Why am I now part of your assignment?"

"Simple," Morris said with a casual shrug. "You're his fiancée now. A witness's immediate family can enter Wit-Sec with him and receive our protection."

Confused, Darby stopped walking and stared at Morris. "Who said I was his fiancée?"

Realizing she'd halted, Connor and Morris turned to look back at her.

"You did," Morris said. "You said he asked you to marry him."

Connor arched an eyebrow, his expression full of hope. "You told him we were engaged?"

"No." She scowled at Morris. "If you'll remember, I told you I said no. As in, not engaged. Don't men ever listen?"

Connor's shoulders dropped, and the light that had filled his face moments earlier faded. Darby's heart pinched, regretting the hurt her denial clearly caused him.

Morris swatted away a mosquito and sent her a cagey glance. "What do ya say we keep that minor detail between us?"

She blinked her disbelief. "Minor detail?"

"As long as Jones and the department heads think you're engaged, they'll continue to protect you and your daughter with the full resources available, until you're all able to relocate, as a family."

Darby stood straighter. "I—"

"Then," Morris continued, "should you change your mind about marrying him —"

"What?" Darby goggled.

He held up his hands, palms toward her. "Sorry, that's personal and for you to decide."

"Darn right." Connor faced Morris with his hands on his hips and a dark glower on his face.

"But I can't relocate with Connor. We've discussed this!"

Morris ignored Connor's glower and spoke to Darby. "'Your task is not to seek for love, but merely to seek and find all the barriers within yourself that you have built against it.'"

She shook her head. "What?"

"Rumi. He was a thirteenth century poet and theologian. My wife has a plaque with that saying in our living room." Morris shrugged. "I figure it fits."

Darby shook her head. "How's that?"

Morris scoffed. "Come on. Maybe you can't relocate, but by convincing the other marshals you were engaged, I've bought you time. Your daughter is getting the best protection available, and you—" his gaze honed more fully on Darby "—have time with him—" he hitched his head toward Connor "—away from distractions for a few days. That's a gift. What do you think Grant would pay for a few more days alone with his wife?"

Air backed up in Darby's lungs. Morris was right. Rather than quibble over the marshal's methods, she should relish the opportunity he'd given her to be with Connor, what might be her last chance to share a beautiful day and a walk in the woods.

Without saying any more, Morris tucked his hands in his pockets and strolled ahead.

Darby and Connor exchanged a long look. Darby's heart kicked hard against her ribs, and another chunk of the protective wall she'd erected crumbled.

Connor held a hand out to her, and she shifted the bag of art supplies from one hand to the other, so she could link fingers with his. They made their way through the woods to a small clearing where dragonflies buzzed around a small pond. A large pin oak had fallen near the edge of the pond, and Connor led her to it. Across the pond, Morris had found what remained of a child's tree house and had climbed up and settled inside. He gave a wave, letting them know he was watching but affording them a few moments of private conversation.

Darby sat down on the fallen oak trunk and stared out over the glassy green water. "It's so pretty here. And peaceful."

Connor pulled out her sketch pad and handed it to her. "Draw it. I want this to be the picture I take with me to WitSec."

She swallowed hard to clear the tightness from her throat. "For what it's worth…" She glanced down at her fidgeting fingers, then back to Connor. "If Savannah weren't sick, if the Gales weren't still breathing down our necks, I'd have accepted your proposal. I want us to be a family."

Bittersweet emotions crossed Connor's face. He drew a deep sigh and exhaled harshly, clearly fighting to keep his composure. "I want that, too. More than you know."

Darby paused in the middle of pulling a drawing pencil from a pouch. "Then why—?" She bit her lip and, feeling reckless and under the constraint of the limited time they had left together, she blurted the question that had plagued her, tormented her since Connor returned. "Why didn't you ask me to go with you when you entered WitSec? Why haven't you asked me to go with you now?" When he sent her a frown and furrowed his brow like the answer was obvious, she waved a hand, cutting him off. "I know the reasons I *can't* go. We've just been through all that with Morris. I want to know why you didn't even *ask* me to go with you, even when you proposed!"

Connor looked stunned. "Darby, I—"

But she wasn't done. Once the floodgate of pain opened, the hurt poured out. "Throughout this whole ordeal, you haven't once asked me to stay with you, to give our relationship a chance. You've said you love me, yet you have no plan of staying with me!"

"Because I can't!" he said, his jaw, his fists, his shoulders all taut. "I can't put you at risk!"

"I know that! God, I know all that! But you haven't even *asked.* You *tell* me how it's going to be. You *tell* me what you've decided. You *tell* me you want Savannah to have your name. But you leave *me* out of every decision that affects us and our future. Just like you have from the moment you faked your death and left me alone to grieve for you and have our baby alone!"

"That's not fair. I didn't know about your pregnancy!"

"Because I didn't know yet! And my being pregnant shouldn't make the difference."

"What? Of course it makes a difference! If I'd known I was a father, I'd have—"

"What?" she interrupted, pointing at him. "You'd have what? Married me? Taken me with you?"

He spread his hands, his expression incredulous and exasperated. "Yes! Of course!"

She inhaled sharply, a searing pain shooting to her core. She wilted, letting the pad and pencil pack in her hands slip to the dirt. "That's what I thought," she muttered, not hiding her dejection and hurt.

Confusion denting his brow, Connor stepped forward and knelt at her feet. "How is that the wrong answer?"

She looked across the still pond, watching a Jesus bug skim across the water and saying nothing for long seconds. Finally he shifted to sit beside her on the fallen tree.

"Darby, please." He rubbed a hand on her back, massaged her neck gently. "I want to understand. Why are you mad? Tell me what you want to hear."

"It's not about what I *want* to hear. What I *need* to hear is the truth. Just the unvarnished truth about us. And I think I just got it." She darted a quick side glance at him and found his face as creased with doubt and confusion as before. Sighing, she turned back to the pond, knowing if she wanted his bald honesty, she owed him full disclosure, too. She took a moment to garner her courage and composure. "When my dad left us, he disappeared without explanation, without saying goodbye."

Connor's thumb strummed the tendon at the back of her neck, his fingers cradling her nape. "I know. And I know how much it hurt you."

"Do you?" She looked at him, searching his golden-brown eyes. "Because I've only come to realize all the ways he hurt me in recent days. Since you came back."

Connor stiffened.

"The thing is, when he left us so abruptly, I felt…more than rejected. I felt like…I didn't matter. I wasn't important. I wasn't loved enough for my father to stay."

Connor groaned sympathetically. "Darby, no. Don't put that on yourself. You are loved, and you are important. To lots of people."

"Just not to you. Not important enough."

She felt the jolt that shot through Connor, making him jerk taut. "Are you insane?"

He reached around her to seize her arms and turn her toward him. He gave her a small shake and drilled her with his stare. "You matter more to me than my own life! That's what all this is about! That's why I gave up *everything* to protect you. How can you say you aren't important to me?"

"Then fight for me!" she cried, her voice torn by a sob. "Give me the chance to be *with* you. *Ask me* to go with you when you leave for WitSec! I don't want to be abandoned again! I want to know I'm enough reason for you to stay even if Savannah wasn't part of the equation."

Connor released her, dragging a hand over his mouth as he rocked back on the tree trunk. His face paled, and his expression was stark, stricken.

Darby squeezed her eyes shut and swiped away the tears on her cheeks with her palms. "I know it wouldn't change anything about the reality of our situation and all the reasons I can't go with you. But it would make a difference in here." She clapped a hand over her heart. She raised her eyes to Connor, her soul stripped bare, her emotions raw and naked. "I just want to matter enough that you *ask* me to go with you."

He took a few more deep breaths, then laced his fingers with hers and kissed the back of her hand. "I'm sorry I hurt you, Darby. I didn't realize…I didn't—"

He paused, a thousand emotions swirling in his gaze when he met hers. Darby held her breath. Waited. Her hope was a fragile bird perched on the edge of a vast abyss.

"I didn't ask you to come with me," he started slowly, softly, his voice heavy, "for all the reasons I've told you. To keep you safe. Because my death had to look believable. Because I didn't want you to have to give up your life, your family." He waved a hand. "All that is true. But if I'm honest—with you and with myself—I also didn't ask you because…I was scared."

It was Darby's turn to be stunned and confused. She wrinkled her forehead and shook her head. "Why?"

"Because I am the control freak you say I am. I could handle living without you if I believed I was making the sacrifice to keep you safe, but I couldn't bear the idea of living without you because—" he stopped and looked away "—because you said no."

Her breath caught. "Connor…"

"I knew how much your family meant to you, how much your art meant to you, and I knew there was a good chance you'd say no. I needed our separation to be on my terms… because I was afraid if I gave you a choice, you'd say no." He blew out a cleansing breath through pursed lips and sent her an apologetic look. "I guess I'm still scared. I know how mad you were over my deception when I entered WitSec. Even though I know Savannah's illness prevents you from coming with me, I don't want to know you might choose your life in Lagniappe over me. You said you couldn't love me again."

Darby blinked slowly, letting Connor's confession roll through her and settle in her bones. A mixture of relief and sadness expanded in her chest.

They sat together in an aching silence as the late spring sun beat down on them. In the pond, a fish jumped, and a bird took flight from a scrub bush nearby. After a few moments, Connor took both of her hands in his and squeezed them tightly. She lifted her head and met the heat and passion in his gaze.

"Darby, I love you with all I am and all I'll ever be. I need you in my life and at my side for always. Will you please come with me, stay with me, no matter what life brings and where fate takes us?"

Love and pain exploded inside her, and a sob hiccupped from her throat. With tears rolling down her cheeks, she captured his mouth in a lip-bruising kiss. He released her hands to plow his fingers into her hair and frame her face with his hands. His fingers curled against her scalp, holding her close as he shifted his lips to deepen the kiss. She slid closer, settling on his lap so that the frantic clamoring in her chest was pressed against the thunderous cadence in his.

He moved his lips along her jaw, over her nose, drying the moisture from her cheeks with his kisses. And for the first time in many years, she felt well and truly cherished.

Digging her fingers into his shirt, clinging to him, to the beautiful moment they had together, she whispered, "I want that. So, so much. I want to stay with you forever." A knot closed her throat. "But I can't."

He stilled. Pulling back, Connor looked into her eyes with a shared grief. "I know."

Chapter 20

A low buzzing woke Darby early the next morning. At first she thought a mosquito had gotten in the bedroom, and she swatted groggily by her ear. But the intermittent buzz continued until the low rumble of a sleepy male voice in another room said, "Yeah, I'm here. What's up?"

Darby pressed a button on her watch to light the face, and even that dim glow was blinding in the dark room. She squinted at the watch, blinking the numbers into focus—4:35 a.m. Awfully early for a phone call. Too early. Phone calls at this hour usually meant bad news. Her heart lurched.

"No, nothing. Why?"

She rolled her head to the side to glance at Connor, but he snored softly, contentedly asleep.

"What!" Morris said, more loudly, the displeasure in his voice palpable.

Darby's gut flipped. So it was bad news. Tossing back

her covers, she crept soundlessly on bare feet toward the door of the living room.

"In her room?" Morris asked, his volume decidedly lower now, almost a whisper. If not for the stillness of the night, Darby would have missed his reply. "Is the girl okay?"

Darby froze, still hidden around a corner in the hall. *Savannah!*

She clapped a hand over her mouth, muffling the mewl of distress that rose in her throat. Her knees buckled, and she braced a hand on the wall, straining to listen.

"Damn it! No, that doesn't sound good." A floorboard squeaked, and the soft thud of footsteps filled the gap between Morris's responses. "What did the note say?"

Darby peeked around the corner and found Morris pacing, his fingers raking through his sleep-mussed hair. Her first impulse was to charge into the room and demand to know what had happened to Savannah, but Morris's next reply stopped her.

"No, I agree. I won't tell them. They'd only freak out. What's done is done."

Darby's eyes widened, and anger roiled inside her. Not tell them? How much of the truth were the marshals withholding from her and Connor? She had a right to know anything and everything that was happening with her daughter! Adrenaline and fury fueled her rubbery legs, and she made a move toward the living room. Then balked.

Her best chance to learn what had happened was to continue listening from where she was, out of view. She pressed her back against the cool wall and tried to hear Morris over the sound of her pulse throbbing in her ear.

"How the hell did he get in there? Where was Hargrove? The family? The nurses?" Morris fell silent, then cursed.

"And you've interviewed everyone who was on duty? No one saw *anything?* How is that possible?"

Darby closed her eyes, imagining a hundred kinds of terror that could have happened. She'd stayed out here at the safe house because she'd trusted the marshals to protect Savannah. But from the sound of it, some form of evil had slipped through the cracks and threatened her daughter. She curled her toes against the hardwood floor, hating her isolation, swamped by a need, an imperative to get back to her daughter's bedside. Even if it cost her her own life. She had to protect Savannah, and she would move mountains to make that happen.

"No problem. You finish cleaning up the situation there. I can stay." The creak of floorboards was replaced by the squeak of a couch spring. Darby hazarded a peek, and sure enough, Morris had sat down on the edge of the sofa, his head down, phone to his ear. "Right." He sighed with disgust. "Keep me posted. Yeah, bye."

Morris keyed off the connection and tossed the phone on the cushion beside him. He stayed in his defeated position, shoulders slumped and head lowered, his hand scrubbing his face for long seconds before pushing to his feet and walking to the front window. Parting the blinds with one finger, he peered out into the night.

Darby debated her options. Morris had always seemed sympathetic to her cause, had shown a personal interest in her well-being, had helped Connor get the art supplies that had filled her hours this week. Maybe she could wheedle some information from him. Maybe it wasn't as bad as it sounded, as bad as she was imagining. Because her imagination was playing some pretty terrifying scenarios in her head. Stabbings, her family taken hostage, more car bombs, poisons injected in Savannah's IV.

Straightening from the support of the wall, Darby gathered her composure, at least outwardly, and schooled her face not to give away the churning in her gut. She stepped into the living room, blinking groggily and trying to look as if she'd just gotten up. "Who was that on the phone?"

Morris whirled around, his expression momentarily startled, but he, too, quickly put on a mask of nonchalance. He grinned and shoved his hands in his pockets. "What are you doing up?"

"I heard the phone. Talking." She tipped her head. "What was it about?"

He twisted his mouth in a dismissive moue and shook his head. "Nothing."

She narrowed her eyes skeptically, feeling her temper and sense of betrayal rise. "Nothing? Someone called at four-thirty to say nothing?" Her voice sounded remarkably calm, considering she was still quivering with fear for Savannah and pique at the marshal's obvious intent to keep her in the dark.

He shrugged. "Yeah. Nothing. Wrong number."

Liar. "Hmm. You always talk that long to a wrong number?"

She held his gaze, and he had the nerve to look her in the eye as he said, "Drunk dialer. I decided to yank his chain a bit before I hung up." He flashed a lopsided grin. "Let him think he'd reached his friend to see where it would go, if he'd catch on."

"Hmm," she hummed tightly, barely containing the anger and hurt that this man she'd trusted could be so completely dishonest without an ounce of regret. "Did he? Catch on that you were *lying* to him?"

A flicker of something crossed his face. The barest twitch in his cheek as he gritted his teeth. But his eyes remained steady, emotionless. Unyielding. "I don't know. I hung up."

She grunted as if acknowledging him and jerked a nod. "All right, then. I'll go back to bed. Good night."

He nodded once. "'Night."

Her body taut and vibrating, Darby stalked back to the bedroom and closed the door. Using only the dim light from the moon through the blinds, she crawled back onto the bed and shook Connor.

"Wake up," she whispered, her voice quiet but urgent. "Something's happened with Savannah, Connor. We have to get away from here."

He jerked awake, sitting up quickly and rubbing his eyes to help him focus. "What did you say?"

She grabbed fists full of the sheets, working to keep her voice quiet, despite the panic fluttering beneath her ribs. "Morris got a call. I overheard his end of the whole conversation, and it was clear that something bad had happened. I heard him ask if 'the girl' was okay. He had to mean Savannah."

In the dim glow from the window, she saw the frown that pulled Connor's mouth and brow. "And what answer did he get?"

"I don't know, but it didn't make him happy. There was something about a note in her room, and he wanted to know how anyone could have gotten into her room." She detailed everything she heard, including Morris's decision not to tell them so they wouldn't "freak out."

"He was right about that much," she said, her hands restless in her lap and her heart hammering. "I'm officially freaked out. We gotta find out what happened. I have to get out of here. I need to be with my baby!"

Connor tossed back the covers and swung his legs to the floor. "I'll talk to Morris, demand to know what's happening."

"I did ask. He denied he got the call. Claimed it was

a wrong number." She squared her shoulders as she rose from the bed and faced Connor. "He flat-out lied to me. Right to my face. Without even blinking." A fresh wave of betrayal and anger swirled through her. "I'm through with the marshals and this protective custody, Connor. I have to be with Savannah. I don't care how dangerous it is. Protecting her is *my* job. I'm her mother!"

Connor stared at her for long pregnant seconds, his body tense and resolute, his mouth grim. "No. It's *our* job. I'm going with you."

They kept the light off, their voices a whisper, so they wouldn't alert Morris or Ramsey that they were awake… and planning.

"So how do we get the car key from that safe without them knowing?" Darby asked, snuggled against Connor on the bed. Her pulse galloped with anticipation as they plotted.

"We don't. Grant taught me how to hot-wire a car when we were in high school. We just need to find a screwdriver around here."

Darby scrunched her nose. "Is that still possible with newer cars? I thought hot-wiring was just for older cars."

"Well, it's trickier for sure, but determined thieves found ways around the safeguards and shared the info on the internet for delinquent teens like Grant to find and practice."

"Grant was a delinquent? I thought Hunter was the wild child of the family."

"Grant had his moments, especially when it came to cars. He loves to tinker and was known to drag race and go for unauthorized joyrides."

Darby digested this new insight on Grant for a moment,

then returned to the topic at hand. "So we're going to steal one of the marshals' cars?"

"Borrow."

She snorted at his semantics. "Then I need to find a way to distract them and buy you time to work your magic."

"Exactly. Whatcha got?"

"I could fake an injury or illness."

Connor stroked a hand over his mouth as he considered it. "They'd wonder why I wasn't helping you and might guess pretty quick it was a bluff without real physical evidence of illness."

"I'm not against cutting myself to get blood for realism."

Connor angled his head to frown down at her. "No. I won't let you do that. Keep thinking."

They spent more than an hour working out details for implementing their plan to sneak away from the safe house undetected. Or at least to distract or detain the marshals long enough to make their getaway. Having an action plan, something to *do* with a goal in mind, gave Darby renewed energy and focus. They spent the morning surreptitiously gathering the tools and laying the groundwork.

Just after lunch, Darby and Connor excused themselves to their bedroom for a nap. After about twenty minutes, Connor slipped from their bedroom into the one the marshals alternately used. When he was in place, Darby got to work.

Standing on the toilet in their bathroom, she screamed.

Both Morris and Ramsey came scrambling back to respond to the commotion, weapons drawn.

"Over there! Get him!" She aimed a finger to the far corner of the bathroom.

Ramsey filled the bedroom door, while Morris ducked into the small bathroom, his body tense. "What is it?"

Darby flailed her arms, keeping the marshals' attention

while Connor slipped out of the second bedroom and hurried to the front door. "There was a mouse!"

Morris relaxed, lowering his weapon. "Geez, Darby, I thought there was a break-in."

"There was! A mouse! Get him," she screamed, trying to sound hysterical.

"I don't see—"

"Now he's over here!" She screamed again and jumped off the toilet, racing for the bathroom door.

Ramsey stepped closer to the bathroom, chuckling at Darby's girlish hysterics and peering in at Morris. "Where's your cat? Why not let him catch it?"

Darby grunted and hitched her head toward the feline lounging on the bed, blinking curiously at the commotion around him. "Fat chance of that. Toby's a lover, not a hunter. Just grab the mouse and throw it out of here!" She darted to the bedroom window and shoved it open. The house alarm, as predicted, shrieked, sending Toby scurrying...and allowing Connor to also open the front door without alerting the marshals.

Ramsey turned toward her. "Close that! We'll trap the critter and take him out the back door."

"Darby, there's no mouse," Morris said, bent at the waist checking inside cabinets below the sink.

"Look again!" She scurried back toward the bathroom, planting a hand on Ramsey's chest when he tried to exit the bathroom. "Help him look!" She shoved him back and slammed the backward-installed door. "And don't come out without that rat!"

She quickly flipped the knob latch, locking the marshals in. Immediately they knew they'd been duped and rattled the doorknob. "Not funny, Darby! Open up!"

Soon enough, they'd give up ordering her to release them and kick the door down. She hurried out the front door, joining Connor on the front lawn where he was already at work jerry-rigging the steering column of the marshals' sedan.

"They're locked in the bathroom," she told Connor as she snatched open the passenger door and clambered inside. "But they won't be for long. Hurry!"

"Almost there." He fiddled a bit more while she anxiously watched the front door, expecting Morris and Ramsey to come charging out any second.

When the engine roared to life, she exhaled the breath she hadn't realized she was holding. "Let's go!"

Ramsey appeared in the front door, his face dark with fury, just as Morris ran around the corner from the back of the house. "Don't do it! Stop!"

Connor jammed the car into gear and peeled down the dirt driveway, spraying dust and debris kicked up by the back tires. Morris gave chase on foot, shouting for them to stop, but Connor quickly outpaced him. He whipped the car onto the small state road and stomped the accelerator.

Darby grabbed the armrest and cut her gaze to the side mirror, where she saw Morris, then Ramsey, stumble to a stop at the end of the dirt drive and stare helplessly at their escaping charges. A pang of remorse poked her. She hated that they'd had to resort to tricking the marshals and making them look bad to their superiors, but she shoved the regret down. Morris had lied to her about Savannah's welfare, about the call he'd gotten. She and Connor were doing what they had to do, what any parent would do, to protect Savannah.

Shifting her attention to Connor, who squeezed the steering wheel with a white-knuckled grip and whose jaw was rigid, she settled back on the seat and buckled her safety belt.

"Look around for something that might tell us where

we are and how to get back to Lagniappe." Connor waved a finger toward the map pockets in the door by her. She pulled out a stack of papers and flipped through them but saw nothing helpful. Next she checked the console between the front seats, storage cubbies on the dash and a file folder she found on the backseat. The file contained surveillance photos of Victor and James Gale. She shuddered, staring down at the faces of the men who wanted to harm her family, who had ordered a contract to kill Connor.

Connor sent her a curious look. "Got something?"

She grunted and slapped the file closed. "Nothing helpful." She stashed the file in the map pocket and tried the glove box. When she saw the compartment's contents, she gasped.

"What?" Connor cut a sharp side glance toward her.

She carefully extracted the handgun she'd discovered and held it up for him to see, her hand shaking and her eyes wide.

"Good!" Connor said, turning his eyes back to the road. "We may need that."

Darby swallowed hard. "Do you really think you could shoot someone?"

"If it came to it, to save you or Savannah. Hell yeah."

She exhaled slowly through pursed lips and set the gun on the seat beside her. Turning back to the glove box, she extracted the next treasure. A cell phone.

"Score." She mashed the power button, and the screen lit. She keyed in Hunter's phone number and listened to his line ring. Once. Twice.

Connor gave her a puzzled look. "Who ya calling?"

"Your brother. I want answers."

Hunter answered on the fourth ring with a leery, "Hello?"

"It's me. And Connor. We shook our babysitters and are on our way to the hospital."

There was a brief pause, then, "Darby? What's going on?"

She lowered the phone, switching it to speaker setting, then said, "That's what we want to know. I overheard Morris on the phone discussing something that happened there with Savannah, but they wouldn't tell us anything."

"You mean the note," Hunter replied, his voice dark.

She and Connor exchanged a worried look, and he said, "Tell us everything. What did the note say? Where did they find it?"

"Is Savannah all right?" Darby added. "Be honest, Hunter. Is she safe? Is she getting better?" Ahead of them, Darby spotted a highway sign, advising of an upcoming crossroad with an arrow pointing left for Lagniappe and right for Alexandria. She motioned toward the sign.

Connor nodded that he'd seen it and turned left at the intersection.

"She's fine, Dar. The doctors have been watching her for changes because of the rat, but—"

"Rat! What rat?" Darby cried.

"The dead one delivered with the threatening note. The intruder left both on the foot of Savannah's bed while she slept. A gruesome little warning for Connor."

A muscle in Connor's cheek twitched, and his mouth pressed into a frown. "Damn it."

Visions of bubonic plague, hanta virus, rabies and other rodent-borne illnesses surrounding her immune-deficient daughter sent a fresh ripple of horror through Darby. "Oh, God," she groaned.

"Darby, listen to me." Hunter's voice sharpened and cut through her straying thoughts. "Savannah is okay. She wasn't hurt. In fact, she's made small improvements every day."

She huffed a huge sigh of relief. "You promise?"

"I swear," Hunter replied. "But you can't come back here. Especially not Connor."

"Why?" Connor asked gruffly.

"Because that's what the note was angling for." Hunter's tone was grim. "It said for you to give yourself up or they'd hurt Savannah."

Darby couldn't help the small whimpering sound that issued from her throat. She squeezed the door's armrest and bit down on her lip.

"Bro, that's why we have to come. I can't give them a reason to hurt my daughter. And I'm sure as hell not leaving her protection up to anyone else. How was this guy able to get past the marshal on duty? All the nurses?"

"I'm not sure. It happened really early in the morning, at the nurses' shift change. Hargrove swears no one but nurses went in or out, which means the Gales had to have bribed or threatened one of the nurses to plant the note and rat for them."

"And where were you?" Connor asked, his timbre condemning. Darby sent him a scolding look.

Hunter sighed, and the breathy sound resonated with despondency. "At home. I went home to sleep last night. I'd only gotten three or four hours a night on that rock they call a sofa in the waiting area outside Savannah's room, and it was showing at work. We almost had a loss time accident at a construction site a couple days ago because of my inattention. I'm sorry, guys. I know I should have been—"

"No, don't blame yourself," Darby interrupted. She knew the hazards of the blame game too well.

Connor pounded the steering wheel with his fist, his

body vibrating with his frustration. "All the more reason for us to come."

"No," Hunter countered. "Stay away. Go back to the marshals' safe house."

"Ain't happening." Connor lifted the gun from the seat where Darby had left it and jabbed the magazine catch. After he'd confirmed that the pistol was loaded, he clicked the magazine back in place and stashed the gun at the small of his back. "This is my fight, and I will fight it."

Darby wet her lips, anxiety roiling in her gut. Was this a mistake? Had she let her fears for her daughter and desperate yearning to be with Savannah muddle her judgment?

"Man, I know you think you have to—" Hunter started.

Connor took the phone from Darby. "It's decided." He disconnected with Hunter, then dialed a new number from memory with his thumb.

"Connor..."

He sent her a quelling look as his call was answered by a male voice.

"James, it's Connor Mansfield."

James? As in James Gale? A prickle of alarm raced down her spine. Eyes wide with panic, she grabbed Connor's arm and mouthed, "What are you doing?"

James Gale hesitated, then said, "Mansfield. What do you want?"

"I want you and the rest of your family to stay the hell away from my little girl!" Connor snarled.

"I told you before I have no interest in hurting your family." James's voice was flat, firm. "Especially not your daughter."

"Really?" Connor's lip curled, and his tone was venomous. "Then explain the dead rat and threatening note left in her hospital room early this morning. My daughter's immunity is compromised because of the transplant, and you put a filthy rat in her room? That's dirty pool, even for you."

"A rat?" James sounded genuinely startled. Surprisingly angry. "Was your girl hurt?"

"If she gets some latent infection or illness because of her exposure to that rat, I'll hunt you and your brother both down and kill you myself!"

"Not if I get to my brother first," James growled. "I had nothing to do with the rat or any threats to your daughter. I've told you I don't condone the injury of innocents, and I meant it. But I'm afraid Victor isn't as merciful."

Darby pressed both hands over her face, struggling to keep her composure. She felt as if the last threads of her sanity—of her life—were coming unraveled. She drew slow breaths and fought to hold herself together, willing Connor to drive faster, get her to Savannah as quickly as possible. *Please, God, don't let Victor Gale hurt my baby!*

"If anything happens to Savannah or any member of my family, so help me," Connor warned James, echoing her thoughts, "I'll—"

"It won't," James said. "I'll see to it. Let me handle my brother."

"*No.* I will not trust my daughter's safety to you or anyone else. She's my responsibility, and I will do what I have to to protect her. Am I making myself clear?"

The unspoken threat in Connor's tone and the vengeance in his eyes stirred a gnawing ache in Darby's gut.

"Perfectly. But remember this—it's still open season on you. Any move you make, you make at your own risk." James's cold, unflinching tone sent a chill through Darby.

"Go to hell," Connor gritted and jabbed the disconnect button. Throwing the phone aside, he narrowed his gaze on the highway, his expression stormy.

Darby's mouth dried, and she reached for Connor's arm,

could feel the tension vibrating in him. "Don't do anything crazy, Connor. I couldn't stand for anything to happen to you. Protecting Savannah is one thing. Going looking for trouble is another. Don't do anything that will paint a target on your back." She squeezed his wrist. "Please, Connor."

He lifted his hand from the steering wheel to twine his fingers with hers and kiss the back of her hand. He gave her a quick glance and sighed. "I can't make that promise. I have to end this. One way or another."

Victor Gale yawned and rubbed his eyes with the heels of his hands. Surveillance was boring, tedious work, but he had every reason to believe it would pay off. He rocked back in the rolling chair stationed in front of the bank of monitors affording the hospital security a view of every entrance and hallway in the building. The security office was tucked away in the basement of the hospital, off the beaten path for ninety-nine percent of hospital employees. Just the same, he'd donned the uniform of the security guard whose body he'd stashed in the security office utility closet, in case anyone glanced through the hall window. When Officer Nance had returned from his early morning call concerning a dead rat and threatening note in the isolation room of a pediatric patient, Victor had been waiting. He figured he had a few hours left before the next shift arrived. He hadn't seen his quarry yet, but he had patience.

If Mansfield got even a whiff of the news that Victor had paid a visit, via one very scared and cooperative nurse's aide, to his kid's hospital room, he should be showing up anytime now. Men like Connor Mansfield—and James, for that matter—were easy to manipulate. Just point a gun at their wife's head or promise harm to one of their snot-nosed brats, and these *family men*—Victor snorted at the term—crumpled like wet paper.

Not him. He wouldn't let anything get in the way of exacting vengeance for Pop's incarceration. He hesitated when that entered his mind. Maybe he was a family man, too. His loyalty was to Pop. Victor shook his head as if to rid himself of the irony. His allegiance to Pop was different. He couldn't say how. It just...*was*.

Victor's cell buzzed, and looky there, speaking of his brother, the whipped bastard...

He raised the phone to his ear. "What?"

"I told you to leave Mansfield's family alone," James growled.

"Yeah, and I ignored you."

James's frustration was palpable even over the phone. "Where are you?"

"Working."

"You're not at the office. I was just there. Where. Are. You?"

Victor didn't answer. He gave the monitors another encompassing glance. Still no sign of Mansfield.

"Victor, I want Mansfield to pay for betraying Pop as much as you do, but not at the expense of a child's life. Stand down. Leave the girl alone. Do you hear me?"

On a monitor, he saw a car speed into the parking garage and jerked to a stop in a spot reserved for staff doctors. Victor leaned forward to watch the scene unfold on the small monitor and grinned when Mansfield and his girlfriend climbed out of the sedan and hurried to the elevator. "I have business to take care of now. Goodbye, James."

Victor disconnected, even as James shouted more warnings and threats. Screw him. If James wouldn't take action, he would. *This one's for you, Pop.*

Chapter 21

Connor darted from the elevator, clutching Darby's hand, and they jogged down the corridor to Savannah's isolation room. Seeing them approach, Hunter and Marshal Hargrove rose from chairs in the visitors' area outside Savannah's room.

As they stumbled to a stop, casting worried glances through the observation window to their daughter, Hargrove gave them a frown of disgust and disappointment. "Morris called earlier. I've been expecting you."

"So have I," said a menacing voice behind them. A man in a security guard uniform stalked toward them, and something about the officer's dark eyes and grim mouth sent an uneasy shudder through Connor.

"Who—?" Darby started.

But in the same instant Connor recognized James's brother, Victor Gale raised a pistol with a silencer and fired two quick shots at Hargrove.

Darby screamed as the marshal crumpled. Hunter and Connor closed ranks, putting themselves between Darby and the assassin's gun.

Victor realigned his aim toward the three of them, clustered in front of Savannah's door.

Connor's pulse slammed into overdrive, and his mind raced. *Protect Darby. Protect Savannah. End this!*

Raising his hands, he shouted, "No! Leave them out of this! It's me you want."

"Exactly." Victor moved his pistol a few degrees, centering his aim on Connor. "For Pop."

Connor dropped, pulling Darby with him, a millisecond before the muffled crack of the pistol. He felt the heat of the bullet whiz past him, heard the thump as it lodged in the wall.

Adrenaline surged in Connor's blood, and he used the burst of energy to spring up and lunge at Victor. His move surprised Victor just enough to buy him a critical second. He charged at the gunman. Tackled him. The pistol fired again, the bullet flying wildly.

"Connor!" Darby's panicked cry reverberated in the tiny waiting room. On some level Connor recognized the sounds of alarm from the nurses' station down the hall. But his focus was on Victor, the gun. Victor's grip on his weapon was steely. He battled Connor with brutal force, slamming him against the floor and cracking the pistol against Connor's ear.

Pain rattled through Connor to the bone, but he ignored it. He had to do something to draw Victor and the danger he posed away from his family and other bystanders in the critical care wing.

With a twist, he landed a punch to Victor's jaw and followed it with a knee to the solar plexus. Victor wheezed and loosened his grip enough that Connor wrested himself free and staggered to his feet. Sucking in a lungful of oxygen, Connor glared at Victor and gritted, "You want me? Come get me."

Darby gasped and struggled against Hunter's hold. "Connor, no!"

Backing toward the exit, he aimed a finger and an unyielding look at Darby and Hunter. "Stay here! Protect our daughter!" With that, he slammed through the stairwell door.

As he'd prayed, Victor gave chase. In a snap choice, Connor headed up the steps, hoping he'd encounter fewer hospital visitors or staff on the stairs to the higher floors. He reached behind him and withdrew the pistol Darby had found in the glove box, flicking off the safety. He'd not drawn on Victor earlier because he hadn't wanted an exchange of gunfire on the pediatric floor, where too many bystanders could get hit with a stray bullet.

"Give it up, Mansfield!" Victor taunted. "We both know how this will end. There's only one way this will be over for your family. When you're dead!"

Connor took the steps two at a time. He could hear Victor's feet pounding the concrete, the sound echoing hollowly in the empty well. He paused and glanced over the railing long enough to draw Victor's fire. Hold his attention and keep him in pursuit. As long as Victor was charging after him, his family was safe. He was buying time for the police to arrive. By now, Darby and Hunter would have called 911. He just had to evade Victor, keep up the chase for a few more minutes....

Another bullet zoomed past his ear, and he jerked back, continued running up the stairs. Sixth floor. Seventh, then...dead end. He'd reached the roof.

Darby's hands shook as she ripped at Hargrove's shirt to find his wound. "Help us," she shouted. "He's been shot!"

The marshal wheezed, coughed and a bubble of blood formed at his mouth.

Hunter held his cell to his ear with one hand while he worked to loosen the buttons at Hargrove's neck. The marshal struggled to breathe, his eyelids fluttering and his gaze unfocused.

Darby's own breathing was shallow and nervous, but she refused to fall apart. She would be no good to Hargrove, or Savannah, if she gave in to the fear pulsing through her. She would be no help to Connor....

She cut an anxious glance toward the stairwell. She knew Connor's motive for leading the gunman away, but his means left him in the assassin's crosshairs. Nausea roiled in her gut, and she whispered a prayer. *Please, God, keep him safe.*

When she finally got Hargrove's shirt open, she blinked in surprise. Not blood. A bullet-proof vest. But the blood in his mouth and his wheezing both pointed to internal damage. The impact of the bullets on the vest could still have caused broken ribs, punctured lungs or bruised organs. "Someone help us!"

A tall man in a dress shirt, suit coat and Windsor tie stepped into her field of vision and bit out a curse. "Where's Mansfield?"

She recognized the man looming over her from Tracy's funeral, the pictures in the marshals' car and a business party she'd attended once with Connor. James Gale. A chill rippled through her.

"Where are Mansfield and my brother?" he shouted, getting right in Darby's face with a lethal and terrifying glower.

Hunter lunged for him. "Get away from her!"

James reached under his suit coat and jerked a handgun

toward Hunter. "Stop right there, hero. My beef's not with you. Just tell me where they are, before anyone else dies."

Hunter growled an anatomically impossible suggestion in reply. But something tickled the back of Darby's nape, something James had said not even an hour ago when Connor had him on speakerphone in the marshals' car. *Let me handle my brother.*

A team of nurses hurried toward them with a gurney and crash cart. Her gaze flashed from the medical staff to Hunter, then back to James. Her mouth dried, and air hung in her lungs. Wetting her lips, she rasped, "The stairs."

Connor yanked on the door to the roof and staggered out into the bright glare and oppressive heat of the Louisiana sun. To his left were massive air conditioner compressors, whirring at full force. He scuttled between the units, using the metal giants as cover as he moved away from the door. Across the tar-and-pebble rooftop, an area had been resurfaced as a helicopter landing pad and a large *X* painted in white to direct the pilot. The medevac helicopter was there, idle and waiting for the next emergency flight. Immediately past the helicopter, he spied a set of double doors, wide enough to accommodate a stretcher and medical personnel.

If he could reach that set of doors…

The creak of hinges called his attention back to the exit he'd just come through. He raised the marshal's gun.

Victor stepped out and cast a wary gaze around the roof. "Come on, Mansfield. I know you're up here." He crept forward another step, glancing between AC units. "It's just a matter of time before—"

Connor fired. Missed. Victor jumped behind an AC compressor, cursing.

"Okay." Victor gave a bitter laugh. "We can do it that way." He fired back in the direction Connor's shot had come.

Crouching behind the nearest compressor unit, Connor gauged his chances of reaching the double doors of the helo pad. Too risky. Too much open space yawned between him and the second hospital entrance. Moving target or not, he decided he was better off staying behind the air-conditioning units.

Victor started moving toward him, his weapon aimed right at the spot where Connor hid. Quietly, Connor scooped a handful of the pea gravel on the roof and flung it in the direction of the helicopter. The tiny rocks hit with an effective plink and clatter, drawing Victor's gaze and changing his course. A pigeon took flight from behind the helicopter, adding to Victor's distraction. Connor held his breath as Victor followed the sounds and edged away from him.

Connor seized the opportunity to circle back, easing from one AC unit to another, moving as silently as he could and praying the rumble of compressors would mask his footsteps.

He'd almost made it back to the stairwell door, had ventured a few steps away from the cover of the compressors when Victor swung around, his gaze locking with Connor's.

The following seconds may have passed in real time, but they slowed, stretched in a surreal blur for Connor.

Victor swung his weapon up. Fired. Connor spun to the side, then flinched as Victor's bullet hit the concrete wall behind him. To his right, the hinges of the stairway door shrieked. The steel door flew open.

Victor's aim shifted abruptly as someone burst through the portal. Connor didn't wait to see who'd stumbled onto the scene. He dove toward the figure that emerged, knocking the newcomer's solid frame to the ground. Shielding them as Victor squeezed off one, two, three shots that peppered the gravel around them.

Quickly, Connor flipped to his back and returned fire. He managed only one shot before his gun jammed.

His gut clenched, and he turned to shout for the person beside him to take cover inside. But his throat froze. The new arrival, the man he'd knocked down, was James Gale.

A shadow fell over him, and Connor jerked his attention back to Victor, who now loomed less than ten feet away. Victor wore a gloating grin as he held his weapon with a two-handed grip, aimed straight at Connor's center mass. "Hey, big brother, glad you could make it for the grand finale."

Connor crab crawled back a foot, but he hit the wall. James lay between him and the stairwell door. When Victor narrowed his eyes preparing to fire, Connor gritted his teeth, braced for the bullet. Images of Darby and Savannah, his parents, his brothers flashed in his mind. Everyone he loved enough to die for. Everyone he wanted to *live* for.

An ear-shattering blast rent the air. The concussion ricocheted in his chest, and a wrenching regret ripped through his heart.

But the cry of pain didn't come from him. He raised a startled gaze, as Victor shouted a curse. Victor clutched his right arm, which bled through the fingers of his left hand. Lifting a furious glare to James he screamed, "What the hell?"

James still held his own snub-nosed revolver leveled at his brother. "Drop your gun."

"Are you insane?" Without waiting for his brother's response, Victor raised his injured arm with his left hand and took aim at James. "You son of a bitch!"

Connor rolled to his feet and sprang forward in one smooth motion. Ducking his head, he rammed Victor with his shoulder. His momentum sent both of them reeling backward, stumbling.

Victor growled with rage and grabbed fistfuls of Connor's hair, his shirt. He twisted and fought Connor's hold. Connor backed Victor against one of the air-conditioning compressors, bending his opponent backward as he reared back with his arm and smacked the jammed pistol into Victor's temple.

Victor blinked hard and shook off the blow. When Connor took aim to thwack him again, Victor jerked his head forward, slamming his skull into Connor's nose. The roof rocked under Connor's feet, and his vision blurred. He felt Victor plant a foot in his gut and shove. His head foggy, Connor staggered back and landed on his butt.

As he was blinking to refocus his eyes, another crack of gunfire split the air. He jolted and watched, stunned, as Victor slumped on the roof. A red stain spread at his heart.

Adrenaline muted Connor's pain, but left his body shaking and his head spinning.

James Gale's shoes crunched in the gravel as he stepped over to his brother's body and stared down at him with a haunted expression. His voice was little more than a murmur when he turned a bleak and angry glare toward Connor. "I told you to leave my brother to me."

Connor pressed a hand to the warmth seeping from his nose and held James's stare. "So I guess you're going to kill me now?"

James's mouth tightened, and he exhaled a harsh breath that made his nostrils flare. "I should." A muscle twitched in his jaw. "When Pop hears what happened to Victor, he'll hire men to come after you."

Connor gave a humorless laugh. "So what else is new?"

James took a slow step toward him. "I'm done. I don't want any part of the killing anymore. That's not the man I want to be, not the person I want my children to see and emulate. I don't want to be in a position where men with a grievance could come after my family." He sighed and looked off over the skyline of Lagniappe, squinting in the bright sun. "I'm done."

Connor pushed warily to his feet. "So my family—"

"Is safe. From me and Pop. I'll see to it. You saved my boy seven years ago, and you saved my life today. I get to go home to my kids and wife tonight. For that, I'll protect your family. But you—" James returned his gaze to Connor. "Pop won't overlook this. He'll blame you." He rubbed the muscles at the back of his neck. "You need to get back in the U.S. Marshals' car and get lost. Hide. Today." James shook his head and pursed his mouth as he glanced back at Victor. "Pop won't forgive this."

Connor clenched his back teeth and nodded. He was back to square one, needing to leave Darby and his daughter behind to protect them from getting caught in the cross fire. Connor's heart wrenched so hard it stole his breath. Giving up Darby and Savannah would be its own kind of death, and he grieved the loss to his bones.

Chapter 22

That evening, the entire Mansfield clan, Darby's sisters, and Marshals Jones, Morris and Ramsey gathered in the senior Mansfield's living room. The mood was somber, funereal. The last time Connor entered WitSec, the marshals had faked his death. This time, Darby felt as if she were the one dying. With James Gale's promise that she, Savannah and the rest of Connor's family would be safe, and the heightened threat to Connor of vengeance from William Gale's thugs, the marshals and Connor decided that the time had come for Connor to disappear again. He'd wanted to wait for Savannah's release from the hospital, but the marshals had convinced him time was of the essence. A new life, a new identity and a new start were waiting for him in an undisclosed city.

In minutes, Connor would climb in the marshals' car, and she'd be alone again. Heartbroken. But she knew Connor's decision to leave was made out of love, sacrifice. Not only to keep him safe, but to ensure no one else in his family died as collateral damage the way Tracy had.

Connor released his mother from a bear hug, wiped his eyes and gave the marshals a tight nod as he started for the door. He gave the room an encompassing glance as he backed out. "I love you all. So much."

A chorus of returned sentiments and sniffles answered him, but Darby's eyes were dry. She was numb, shaking inside, unable to draw enough air into her leaden lungs. Connor's gaze connected with hers, and he held his hand out, silently asking her to accompany him to the car for one last private moment.

Somehow she made her feet move and followed him to the door, then outside into the suffocating humidity and fading daylight.

Connor had stopped by Savannah's hospital room one last time before his meeting with the family, and Darby hadn't been able to watch the tender goodbye. Savannah had been asleep, unaware, but the heartache and misery on Connor's face as he kissed his daughter's forehead and whispered words of love had been more than Darby could bear.

She walked stiffly to the end of the sidewalk, her breathing no more than shallow, desperate pants. *Don't go. Don't leave me!*

Eyes bloodshot with grief, Connor drew her into his arms and rubbed her back. "Come with me?"

Darby shuddered, and pain lanced her heart. She swallowed hard, searching for her voice. "I can't."

Connor kissed her eyelids and stroked a hand over her hair. "I know. But I couldn't leave this time without asking. So you'd know…" He didn't finish. He didn't need to. The gesture meant the world to her, and she'd treasure the knowledge that Connor loved her, that he wanted her with him. That she mattered.

As he pulled away from their embrace, she offered him a parting gift, as well. "I'm going to tell Savannah who you are. That she has a father who loves her more than anything. Who not only gave her life, but who risked his own to save her, to heal her. I'll tell her all about you. I promise."

Connor drew a sharp breath, and moisture filled his eyes. "Thank you."

Marshal Jones circled the front fender of the car and opened the driver's door. "It's time."

Darby's fingers curled into the muscles of Connor's back, clinging to his shirt. *No. No!* She couldn't lose him again! "Connor..."

His lips crashed down on hers in a deep, possessive kiss, a lingering, tender goodbye that she would hold in her heart forever.

As Connor stepped back, his hand slid along her cheek. "I love you, Darby. I always will."

Her throat squeezed so tight with emotion that no sound came out when she tried to speak.

Connor climbed in the backseat of the marshals' car and closed the door, and Jones backed down the driveway. A sob wrenched from her chest as the taillights disappeared down the street, and she rasped, "I'll always love you, too."

She jolted when Marshal Morris stepped beside her and gave her shoulder a comforting squeeze. "I'm sorry. I know this is hard for you."

She wrapped her arms around herself, suddenly icy cold despite the Louisiana heat. "Hard doesn't begin to describe it."

Darby couldn't bring herself to go back inside yet and face all the well-meaning hugs and words of condolence.

See the pain so like her own in Julia's eyes. Hunter's bravado. Grant's grief-ravaged face. So she stood on the sidewalk, staring blankly, and Morris stayed with her, offering his silent commiseration. In the quiet of the approaching evening, a keening ache raked her, much like the emptiness and pain she'd known when her father had deserted her years before. Leaving her no option but heartache and rejection. No option…

A stubborn refusal to allow her life to be forced down this path of misery again roared to life. Adrenaline hardened her resolve. This was wrong. She couldn't let this happen!

She thought about the hurt she'd harbored since her father's desertion, the resentment she'd felt when she'd learned of Connor's deception, the fear of offering her whole heart to him because of their impossible circumstances. Had she let her insecurities and old wounds keep her from doing everything in her power to surmount the obstacles between her and Connor? How could she give up on something as important to her as Connor's love?

"I can't accept this," she said, voicing the determination that was gaining ground in her mind, her heart. "There has to be a way to make this work."

Morris shoved his hands in his pockets and sighed. "Darby, we've explained why—"

"I know what you've said! Savannah's medical needs made it impossible for her to be hidden in WitSec. That's why we aren't going with him. The only reason! But I can't accept that. I can't give up without trying!" She grasped Morris's arms and shook him. "Isn't there any way, any way at all, that we can make this work?"

"Darby, if there were, don't you think I'd—?"

"No ifs! I can't lose Connor again. I'm tired of life happening to me. My father left me, and I could do nothing about it. Connor faked his death and gave me no choice in it. My daughter got cancer, and I could do nothing for her. But this time… This time I won't accept 'no' for an answer! You have to help me find a way to hide Savannah in WitSec so we can be with Connor. Please!"

Morris's eyebrows furrowed. "A family like yours should be together. I agree. After all the risks he's taken, the sacrifices he's made, I think Connor deserves to see his little girl grow up, but—"

"No!" She gripped his arms and pinned a hard look on him. "No buts. Just say you'll help me find a way to make this work!"

Morris glanced away, swiping an agitated hand over his face. "I don't know where we'd begin. We'd have to be able to eliminate all the risks to you and make sure all your ties, all of Savannah's ties to this life are severed."

"I don't care how long it takes or what I'd have to give up. My place is with Connor. We should be a family, whatever it takes. However long it takes. I won't quit looking for a way to be with him. All I ask is that you promise to help me."

Morris scowled and shook his head. "It would take so much—"

"Marshal!" She fisted her hands and drew back her shoulders. "'Your task is not to seek for love, but merely to seek and find all the barriers within yourself that you have built against it,'" she quoted, and he snapped a startled gaze to her.

"Rumi," he whispered, letting her know he remembered the walk in the woods when he'd first shared the poet's wisdom.

She nodded. "I'm trying to remove the barriers. Please, help me. I belong with Connor. Savannah belongs with her father. Help me find a solution."

Morris raised his chin, squared his shoulders. "No guarantees that we'll find a way to make it work, but...I'll do my damnedest."

Hope blossomed in her chest and filled her with a radiant joy. "Good enough. I can work with that."

Six months later

John Lancaster answered the door of his suburban home and found Marshal Morris standing on his porch with an adorable four-year-old girl in his arms. Her cheeks were thin but rosy, and she had a head of short brown hair the same color as his. Her golden-brown eyes twinkled when she saw him, and she chirped, "Hi, Daddy! We're here!"

John laughed. "So I see!" He pulled his daughter into his arms and hugged her tightly. Over his daughter's shoulder, he met the gaze of the auburn-haired woman beside Marshal Morris. The beauty gave him a playful grin and, juggling a tabby cat he knew well, held out her hand, "Allow me to introduce myself. My name's Karen. I'm your fiancée."

He took her hand, but instead of shaking it, he tugged her into his arms, squishing Toby between them, and bent his head for a kiss. "Indeed you are, my lovely." He glanced back at his little girl, marveling at how happy—how healthy—she looked. "And who are you?"

"I'm Savannah, silly!" The girl giggled.

He cut a glance to Darby...er, Karen...for confirmation. She set Toby on the ground in front of the open door, and the cat trotted inside as if knowing he was at his new house and ready to claim it. "It's less confusing for Savannah to let her keep her name," she said.

"Gotcha." He smiled, bent to give his fiancée a lingering kiss, the first of many to come.

Raising his gaze to the marshal, he asked, "And you're sure they'll be safe with me? What about Savannah's medical records?"

"What records?" Morris gave him a sly grin and tugged Savannah's earlobe. "She looks pretty healthy to me."

He smiled at his daughter, his chest full to bursting with love and happiness. "Same here, but…"

"Dr. Reed checked her out and ran tests the day before we left," Dar—er, Karen said. "She's still in remission. There's every hope she'll stay cancer free, but you and I will need to be vigilant and watch for any signs of relapse. If she does get sick again…" She shuddered visibly at the mention of it. "We'll find a doctor here to treat her. We'll start from scratch."

"We vetted this situation fully, John." Morris grinned when he used the new alias. "You have the full resources of the U.S. Marshals behind you and your family. We haven't lost a witness in our program yet, and I don't intend to let anyone in your family be the first."

"Oh, my God," he said, heaving a sigh of disbelief. "I can't believe this is happening."

"Believe it." The woman he'd loved since college leaned close to him and whispered, "I never quit working to find a way to be with you. I couldn't accept being without you. I loved you too much to lose you again."

He kissed her hard and squeezed his daughter and fiancée in a group hug. "I am the luckiest man in the world. And the happiest. I love you, Darby."

"Karen," she whispered, and he winked.

"Right." He swept a hand toward his front door. "Welcome home, honey."

* * * * *

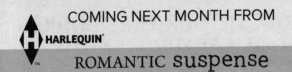

REQUEST YOUR FREE BOOKS!
2 FREE NOVELS PLUS 2 FREE GIFTS!

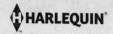

ROMANTIC suspense

Sparked by danger, fueled by passion

YES! Please send me 2 FREE Harlequin® Romantic Suspense novels and my 2 FREE gifts (gifts are worth about $10). After receiving them, if I don't wish to receive any more books, I can return the shipping statement marked "cancel." If I don't cancel, I will receive 4 brand-new novels every month and be billed just $4.74 per book in the U.S. or $5.24 per book in Canada. That's a savings of at least 14% off the cover price! It's quite a bargain! Shipping and handling is just 50¢ per book in the U.S. and 75¢ per book in Canada.* I understand that accepting the 2 free books and gifts places me under no obligation to buy anything. I can always return a shipment and cancel at any time. Even if I never buy another book, the two free books and gifts are mine to keep forever.

240/340 HDN F45N

Name	(PLEASE PRINT)	
Address		Apt. #
City	State/Prov.	Zip/Postal Code

Signature (if under 18, a parent or guardian must sign)

Mail to the **Harlequin®** Reader Service:
IN U.S.A.: P.O. Box 1867, Buffalo, NY 14240-1867
IN CANADA: P.O. Box 609, Fort Erie, Ontario L2A 5X3

Want to try two free books from another line?
Call 1-800-873-8635 or visit www.ReaderService.com.

* Terms and prices subject to change without notice. Prices do not include applicable taxes. Sales tax applicable in N.Y. Canadian residents will be charged applicable taxes. Offer not valid in Quebec. This offer is limited to one order per household. Not valid for current subscribers to Harlequin Romantic Suspense books. All orders subject to credit approval. Credit or debit balances in a customer's account(s) may be offset by any other outstanding balance owed by or to the customer. Please allow 4 to 6 weeks for delivery. Offer available while quantities last.

Your Privacy—The Harlequin® Reader Service is committed to protecting your privacy. Our Privacy Policy is available online at www.ReaderService.com or upon request from the Harlequin Reader Service.

We make a portion of our mailing list available to reputable third parties that offer products we believe may interest you. If you prefer that we not exchange your name with third parties, or if you wish to clarify or modify your communication preferences, please visit us at www.ReaderService.com/consumerschoice or write to us at Harlequin Reader Service Preference Service, P.O. Box 9062, Buffalo, NY 14269. Include your complete name and address.

HRS13R

SPECIAL EXCERPT FROM

H HARLEQUIN

ROMANTIC suspense

When an arms dealer tries to kill his neighbor, bounty
hunter Lincoln Ivy steps in, only to learn the redheaded
spitfire isn't who he thinks she is.

Read on for a sneak peek of

ARMED AND FAMOUS

by Jennifer Morey, available February 2014 from
Harlequin® Romantic Suspense.

Maddie barked and moved closer to Remy, protecting her.
Remy stepped outside and the dog did, too. Remy was tempted
to run.

Wade, appearing at the open door, aiming his gun, stopped
her. Maybe Maddie would go next door, or her barking would
alert Lincoln.

She reentered the house and closed the door before Maddie
could follow. Her heart wrenched with the sound of frantic
barking.

"In the living room," Wade ordered her.

Maddie's barking stopped. She was running next door.

"You've been sneaking around again," Wade said, stepping
close to her with dangerous eyes. "What were you doing at my
store three days ago?"

"What are you talking about?" She played ignorant, the
same as she'd done the last time he'd come accusing her of
spying on him and his friends. That time she'd followed him
when he'd met some men she hadn't recognized. Nothing had

been exchanged, but she suspected he'd gone to discuss one of his illegal gun deals, deals that he expected her to execute for him.

He leaned close, the gun at his side as though he didn't think he needed it to keep her under control. "You know damn well what I'm talking about. You're supposed to be working with me, not against me."

"If working with you means breaking the law, I'll pass."

With a smirk, Wade straightened. "You've already done that. And if you don't start doing what I tell you, the cops are going to find out."

Because he'd tell them. Soon, he wouldn't be able to threaten her like this. Soon, she'd be able to call the cops herself and have *him* arrested. But for now she had to be patient.

Remy spotted Lincoln at the back door. She'd left it unlocked for him, hoping he'd retrace Maddie's path. Sure enough, he had. Wade's back was to him. Careful not to shift her eyes, she used her peripheral vision to watch Lincoln enter.

"I'm only going to ask you once more," Wade said.

Before he could repeat the question, Lincoln put the barrel of his pistol against the back of Wade's neck. "Put the gun down."

**Don't miss
ARMED AND FAMOUS
by Jennifer Morey,
available February 2014 from
Harlequin® Romantic Suspense**